Christopher Fowler is the author of twenty novels and once
tions of short stories, including *Roofworld, Spanky,* and *Full
Dark House*. He lives and works in central London, and would
be more prolific if he didn't go out so much.

Serpent's Tail publishes three collections of his stories, *Personal Demons, The Devil in Me,* and this, his latest, *Demonized*.

Visit www.christopherfowler.co.uk.

5

Also by Christopher Fowler and published by Serpent's Tail

Personal Demons
The Devil in Me

DEMONIZED

◆

SHORT STORIES
BY
CHRISTOPHER FOWLER

Library of Congress Catalog Card Number: 2003111415

A complete catalogue record for this book can
be obtained from the British Library on request

The right of Christopher Fowler to be identified as the author of this
work has been asserted by him in accordance with the Copyright,
Designs and Patents Act 1988

Copyright © 2003 Christopher Fowler

First published in 2004 by Serpent's Tail,
4 Blackstock Mews, London N4 2BT

Website: www.serpentstail.com

Phototypeset in 10.5pt Sabon by Intype Libra Ltd
Printed in Great Britain by
Mackays of Chatham plc, Chatham, Kent

10 9 8 7 6 5 4 3 2 1

CONTENTS

FOREWORD:
INTO DARKER FICTION

'Absence doesn't make the heart grow fonder; it makes people think you're dead'

– James Caan

I read the other day that English writing is dead, which came as a bit of a shock, because I thought I still had a pulse. What the article meant, I imagine, is that the kind of English writing the critic would like to read is dead. True, we rarely produce those expansive Homeric sagas which US novelists publish with such regularity, but English writing is very much alive and well; it's just not always where one expects it to be. Many English authors I admire work outside the mainstream categories, and perhaps the true picture of anything lies in its barely registered peripheries.

What you have here is a dispatch from what has become a strange side-alley to the house of fiction. After enjoying well over a century of immense popularity, tales of mystery and imagination have spread their wings and transmuted into Dark Fiction, a genre that allows far greater freedom to explore new themes. The English fascination with black humour, cruelty, cynicism and leading men of weak character places us in a strong position to lead the left field. Yet, right now, it's hard to find editors who will buck the company line to venture into darker territory.

Our great-grandparents had ghost stories; peculiar tales

narrated by clubbable men who commenced after knocking their pipes out on mantelpieces and pouring themselves large brandies. '*And he never spoke another word to the end of his days*,' says the narrator meaningfully at the end of such tales. Now they have gone the way of the western or the locked room mystery, consigned to the second-hand book stalls of history. Quite right too; the world's a frightening place and nostalgia isn't what it used to be. There are plenty of darker new tales to write, especially in a nation that obsesses about celebrity sex, the price of cocaine and new shades of nail varnish while its secret population sleeps on deadly streets.

This collection sets out to provide a little more darkness in short form. Darkness of the soul, of the cynic, of the less-than-happily ever after, because Bridget Jones doesn't always find her prince and life tells you tongue-swallowingly terrible lies. I seem to have set up my stall as the literary equivalent of Guinness or Marmite; something you didn't think you'd like, but hopefully become addicted to. The first trick is to make each short story cheerful enough to keep you from slitting your throat. The second is to take you with me as I gently move the goalposts.

Aristotle said, 'Hope is a waking dream,' and as we search for new things to demonize, the line between wakefulness and nightmares is blurring. Ideas for stories can arrive after particularly circuitous routes through fact and fantasy. Before I wrote the first tale here, an old schoolfriend sent me an old end-of-term photograph with the eventual destinies of our classmates added beneath each face. The three most popular categories were 'In His Grave', 'In Prison' and 'In Insurance'. A few days later, a journey across France in a collapsing classic car resulted in a nightmarish trip around the hairpin bends of the storm-swept Mont Blanc with a puncture, no alternator and no lights. Somehow these unrelated events conflated into 'We're Going Where the Sun Shines Brightly', although I wonder how many people will still appreciate the movie references.

Some stories were commissions. 'Dealing with the Situation'

began as a Christmas story for the *Big Issue*. Few magazines buy fiction these days, and I rarely turn down the opportunity to produce something if asked. The *Big Issue* has certain rules you need to follow, the main one being Do Not Write About Drugs. This is because the vendors get knocked down by easily confused readers looking to think the worst of them. Another was commissioned (and written in record time) for the *Dazed & Confused Annual*, who published the piece and forgot to pay me, threw a launch party for the book and forgot to invite me, and forgot to send me a finished copy. I tell you this in case you're thinking of becoming a writer.

As in previous collections, there's an 'Odd One Out' tale, in this case 'Emotional Response', written for my friend Sally, who asked 'Can't you write a nice love story, just for a change?' Sally, I gave it my best shot. The story 'Personal Space' was written in a single sitting, something I've never done before and wanted to try as an experiment. Unfortunately it happens to be based on fact, and the true-life ending was much grimmer.

I usually rewrite stories when it comes to placing them in a collection, in order to create a 'definitive version'. Last year I took a walk in an ancient Malaysian jungle, a bookish Englishman poorly prepared to experience the rougher edge of nature. I certainly didn't expect to emerge with my skin covered in welts and my socks filled with blood. Consequently, I wrote 'The Green Man', turning to the once-popular sub-genre of the English tropical story, a tradition that peaked with Kipling and Wells and hasn't been seen much since Carl Stephenson's 'Leiningen Versus the Ants'. Evelyn Waugh's 'The Man Who Loved Dickens' is probably the most reprinted example – it's a chapter from his satirical novel *A Handful Of Dust*, but so fine in its construction that it has often appeared as a free-standing horror story. It's odd how many English writers are sensitive to the surreal and the mysterious. As inhabitants of a grey, damp world, I think one is drawn to seek out the exotic.

In 'Breaking Heart', which was written to be performed at

an 'Anti-Valentine' event at Borders, the character of Emma is my friend Amber, whose experiences as Cinderella I ruthlessly used. 'Cairo 6.1' is my one hundredth published story, and I suppose represents some kind of conclusion, or perhaps a fresh beginning. Like many writers, I've still never written a story I'm completely happy with, but I hope to continue mining the seam of Peculiar English until I come up with an unflawed gem.

Peculiar English coincidentally describes the annual BFS Christmas bash, held upstairs in the Princess Louise pub, High Holborn, London. The British Fantasy Society is not solely for writers who provide alarmingly detailed maps of elf shires in their novels. It's a club for anyone who chooses to stray from the straight, narrow path of reality-mirroring fiction. Okay, there's a preponderance of big jumpers and draught stout at such events, but everyone's surprisingly sane and likeable, and – unlike some other professions – there are almost as many women as men. Still, they're all finding that publishers are less willing than ever before to take chances, even though it's now possible to laser-print ten copies of a book to meet specific demand. This should have led to more choice, not less. All the more reason for me to be grateful to trend-bucking companies like Serpent's Tail.

Of the stories here, you'll find five outright happy endings, seven dark conclusions and a number of split outcomes. To me, that seems an even-handed reflection of what life deals out.

It feels like I've been away for ages. Actually it was just over two years, during which time I never stopped writing. It's good to be back in the world of Darker Fiction.

WE'RE GOING WHERE THE SUN SHINES BRIGHTLY

'No more fairy stories at nanny's knee; it is all aboard the fairy bus for the dungeons'

– Geoffrey Willans

'He's just an innocent,' said Steve, lighting a grubby dog-end. 'You have to fall from grace before you can understand anything adult. He had no idea that she wasn't interested in him. She was really old, thirty at least.'

'And he was still chasing her around the bar when you left?' I asked.

'Cyril will try to shag anyone.' Steve examined the end of his cigarette with distaste. 'Because he's a pathetic virgin.'

'Thirty, and she still turned him down?' I wasn't about to mention that I was also a virgin.

'She had a face like a rag and bone man's horse, and it didn't put him off. The whole thing was creepy.' Steve swallowed smoke and had a coughing fit. 'Roll on summer holidays.'

'Roll on summer holidays.'

We were on our fag break, up near the roof of the Aldenham Bus & Coach Overhaul Works. Through the hangar doors you could see it was grey and raining. Looking to the horizon was like going blind.

'We'll have two weeks to get him laid then,' said Steve, once he'd got his breath back. 'If he doesn't get a bird soon he's going to do himself a mischief.'

If he does get a bird, I remember thinking, *she'll be the one he'll do mischief to.* Cyril had scary energy, undirected, uncontrolled. I assumed it was because he was young; we all were.

The Aldenham Bus & Coach Overhaul Works was built on the site of an old aerodrome. The aircraft hangars that had once housed Mosquitos and Hurricanes had been converted to contain transport machinery. The uneven concrete squares of the runways were pock-marked by pools of iridescent water. Beyond were the wet green hedgerows that shielded the factory from the arterial road. The glory of war days still haunted the horizons of the surrounding meadows, a taunting memory of something noble and exciting.

I was one of the youngest workers. I hated the job, the old men who smelled of roll-ups and sweat, the acrid air of filing-dust and rust, the sinus-sting of spray-paint that hung in the thick air, the machines that shuddered and punched panels from sheets of steel. The sheds churned with the thought-destroying thump of the presses, like the noise of an endless summer storm, its sound condensed and released by the high whine of pistons. Everything around me was black and brown and shades of grey, drained of any sensation other than the slam of the safety barriers and the shake of steel sheeting that vibrated through the soles of your boots.

I wasn't stupid. I didn't think that working in this place was all there was to life. I sensed – but had no way of knowing for sure – that the world beyond the factory was filled with mysteries. I'd been growing increasingly restless at home. I lay on my bed, listening to the strikes and reprisals of my parents' conversation, and felt that somewhere, away from the odour of unused rooms and beeswaxed sideboards, away from the bitter tang of factory metal, there were beautiful girls who laughed and threw themselves recklessly into the arms of boys the same age as me. I wasn't going to be like Cyril, getting drunk and chasing world-weary old boilers around pubs all night. I was going to make something of myself.

I wasn't alone in my dreams. There were four of us; Steve had thick square glasses and worked weekends in a hardware store, saving every penny he earned for plans he had no imagination to realise. Cyril was skinny and blonde and never took off his cap, and went on about girls in a voice that cracked like someone skating on unsafe ice. Don wore his hair in a perfectly greased quiff, and spoke in an attempt at a refined voice. His clothes were always perfectly ironed. He was too worried about what other people thought to ever let himself relax, and insisted on calling us 'fellas'. 'Hey, fellas, I've got a great idea,' as though he was in one of those youth films from the sixties that now look as though they come from another world, Planet Polite. But of course it was the sixties, we were teenagers, and none of us had a clue about the corruption of time.

It was Don's 'Hey, fellas, I've got a great idea,' that started it. His idea sounded hopeless, especially as we had only seven days to go before the start of our summer holidays. Steve and I were on a fag break, sitting waiting for Don, when we saw him driving toward us through the rain, and at that moment we realised dreams were possible, and our monochrome world turned into Technicolor.

Don had heard that London Transport might be willing to sell one of their old Routemaster buses, and managed to persuade them to let him have it on the condition that we did it up, because its seats were slashed to bits and its engine was knackered. And it was my idea to have some of the blokes at the factory overhaul the engine and convert the interior into something more liveable, so that it ended up looking like a double-decker caravan, even though we kept the red exterior and the number above the destination board that proclaimed it to be a Number 9 heading for Piccadilly.

Suddenly we had a chance to fulfil our dreams, and there was a way to escape the troglodyte days of the English summer. We no longer had to make do with the bandstands, chip-shops and smutty postcard racks of the South Coast. We would fix up the bus and head for the South of France, where the sky was wide, the sea was warm and the promenades were filled with the scented promise of sex.

We only managed to get the bus roadworthy by paying mates to work late, so that by the time we were granted our licence we were almost broke, but we were so determined to escape that nothing was going to stop us. On a drizzling Saturday morning we headed for Calais with some half-baked idea that we might even get as far as Greece before having to turn around. Cyril thought if we proved the journey was managable to the bus company they might allow us to take fee-paying guests on charter trips, but we hadn't thought any of it through. It just seemed possible; everything is possible when you don't know the drawbacks. Opportunity can present itself to innocents just as much as it can to the corrupt, and we had an advantage: we were the young ones.

It seemed that the sun began shining at Calais, and as the bus laboured to leave the hills of the town we saw only empty sunlit roads ahead, tarmac dappled in the cool green shadows of the trees. We didn't reach Paris until dusk the following day (the bus's top speed was none too impressive), and went bouncing off to meet girls in the bars of Montmartre. We didn't get to meet girls; we attempted conversations with a few, but they couldn't – or wouldn't – understand us, and in the process we became paralytically pissed, probably due to our over-excitement at being somewhere new. The first real way you can separate yourself from your parents is by choosing who to have sex with. It's an act of rebellion and even betrayal; that's why it's so easy to be a coward and behave badly about the whole thing.

That night we slept like the dead, sexless and still innocent, in the bus, and left for the south late the next morning, nursing beer-and-brandy hangovers. It was a beautiful journey. The roads were less crowded then, and you had time to look around. Just outside Avignon, where the distant walls of the gated city could be glimpsed, we saw a pretty young girl seated in a red MG with a steaming radiator, and stopped to help her. The car was old and the seals would be hard to repair, so I suggested that she come with us. We could phone ahead for the parts, I explained, and Don would replace them for her on the way back. The girl, Sandy, agreed so readily that I knew she had her eye on one of us, but which one? She had bobbed black hair and black eye-shadow, a short pleated skirt and white kinky boots. She was so at ease in our company that she made us look like children.

By the time we reached Marseilles, I knew she fancied Don, and that night, stopping on the starlit road to St Tropez, I was sure she would sleep with him. Steve seemed the most put out, and sulked until we took him drinking in a bar that played samba music and was filled – for some reason I now forget – with loud Brazilian girls. They laughed at everything, downing as many drinks as we did, and then picked us off like sharp-shooters attacking targets.

The one I took back began to undress me while we were still in the street. We made awkward, squeaky love on one of the bench seats upstairs in the bus. She freed me from more than my parents; she freed me from England, and all of my embarrassing, desperate memories. I can't remember ever being happier. In the morning she left with her shoes in one hand, and a kiss blown lazily over her shoulder.

On that first morning after my fall from grace, everything looked different; the sky was an angry blue that hurt the eyes, the air was pungent with wild lavender and the sea was filled with whining white motorboats. As we set off toward Nice, Cyril worked out routes that avoided heavy inclines, bypassing the dramatic bulk of the Massif d'Esterel because the bus over-heated easily. We avoided the fire-ravaged scrubland sur-rounding St Raphael and Fréjus, staying mostly to the main roads, but there was a point where the throb of the engine began to exacerbate our hangovers, so we took a turn-off through the pines, firs, olive groves and mimosa trees, looking for a spot where we could buy a beer and a baguette.

'The Romans planted these trees beside the roads so that their footsoldiers could take shelter,' Don pointed out. 'Now motorcyclists keep slamming into them and killing themselves.'

The conversation kept returning to death. The rest of us were no longer virgins. Only Cyril was left, and suddenly it looked like he was the odd one out. He grew nastier as the day progressed. It was as though we were in on a joke that he wasn't being allowed to share.

The sharp morning air felt electrically charged as we sat in a meadow waiting for the bus's radiator to calm itself. Steve talked about what he wanted to do with his life. He had no intention of staying in a hardware store forever, selling locks and drill bits. He wanted to go to art college and learn how to paint. He had started drawing, and had been encouraged by the sale of a picture. Cyril liked working at the depot but saw it as a temporary job, something to do before he discovered what really interested him. I wanted to be a musician. I'd traded some time in a recording studio and was in the process of putting together a demo tape, but work always got in the way. Don wanted to set up a business of his own in the city, something to do with owning a chain of bars. He'd worked out a business plan of sorts, and was on the lookout for investors. By the time we hit the road once more, we had sorted out the rest of our lives.

'So you don't mind what you do so long as it makes you rich.' Don and I wound each other up whenever we discussed the future. It was that stupid argument you have about keeping your scruples once you were rich and powerful, as if you had a choice.

'I'll still have principles, obviously,' he replied, resting his arms on the great black steering wheel and taking his eyes from the road to look at me. 'If you give up what you believe in, you'll be poor anyway.'

'Nice sentiment,' Steve agreed, 'I only hope you manage to keep it.'

'I don't want to turn into my dad,' said Cyril, 'pissed all the time and talking about the good old days, like there was some kind of magical time when he didn't behave like an arsehole.'

'If we all unite with a single political conscience, the young have enough energy to rebuild the world,' offered Sandy, in one of those general French-influenced statements calculated to annoy everyone. But there were riots in Paris that year, so I guess she was just expressing a widely-shared viewpoint.

'You're forgetting one thing,' Steve pointed out. 'The young lack power and money, and once they finally have them, they don't want to change the world anymore, they want to keep it all for themselves. The rich get away with murder.'

Before we could move onto eradicating Third World hunger, Sandy reminded us that she wanted to visit Grasse because she had heard they made perfumes there, and she wanted to buy some bath salts. According to Cyril's map the road was too narrow, the bends too sharp for the bus to handle, so we turned around and coasted onto a long flat road that cut between two plains studded with ochre rocks, lined with rows of dark cypresses. For a while we saw scattered farmhouses in the distance. Then there was nothing but meadowland and woods.

It was as we entered the tunnel of trees that the mood changed. The sunlight was fragmented here, and the black tar road, frayed into earth at its edges, was shadowed in wavering green. The air cooled and for the first time I noticed birdsong, not along the road itself but beyond it, back in the sunlight. It was my turn to drive. Don and Sandy were sitting upstairs. Cyril and Steve had finished their card game and were staring vacantly from the windows when the engine started to noisily slip gears. The bus coasted on to the lowest point of the road, and I knew it would not make the next rise. We came to a stop in the deep green shadows, and I put on the handbrake.

'What's happened?' called Steve, springing up into the driver's cabin.

'I don't know,' I admitted. 'It feels like we've gone into neutral. Take a look under the bonnet, would you?'

Don and Sandy came down from upstairs, and watched as Steve stripped off his shirt and slid beneath the bus. After a couple of minutes he emerged wiping grease on his jeans.

'There's a small rubber grommet that holds all the gear cables together,' he explained. 'It must have perished, so that when you shifted gears it broke and the cables came loose.'

'Is it fixable?' I asked.

'If you can find me a length of flex I can tie the cables together temporarily. It'll be fine so long as you don't put it into neutral. If I can find a truck garage in Nice I'll probably be able to get a ring of about the same diameter. Maybe I can make a temporary one.' He climbed back under the bus to take another look. The mistral tugged at the high branches above our heads. The trees made a strange lonely sound.

'Did it suddenly get cold?' Sandy hugged her thin arms. Don came over and wrapped a sweater around her shoulders. 'It's going to be dark soon. Look how low the sun is.'

'Nothing to worry about,' I promised cheerfully. 'If Steve can't fix it we'll get a lift from someone.'

'Who?' asked Sandy. 'We haven't passed another vehicle in at least an hour. There's no one around for miles.'

'Don't be such a worryguts,' said Cyril, swinging around on the platform pole. 'There's bound to be someone along eventually.' He cocked his head comically, but there was nothing to be heard except the rasp of crickets. Steve's legs stuck out from under the bus. Every once in a while there was a clang of metal and he swore. Finally he emerged, smothered in thick black grease.

'I've managed to tie the cables up, but I don't know how long it'll hold.'

'What did you use?' asked Don.

'I found a packet of rubber johnnies in your bag.'

'You've been going through my stuff?'

'You'd only used one. It said "Super Strong" on the box. Let's hope they're right.'

A pale mist was settling across the fields like milk dispersing in water. We set off carefully, determined to change gear as little as possible. 'How can we best do that?' I asked Don, who was driving.

'Stick to this low route, I guess. It looks flatter, but if anything comes the other way they'll have to go off-road to get around us.' Tree branches continually scraped the roof of the bus. We crawled through a number of derelict villages, past peeling stucco walls, dark doorways and dry fountains. The road became even narrower.

'We could get stuck and not be able to turn around,' warned Cyril, scrutinising his map. 'This road isn't even marked.'

'What else can we do?' I asked. 'If it gets too much, we'll have to stay here the night and walk to a town in the morning.'

'You'll be lucky. There's fuck-all for miles around and we're out of food.'

The bus crept around a tight bend into another tunnel of trees. 'What's that up ahead?' I pointed to the side of the road. A dusty silver Mercedes saloon was badly parked there. I could make out some movement in the shadows.

'What?' Don peered through the windscreen. 'I can't see anything.'

'Neither can I,' complained Steve.

'You need your eyes tested. It's got English number plates.' A sticker on the boot of the car read: 'Come To HOVE'. There was a straw hat on the back window ledge, the kind Englishmen buy when they go to France in the mistaken belief that it makes them look sophisticated. I nudged Don's arm. 'Pull over. It's our lucky day.' He pulled up the brake handle and left the motor idling.

'I'll go and talk to them.' I jumped down from the rear platform and ran on ahead. Evidently the two men inside had not heard me approaching because they looked startled when I knocked on the window of the car. The driver, red-faced and pot-bellied, wearing a blue striped shirt that was too tight to adequately contain him, jerked his head around and studied me with unfocussed eyes. His face was broken-veined and double-chinned. He collected his wits for a moment before partially lowering the electric window. The other man was grey-haired and thin, with a prominent sore-looking nose and a sharp Adam's apple. He remained hunched over the back of the passenger seat with his arms extended to the floor. A chill blast from the air-conditioned interior fanned my face.

'Yes, what is it?' asked the driver in English, as though impatiently answering the door to an unexpected neighbour.

I'd been about to ask him for help, but from what I saw it looked as though the situation might be reversed. The overweight man looked angry and frightened. Clearly, my intrusion wasn't welcome.

'You're English,' I said stupidly, as if this made us all part of the same club. I peered across at the other man, who now raised his head. He looked ill, or drunk, or both. A livid gash on his cheek was spackling blood onto his yellow T-shirt and the leather seat back. Both men were in their late forties. Having caught them doing something they didn't want anyone to see, I could only ramble on with my original request for help.

'We've broken down and, well, I was hoping you might be going near a village where I could call out a mechanic, and get him to fix—'

'I don't know, hang on.' The fat man turned to his companion, who was struggling upright in the passenger seat. 'Michael, this chap wants a lift.' He gestured impatiently at the man's head.

Michael looked in the wing mirror and hastily wiped his bleeding face with an oil rag. 'No, we're not going there,' he began in some confusion. 'Fucking hell, Sam, can't you deal with it?' He turned back to me. 'Now is not a good time, kid, so piss off, will you?'

Sam, the overweight driver, shifted uncomfortably in the driving seat. 'Look, I'm sorry, we're a bit tied up and, ah, can't really help you.'

Their attitude annoyed and puzzled me. They were the ones in the brand new air-conditioned Mercedes and they couldn't even give me a lift? 'It's just that I think we'll be stuck here all night if I can't get a lift to a town,' I explained, 'because no cars have been past for—'

'What part of this conversation didn't you understand, you little prick?' shouted the sickly man suddenly. He writhed about in the seat and kicked open the car door, storming around to my side. He made a grab for my shirt but I ducked back. As I did so, I saw that the rear passenger door was open. A large material-wrapped bundle on the back seat seemed to be slowly sliding out of the car and into the ditch at the side of the road. Something smelled bad.

The fat man manouevred his way out of the car, and pulled his partner aside. 'For Christ's sake, he's just a kid, leave him alone.'

I stared back at the moving bundle, half in the car, half in the road. There were brown leaves and arrowhead-shaped pine needles stuck to it, and it had begun to make a low gurgling noise.

I looked back along the avenue of rustling cypress trees, but the others must have stayed on board, and it was now too dark to even see the outline of the bus.

'Go back to your vehicle, pal. There'll be someone along soon. Just forget you ever saw us, all right?'

'Sure, no problem.' I backed cautiously away. I didn't want trouble. These guys looked burned out and messed up about something, and I really didn't want to know what they'd been doing. Secret cruelties occurred in lonely spots like this.

But as I turned and passed the rear of the Mercedes I couldn't help looking back at the shifting sack, only now I saw that it was a person unballing itself from a foetal position, because a head had appeared. It was a middle-aged woman in a grey cardigan and a dark blue flower-print skirt. Her hair was the same colour as the leaves in the ditch she was heaving herself into. I realised that she was making the gurgling noise because when she looked up at me and tried to speak, blood swilled over her yellow bottom teeth and ran down her chin, forming a scarlet stalactite. She looked desperate and determined to crawl out of the car by dragging herself forward on her elbows. 'What's wrong with her?' I couldn't stop myself from asking.

Now the fat guy, Sam, was coming at me with his thick Mont Blanc wallet open. He was pulling out notes, separating them and counting them at the same time, the way bank tellers do. His breath was hot and sour with brandy. A blood vessel had burst in his right eye, clouding it crimson. He thrust the cash at me. 'Just take these and move on, son.' He checked himself, made a quick calculation, decided he had under-bribed and added several more notes from the wallet. He held his hand further out, like a child trying to feed a zoo animal that's known to bite. 'Go on, take it.'

'I don't want your money,' I said. It was his quick recalculation of the amount that disgusted me. 'What the hell have you done to her?'

'It's his wife.' Sam gestured over at his bony-faced companion. 'She drank too much.'

'What's wrong with her face?'

'He hit her.' The companion's protests were overridden. 'It was sort of – a game – that got a bit out of hand, that's all.'

I looked down at the woman as she pulled herself forward on her elbows, her fat rump slipping off the leather seat and toppling her into the ditch beside the car. It crossed my mind that if I bent down to help, I might be overpowered by the two men. The skinny one had a screwdriver in his hand. We stood silent in an awkward stand-off as she whimpered and spat between us.

'We can take care of this ourselves, sonny.' Sam's money-hand hung half-proffered at his hip, as though he was still hoping I'd take the cash, but was also reluctant to part with it.

'Just tell me what happened. I'm not going until you do.' I kept an eye on the other one, sensing he was the more dangerous of the two. I was just a kid making brave noises, trying not to betray my fear.

'She was fucking me about, that's what,' shouted the skinny companion. The gash on his cheek had reopened, and was dripping on his T-shirt. 'Now either you help us, or you join her.'

'We're not going to make this worse, Michael.' The over-weight driver dragged a handkerchief from his pocket and mopped his sweating forehead.

'That's it, keep using my fucking name. This is all your fault, you're never man enough to see it through, I always have to finish everything you start.' He gave the crawling woman a vicious kick in the gut, and another in the head. She began whimpering more loudly, and tried to draw in her arms and knees as protection, but the amount of haemorrhaged matter she was leaving behind her as she moved suggested that her internal injuries were already serious. She was missing a sandal, and the back of her skirt was caught up in her pants. She was dying, and it was so undignified.

Michael dropped to his knees and started to do something that caused the woman to shriek. When I dared to look, I saw that he was banging a screwdriver into her ear with the flat of his hand. I gave a yell, ran forward and stood beside her, flinching with indecision as Sam opened the car boot and removed a large yellow sponge. He returned to the back seat and began wiping smears from the cream leather upholstery while Michael kicked at the end of the screwdriver with his foot.

The scene was tripped into my memory like some distant, grotesque photograph of a forgotten crime; the red-faced driver carefully wiping the seats, his stomach pushing over the belt of his trousers, studiously ignoring his screaming companion who, deranged with anger, was leaping around a body with a screwdriver sticking out of its head, a pathetic victim-thing that looked no longer human, just a squirming sack wrapped in pleated floral material. The shiny silver Mercedes still gleamed in the dying light of the day, half lost in the deep cool verdure of the arched trees. Beside its rear tyre a stream of crimson was filling the ditch beside the road.

I ran for help.

I told myself that there was nothing else I could do. I ran without looking back, into the deeper darkness of the tunnel, then out onto the brow of the road where the bus had stopped. Its engine was still running, and its headlights suddenly came on. Sandy and Don were standing beside the boarding platform as Cyril and Steve ran forward.

'Where the hell have you been?' asked Steve. 'We came looking for you.'

'Just beyond the end of the road there.' I gestured back into the darkness.

'That's where we looked,' said Cyril, who clearly didn't believe me.

'I was beside the Mercedes.' I barely knew how to start explaining what I had seen, how I had hopelessly failed to intervene.

'What Mercedes? There was no car.'

'Don't talk shit, it's right there.'

'No, mate.'

'Come with me.' I grabbed at Steve's sleeve, pulling them all forward in turn. 'Before they get away.' We walked through the tunnel of branches to the spot where I had encountered the travellers and their victim, but there was no sign of the Mercedes, and now it was too dark to find the bloody ditch.

'They must have pushed her body into the woods,' I cried. 'Help me. She could still be alive.'

I was still shoving into the brambles when I felt their hands on my arms, pulling me back toward the bus and the star-pierced night.

Nothing went right after that. We slept in the bus and searched the road again the next morning, but found nothing. Don hitched a ride to the nearest town and got the bus repaired. I argued with the others, went to the police and eventually convinced them to listen.

Two doubtful gendarmes took me back to the place where I thought I had seen the Mercedes, but we couldn't find the spot. One stretch of road looked just like the next, and after a while they stopped pretending to believe me. The rest of the holiday was a disaster. Sandy angrily returned to her car without us. We went on, drunkenly rowing until the bus broke down again. This time it defied all attempts at being repaired, and we had to leave it behind. The last time I saw the big red bus it was sitting in a lay-by near a cement factory, abandoned to the corrosive air.

We took trains and a ferry home.

After that, the four of us drifted apart. We went back to our real names. Those others belonged to characters from the film we were copying.

'Don' died of a drug overdose when he was twenty-eight. 'Steve' just disappeared. Only 'Cyril' and I are still in contact, although now he goes by his real name – Michael. I'm still plain Sam. I'm no longer a skinny kid, and have put on quite a bit of weight. I have to buy a lot of business lunches to keep my clients happy. Our company's deep in debt, and once the auditors start investigating, we'll all be in trouble. Michael has gone grey and looks ill. He's married to a woman he hates, and I'm having an affair with her behind his back. We drink too much.

We lie too much. We're going on holiday together in the Mercedes, driving through France.

I was seventeen when I met my degraded mirror-image. I am forty now, and hardly a day passes when I don't think of that sunset evening in the forest. I have already created the circumstances that will return me to that dark spot. I saw the man I have become, and there is not a damned thing I can do about it now. Once you fall, you never get back up.

But as the shadows of fate close in around me, how I miss the bus, the freedom, the laughter, the purity that lasted until my first summer holiday.

HITLER'S HOUSEGUEST

It was a good deal prettier than I had imagined. The schloss is above a deep green valley surrounded on three sides by verdant Austrian territory. In the distance I could see the great blue double-hump of Mount Watzmann, its crest thick with the first snows of approaching winter. To the south lies the Königsee, a picturesque Alpine lake of the kind that finds favour in the Führer's paintings.

Although it is now a town of leisurely pursuits, Berchtesgaden was once the home of salt mines, and later became the summer residence of inbred Bavarian kings. There has been much mad blood, bad blood here.

My coach brought me to the cable railway linking the town with Obersalzberg, five hundred metres above it. It had been snowing heavily for some minutes by the time we arrived before the elegant façade of the residence. My host's servants were waiting in the courtyard to greet us, their hands and faces translucent with cold, and the snow that had settled like white epaulettes on their shoulders told me they had been standing there since it started.

I knew that, apart from the Berghof, here were the private homes of Hermann Goering, Martin Bormann and other Nazi leaders, that the grey concrete lumps on the hillside were their air raid shelters, their barracks, their secret installations. The people are told that my host lives a simple, unostentatious life. How easily they are taken in. I have heard his retreat described as a 'chalet'. Berchtesgaden is as much like a chalet as Dracula's castle. Red and gold are not so predominant here as they are at the rallies, with their endless dreary banner flags, acres of red stamped with black swastikas.

The liveried houseboys stepped smartly forward and took our luggage. I had but one small leather case, and was loath to let it leave my side, but there was the matter of security. I was told that it would be delivered to my room, but not, I was sure, before its contents had been thoroughly searched.

'Anthony Pettifer?' I heard my name called. In the light of what I knew about Hitler's roll-calls, the sensation was a chilling one. I stepped into the marble foyer, and was greeted by an austere, sharp-faced gentleman by the name of Herr Kettner. Each of us was formally greeted in turn. No English was spoken; no allowance was ever made for the presence of other nationalities.

'The Führer regrets that he cannot be present for dinner this evening. Urgent business calls him back to Berlin. We hope, however, that he will be able to return tomorrow.'

Kettner informed us that he was the head of the household, but he had the bearing of an SS guard. He showed us into the main dining room. There were four of us: myself, supposedly representing *The Times*, an American property magnate called Cain, the Berlin press officer Schwenner, and, of course, the radiantly beautiful Virginia Pernand, with whom I had once had an affair.

'You see, of course, how the Führer appreciates comfort,' said Kettner. 'Only the best is good enough for him.'

The dining room astonished me. It was easily sixty feet long and forty feet wide. A huge oak table ran down the centre, and sat upon a vast Persian rug. Four etchings by Albrecht Dürer hung on the softly-lit walls. I had been told that the room in which Hitler usually received his guests boasted a spectacular view over the Alps, and housed his aviary of rare birds, but on this occasion the room was not in use.

'Berchtesgaden has fourteen rooms for guests, but you four are the only ones invited this weekend,' said Kettner, with a hint of warning in his voice. 'Each bedroom has its own private bathroom. Dinner tonight will be served at eight o'clock precisely.' He stopped at the foot of the great staircase and struck a commanding pose, as though preparing himself to be photographed for some kind of Berlin *Nacktkültur* magazine. I saw the rest of his staff hold their collective breath.

'One more thing.' Kettner felt inside his tunic and pulled out several typed sheets of paper. 'These are the instructions the Führer demands that his guests obey so long as they are under this roof.' He handed one sheet to each of us. I glanced down at mine and read:

Instructions To Visitors

1. Smoking is forbidden, especially in the bedrooms.
2. You will not talk to servants or carry any parcels or messages from the premises for any servant.
3. At all times the Führer must be addressed and spoken of as such, and never as 'Herr Hitler' or any other title.
4. Women guests are forbidden to use excessive cosmetics and must on no account use polish on their nails.
5. Guests must present themselves within two (2) minutes of the announcing bell. No one may sit at the table or leave until the Führer has sat down or left.
6. No one will remain seated in a room when the Führer enters.
7. Guests must retire to their rooms at 11:00pm unless expressly asked to remain by the Führer.
8. Guests will remain in this wing and on no account enter the domestic quarters, the offices, the quarters of the SS officers or the political police bureau.
9. Guests are absolutely forbidden to discuss their visit with strangers. The conveying of information about the Führer's private life will be visited by the severest penalties.

There were several other clauses and codicils in the same fashion, all of which left me with a problem – how to get through the weekend alive. You see, I was here at the schloss under false pretences. My identification papers were real enough, but I was no longer employed by *The Times*. Indeed, they had barred me from ever working for them again, thanks to a little misunderstanding over expenses that occurred on a junket to Nice. I was here to see Greta.

I first met Greta Kehl in a hotel in Vienna, before she came to work here at Berchtesgaden as a housemaid. Over the course of my stay there I had come to know her well, and we had become lovers. At the end of the month I had asked her to come away with me, but, pursuing some strange destiny of her own, she had refused my offer, accepting a transfer to a Bayern-based cleaning company. In the weeks that followed, her face haunted my sleep. I knew that we should be together, but needed to convince her of my heartfelt intentions. My letters, addressed to the agency in the town, were returned unopened.

Luckily my skills as a journalist stood me in good stead, and I located the address of her parents in Salzburg. Mr Kehl informed me that his daughter had become a committed fascist, and longed to serve the Führer, but his wife prevented him from giving me details of her appointment.

It was a simple matter to check with the agency – I flattered the matron who ran the office with the thought that I would like to write a profile on her – and ascertain that Greta was employed at the schloss. I still possessed my journalist's union card (although it had been cancelled) and was able to pull off a couple of favours, albeit with an element of blackmail, that had me placed on the waiting list of visitors to Berchtesgaden.

And so I had arrived in Hitler's private residence, with forged credentials and a story that could be demolished with a simple phonecall, determined to woo back the girl I had lost in that Vienna hotel. The first of my problems was gaining access to the staff quarters from which we had expressly been forbidden.

I then had to persuade Greta of my good intentions, and ensure that she did not attempt to raise the alarm and have me thrown to the SS guards.

I had another cause to be worried. In a house governed by a constricting code of acceptable behaviour, one could not afford to drop one's guard for even a second, and as a registered sufferer of Tourette's Syndrome, I was worried that the stress, fatigue and anxiety created by my surroundings would bring on an attack.

I had been a sufferer of Tourette's Syndrome for six years, since I was eighteen. It is an inherited neurological disease that manifests itself in sudden violent involuntary motion, tics, grimaces, flapping of the arms, barking cries, jumping, jerking, spitting and the uncontrollable shouting of obscenities. Very little else is known about this most anti-social of all illnesses. As you can imagine, I was praying not to run into any of Herr Hitler's staff while in the grip of an attack.

I had found that bouts could be brought on by the consumption of certain foodstuffs, and might last for days. During this time I was liable to injure myself and others. I resolved to be very careful about my meals over the weekend, and eat as little as possible.

My bedroom contained a signed copy of *Mein Kampf*, and several pornographic French books imported from Paris. Above the large, hard bed a sinister portrait of Hitler dominated the room. I went along the corridor to visit the little Berlin press officer, Schwenner, and found his room to be identical, down to the hand-stitched bedspread and the way the towels in the bathroom had been folded.

Schwenner had absolutely no desire to be here. He had been invited because Goebbels had insisted upon it, and there was simply no way of refusing. Like me, he was under no illusions about our host. He, too, had seen the frenzied adulation of the motorcade crowds, just as he had seen the beatings on the streets. But we were bystanders, because it was a larger history beyond our control, and we needed to stay alive in order to bear witness.

Our group – one of many such groups organised to visit the schloss that year – had been chosen in order that we might spread the word about Hitler's good works. This was to involve spending the whole of Saturday listening to a series of boring lectures given by various high-ranking propaganda experts. The next day there would be more lectures, and we were to leave late on Sunday afternoon. But I had every intention of disappearing under cover of darkness and taking Greta with me.

The house was stuffed to the point of vulgarity with famous paintings and tapestries, all of them on permanent loan from Germany's greatest museums. When I heard the dinner-bell sound, I was still struggling to get into my bow-tie, and was forced to rush. According to Schwenner, there had been stories circulating at his press agency of guests who had failed to arrive at Hitler's meal table on time. What happened to them was never known; they vanished late at night.

As I made haste toward the stairs, I saw Virginia approaching, resplendent in an emerald silk gown. 'I'm not used to coming down to dinner without makeup,' she complained. 'The maid came to my room and warned me about earrings; we're not to be seen wearing them. I know he likes his farmgirls natural and rosy-cheeked, but this is too ridiculous. Why are you here, by the way? I thought they fired you.'

'Special assignment,' I quickly replied. '*The Times* wants to know whether Hitler is sincere about appeasement.'

'Well, you won't be any the wiser after this weekend. I don't suppose the Führer will even put in an appearance. He hardly ever does these days, you know. Not that it makes much difference. One wrong foot in front of any of his staff and you're for the chop; everything gets reported back.'

The dinner was served on finest Dresden china. When Hitler himself was present, solid silver plate from the Jewish merchants of Nuremberg, stolen by Himmler's agents, was elaborately arranged along the table. I looked at the meal in alarm; the simple peasant fare we had heard so much about was nowhere in evidence. There were rich pâtés, soups, game and pork courses, the very foodstuffs doctors had warned me to stay away from. I tried to eat as little as possible, but servants surrounded us, watching our every move. Six members of the SS guard were present, making a total of ten diners, and a servant for every guest. I saw with a thrill that the maid standing to attention behind Cain's chair was Greta. I had forgotten how pale her skin was, as fine as the Dresden from which we ate.

I tried to think of a way to attract her attention. The conversation from Kettner and the other SS men was stultifyingly dull. They were discussing grain imports and railways. Everyone was being careful to avoid the Jewish question. I felt ashamed about this; how complicit did this make us, if we could not even bring up the subject in an oblique fashion?

We were just placing our knives and forks together (we were carefully watching each other to make sure that nobody finished late) when I saw that Greta had recognised me. Her hand flew to her mouth, and she only just managed to turn her expression of surprise into a discreet cough. Kettner glared sharply at her. She avoided my gaze for the rest of the meal. When guards took the male guests off to the smoking room, the servants filed out into the corridor. They would not clear the table until the doors were closed between us. I made sure I was the last one to pass into the smoking room. I had but a few moments in which to act. I grabbed Greta's wrist as she passed before me.

'Why are you here?' she whispered angrily.

'I came here for you,' I hissed back. 'I love you. I'm sorry about Vienna, I was a fool. Please forgive me. I am leaving in the small hours of Saturday night, and I want to take you along with me.'

'I can't. Do you know what happens to people who try to get away from Berchtesgaden?'

'I'll protect you,' I promised uncertainly. 'I can get you out of the country.'

'And what of my family? You think I can just leave everything behind because you suddenly want me?' Her grey eyes narrowed angrily.

'I beg you, at least consider my offer.'

'Go, go in before they miss you.' She pushed me in front of her just as the head butler turned into the corridor.

We seated ourselves in front of a gigantic ugly fireplace and were offered cigars as Kettner launched into another interminable description of the Führer's plans for 'rehabilitating' those industrialists who failed to comprehend the glories of the coming world order. We were indeed fortunate, he explained, because the Führer had confirmed that he would be dining with us tomorrow night.

As Kettner spoke, I felt the first warning twitch of Tourette's settling over me. My skin prickled hotly, and a muscle in my face began to twitch. I stilled it by resting my fist against my cheek in what I hoped was an attitude of relaxation. Only Schwenner seemed to notice that there was something wrong. At ten minutes to eleven, Kettner checked the mantelpiece clock, clapped his hands and packed us off to bed as though we were schoolchildren. 'I must insist that you turn out your room lights no later than ten minutes past the hour,' he warned.

'Did you see the way Kettner looked at my dress?' asked Virginia as we returned to our rooms. 'Highly disapproving. I thought he was going to say something. Wait until he sees what I'm wearing for the Führer tomorrow. I've brought my best jewellery with me. My mother's sapphire necklace and a pair of matching earrings.'

'Just be careful,' said Schwenner. 'People are being shot for expressing "decadent" views. It doesn't pay to look too glamorous.'

'Darling, they can't do anything to me,' she replied airily, reaching her door. 'In fact, I'm going break Rule Number One right now and have a cigarette in my bedroom.'

'I suppose you think you're safe because you know too much. Well, we *all* know too much. It's just that you have the means of distributing the information.' Virginia was an overseas correspondent for the BBC. 'I bid you goodnight.' Schwenner waited until Virginia had shut her door, and turned to me. I could hear the servants on the stairs not far behind us.

'What was wrong with you tonight? I saw your face.'

'Muscular spasms, that's all.' I tried to make light of it. 'I'm over-tired.'

'Well, if you're sure.'

I could tell by the look on the little press agent's face that he didn't believe me. A few minutes later, the maids came around to check that our lights were out. I contemplated tiptoeing down to the kitchens to search for Greta, but the lights had been turned off throughout the schloss, and I was not yet familiar enough with the layout to safely find my way back in the dark.

Frost formed on the inside of the bedroom windows. I awoke with muscles aching, my limbs numb with cold. Someone was knocking sharply on the door. 'It's seven o'clock, sir,' called the maid. 'Breakfast will be served in fifteen minutes.'

During the night, someone had entered my room and neatly laid my morning clothes out in the dressing area of the bathroom. I resented the intrusion, but at least it allowed me to reach the table on time. Cain and Schwenner were already helping themselves to the vast platters of eggs and cold meats, but there was no sign of Virginia.

'She's gone,' whispered Schwenner, passing behind me with his plate. 'The SS guards took her away in the night.'

'How do you know?' I asked.

'She was in the room next to mine. I heard them come for her at around three o'clock. They didn't even allow her time to pack. Her bedroom door was open this morning, bags gone and bed made up fresh, just as if no one was ever there.'

'Do you think she's all right? I mean, surely they can't do anything.'

'She drank too much at dinner. And she smoked in her room. I could smell it. I hope they'll just deport her. People go missing so easily these days. The Gestapo have a little trick of releasing you but muddling your papers, so that you're arrested by someone else. Who knows where she'll end up?'

'But surely the BBC won't allow—'

'They'll do exactly what they're told. Eat up, here comes Cheerful Charlie.'

Kettner was making his way past the buffet. Despite the early hour, he was in full dress uniform. 'I trust you slept well,' he announced. 'We have a full day, commencing with a talk from one of our leading economic experts at eight o'clock precisely. You will find seats and documentation laid out in the drawing room.' No mention was made of Virginia's disappearance.

The economist, a rotund man in a cheap grey suit reeking of body odour, had greased-back hair above pale side-stubble, and a complexion like a burst sausage. His keenness to explain the workings of an economy based on a two-tier system of first and second-class citizens was fascinating in an offensive way, and typified the blinkered philistinism of the regime. The chairs were hard and the room was cold, but at least we would stay awake that way. I discreetly checked my watch and kept an eye out for Greta.

At eleven, she appeared bearing a trolley and served us with bitter coffee. By now, even Kettner had lost interest and left the room. Two SS guards remained at the door. There was never any effort made to disguise the fact that we were prisoners in the schloss. I used Kettner's absence as an opportunity to speak with Greta.

'Have you had a chance to think about my offer?' I asked as I accepted a cup from her.

'I can't,' she whispered, nervously watching the guards, aware that I was breaking Hitler's second guest rule.

'Let me worry about that. All you have to do is be ready to leave at a moment's notice.' I saw the nearest guard look up at us, his eyes narrowing beneath his cap, and felt a muscle in my right arm involuntarily jump, causing me to tip the cup on its side in the saucer. Coffee splashed onto the table.

'I'm awfully sorry,' I apologised, but the last word turned into a bark and I was forced to fake a coughing fit. An attack of this severity, I knew, could last for several days. Schwenner came over and touched my shoulder. 'Are you all right, old man?' he asked.

'The coffee was too hot,' I assured him. When I looked back, Greta had slipped from the room.

The day dragged past, one dull lecture blurring into the next: the smelting of iron ore, electricity consumption, production targets for the manufacture of jute and sisal. The question-and-answer sessions at the end of each talk grew shorter and shorter as we became enervated, weighed down by the bulk of statistics paraded before us. We were careful to be seen making copious notes, because we knew that our behaviour would be reported to the Führer.

As the hour for my dinner with Adolph Hitler approached, weariness and tension increased the strength of my muscular attacks. I decided to take Cain and Schwenner into my confidence, and explain the symptoms of my illness.

'You mean you could just start cussing at Hitler?' Cain complained incredulously.

'It's possible,' I warned him. 'It's important that nothing stresses me.' They eventually agreed, with some reluctance, to cover for me should an attack become serious.

'He's not come back to see us, he's here to ask advice from Ossietz,' said Schwenner. I had heard that Karl Ossietz was Germany's Rasputin, Hitler's astrologer. There were said to be five rooms in Berchtesgaden that were never photographed, apart from the 'Eagle's Nest', Hitler's private retreat high above the main building. The most important of these was the Chamber of Stars on the roof, which had a ceiling of dark blue glass showing the movements of planets and constellations. The astrologer had predicted a long and happy reign for the Führer, but no one was allowed to speak of Ossietz, on pain of death. Given the loss of control caused by my condition, I tried to forget that I had ever heard his name.

And so we attended dinner.

Hitler was smaller than I had expected, rather drab-looking and unimpressive. It was hard to imagine that this was the man upon whom the eyes of the world were riveted. His handshake was surprisingly weak and soft, without any real strength, his eyes queerly penetrating, endlessly suspicious. There was no hint of humour, curiosity or humanity about him. Having curtly greeted us, he took his seat at the head of the table and sat immobile as he was served different food by a waiter we had not seen before. Presumably this was to safeguard the risk of poisoning.

As the meal progressed he questioned each of us in turn, as though checking that we had been paying attention through the day. And yet, it was clear that he hardly heard our answers, which was just as well, as at one point I found myself inserting the word 'arsehole' into my reply. Greta's presence behind my chair was making me uneasy, and this in turn exacerbated my symptoms. As the soup plates were cleared away, she deftly slipped a piece of paper onto the napkin spread across my lap. I felt sure that someone must have seen, but the Fuhrer was in full flow, and the attention of the room was entirely focussed on him. I used the moment to unfold the note and read it. *Meet me in the kitchen at midnight.*

I crushed the paper and slid it into my pocket, excited that she had at least agreed to discuss the idea of coming with me. She had forgiven me for my disgraceful behaviour in Vienna, and was now prepared to place her future in my hands. I knew that she was due to finish her first duty-period tonight, and would be allowed home briefly to the town in the valley, which meant that she had a ticket and the necessary identification. We would board the train from the schloss before anyone had a chance to miss us.

I tried to pay attention to our host, who was now glaring at a salad and eating in silence. As I did so, I fought the urge to burst out with a string of filthy epithets. It was becoming harder and harder to control myself, the result of the rich food I had eaten and the increasing tension of the situation.

'And so, Mr Cain,' said Kettner suddenly, 'I understand that you are purchasing a great amount of property between Köln and Bonn. I am told your profits are set to increase as the Jews move out of these cities.'

I was shocked. I had not imagined Cain to be a war profiteer.

'Surely you would not suggest that such buildings should be left empty, to rot and collapse,' said Cain indignantly. A foolish move on his part, I thought, to betray any strength of feeling.

'Perhaps not, but surely these houses should be appropriated for use by those who further the glorious cause of the Fatherland rather than those who seek to line their own pockets. Before purchasing any more, I would make sure your own house is in order.' A chill draught crept across the room as everyone concentrated intently on their food.

The Führer lowered his cutlery after taking only a few bites, and waited impatiently for his plate to be removed. He stared at each of us in turn, then, nodding a curt goodnight, rose and left the table, closely followed by his guards.

Cain breathed a sigh of relief. Schwenner took a nervous draught of his wine. I muttered a stream of obscenities and allowed the muscles in my arms to bunch. My left eyelid had begun to flutter uncontrollably.

'Well, gentlemen, I don't know about you but I'm exhausted,' sighed Cain, tension trembling his voice. 'I suggest we retire to our bedrooms.'

*

I had set the alarm on my clock for fifteen minutes to midnight, but was too nervous to fall asleep. By the appointed hour, the lights were out all over the schloss – with the exception of the brazier that burned day and night in the room next to the dome on the other side of the building, where Hitler sat studying the stars with his astrologer. According to Schwenner, Ossietz was due in from Berlin. The press agent sensed that something was up. He had heard that Hitler's most trusted adviser spoke to few of his staff, and was hated by all of them. Goering, it was said, refused to stay in the same room with him. When ill-omens were received, the Führer was preoccupied and quarrelsome, dangerous to be near. His astrologer was expected to deliver a pronouncement, and who knew what trouble his predictions might cause?

The clear mountain air ensured that the grounds were bright with starlight. I knew that it would be difficult crossing the courtyard to the gates of the property. I had allowed for an escape route once we were free of the schloss, but had been unable to make plans covering the interior of the building.

The kitchens – what I could make out of them in the dark – were magnificent. Everything was electric, and of the latest design. Here was final proof that the Führer was a stranger to frugal living. In the far corridor leading to the gardens beyond, a grey-uniformed guard sat with his back to me. I crept across the flagstones, trying not to let the metal tips on my soles connect with the floor. A shadowed figure wearing a midnight blue dirndl beckoned to me. The traditional dress accentuated Greta's slim form. She raised a white arm in the moonlight and held a finger to her lips as I approached.

'I'm pleased to see you have reached the right decision,' I could not help telling her. 'I knew you would agree to come with me, and have planned everything accordingly.' Greta pulled me back into a corridor leading to the servants' quarters. I suddenly found myself walking on bare boards, surrounded by scabbed plaster walls. Clearly, the wealth of the Third Reich did not extend to those who served it at a lower level.

'We must act quickly,' I said anxiously. 'The last train back to town leaves in less than fifteen minutes.'

Greta reached up and sealed my talkative lips with a dry kiss. 'I'll lead the way. I know every inch of this place.' She moved ahead in the darkness, scurrying through the rear corridors until I sensed that we were passing behind the main dining hall. I realised now how much of the building was fake; the great stone fireplace, for example, was backed with plastered lathes, little more than an elaborate stage prop. Greta turned at the end of the passage and ascended a steep flight of steps. The muscles started to tingle uncontrollably in my arms and throat.

'Are you sure this is right?' I called to her softly, but she was too far ahead to hear. We emerged on the first floor at the rear of the building, just past the first set of guest bedrooms. I jumped forward and caught Greta's wrist as she was about to climb another set of stairs. 'We need to go down to reach the courtyard, not up.'

'You cannot go across the courtyard. It's constantly watched, and our footprints in the snow will betray us. The only safe way out is to the back, against the mountain wall.' It was obvious now that I thought about it; the slopes that led to the 'Eagle's Nest' were in the shadow of the mountain, and would be harder to patrol. We could make our way around and join the road further down. But in taking this route, I noted that we were dangerously near Hitler's private observatory, and the light still shone within its blue glass dome.

We reached a corridor clearly intended for private use by the Führer himself. Its walls were covered with gold-painted astrological symbols and designs taken from the zodiac. No more than four strides away stood the wide door behind which Hitler conferred with the constellations. There was only one other exit, through an arch sealed off by another oak door. Greta opened it, and revealed a sloping corridor leading into darkness. She paused beneath the arch as though lost. Gathering her thoughts, she turned and placed a cold hand over my heart.

'I can take you no further.'

'What do you mean?' It was then that I noticed the emerald necklace glittering at her throat. I reached out to touch it. 'That belongs to Virginia.'

'I suppose you had her as well. She doesn't look so pretty now.' Her cruel smile was halfway in shadow. She pushed my hand away. 'Now you must stay here.'

'But I thought you were coming with me.' Electrical impulses raced through the nerve-endings in my hands, shaking my fingers spasmodically.

'Do you seriously think I would betray my party for a weakling Englishman?' she hissed.

'But you can't leave me here!' Neurological tremors rippled deep in my musculature, and I began to shake.

'Give me your watch.' Her hands clawed at my wrist as I tried to prevent her from unclasping the leather strap. My own hands were beyond my control now.

She was still trying to prise open the buckle when the door to the astrology room opposite started to open. With a small cry of terror, Greta shrank back and ran off into the darkened passageway, pulling its door shut behind her. I was left alone in the zodiac corridor as Adolph Hitler emerged from his star chamber.

He was still dressed in the grey suit he had worn to dinner, and although his tie was slightly loosened he still seemed paralysed with formality, as postured as a waxwork dummy. Behind him, within the chamber, I could see the figure of another man, whom I assumed to be Ossietz.

Hitler walked slowly forward along the centre of the corridor, the forefinger of his right hand resting against his dark chin, his eyes downcast, his pace measured. A single strand of his impeccably greased hair had slipped over his forehead. The anxiety I had been feeling all night turned into a wave of wild terror as I realised that I was blocking the Führer's path.

My heart felt as though it had stopped beating. Bitter teardrops of sweat condensed on my brow. An unrestrained string of babble rose in my throat. I bit the words off as the muscles around my mouth fought for dominance. The Führer was staring right at me.

'Hairy cocks,' I barked at Hitler. 'Fucking shitty hairy fanny arse cock tits.'

The Fuhrer widened his dead, pale eyes.

I realised that he was not staring at me, but through me. He was seeing something in his mind's eye, something so vast, so unimaginable, so nightmarish that his present surroundings were completely invisible to him. He looked as though his soul was being seized and squeezed by the Devil himself.

Hitler walked on, seeing only the vision in his head. Grabbing the moment, I fell into the corridor at my back, yanking open the door and closing the latch behind me. I had already planned to leave my belongings in my room. Now I flew as fast as my shaking legs would move, toward the rear mountain-wall exit that Greta had described.

I ran through the darkened side of the grounds, and caught that departing train with seconds to spare. I felt sure that guards would appear at the last moment to pull me out of the carriage. As I fled Germany, I wondered what the Führer had been told by Ossietz that could turn his eyes so deeply into the void. I wanted to know what he had seen inside himself.

During the months that followed, when the world witnessed what one man was capable of doing, I discovered too many answers.

DEALING WITH THE SITUATION

'Because it won't turn off, that's how I know.'

She switches the cordless phone to her other ear, holding it in place with her shoulder while she picks up Emma and checks her knickers. It's her youngest girl's first full week out of disposable pants and she has to keep watching for accidents. The flat is cramped, too small for a woman with three small daughters, but where else could they go?

'I mean it'll turn a bit but it won't go all the way. There's no need, I've tried it a dozen times. All right, stay on the line.' She doesn't want the plumber to hang up because it took her three days to get hold of him.

Angie sets down the baby and the phone and tries the tap again. It makes a horrible squealing noise like tyres on wet tarmac, but it won't turn off. Water is churning around the U-bend with a low vibration that suggests something metallic has entered the pipework, a fork perhaps.

Angie picks up the phone again. 'Well, of course I don't want to leave it running, it's emptying my hot tank. No, I don't know what the other noise is, that's something separate.' She scans the kitchen for children, her gaze sweeping like a prison guard's searchlight. Emma is sitting on the floor, hypnotised by a tangle of tinsel. Victoria is at the table, quietly colouring in a Christmas star, her pale legs kicking the chair. Melanie is helping Mummy with the laundry, an exercise that consists of pulling clean wet towels out of the washing machine and dumping them on top of the cat's food bowl. Angie hadn't intended to name her children after the Spice Girls, but nobody pointed out what she'd done until after John died, and then she was so embarrassed that she decided to keep quiet.

The kitchen is a hopeful yellow, but the hope has started to peel and needs repainting. An imbecilic DJ chatters on the radio, something about Santa being an alien, but it's too far away to switch off from here. Someone upstairs is hammering. Angie pushes a dangling strand of blonde hair from her sightline and peers down the plug-hole. 'I just told you, the clanking thing is nothing to do with the washer, I think one of the kids put something – no, I want you to fix the leak. I need to run baths and I'm sick of boiling kettles, and – well, I know what the date is but when *could* you come?'

Melanie is dragging wet towels across the room, but they're caught on the cat's bowl, which overturns, sending water and ripe jelly-caked meat across the tiles. Angie snatches the towels from her and nearly drops the receiver as the call-waiting signal sounds in her ear. 'I'll have to ring you back. Give me your mobile number.' She throws the towels into a corner, they'll have to be washed again, and takes a crayon from Victoria's box, causing the girl to scream in annoyance. Angie writes the number in crimson on the white counter beside the sink and takes the other call.

'Lucy? No, of course it wasn't, I don't even want to think about dating again, it was the plumber. Well, that's because I was holding for a long time. I've got no hot water and he says his van's broken down, plus Christmas Eve makes it double time. I wish they'd admit they've taken on too much work instead of going for sympathy – are you crying?'

Her older sister is often crying. She only exists in two states, tears or joy, both in the land of hysterics. Lucy is 'unlucky with men', that's how their mother describes it. What this means is that Lucy, who is forty-two, hefty and panicking about her baby clock, loves men so intensely that just being with her can suck all the air from the room, and her partners leave in order to start breathing again. 'Why, what did he do to you? Uh-huh, I'm listening, go on.'

Angie chucks the crayon back into her middle daughter's box in order to stop the yelling. She tries to concentrate on Lucy's problems, but they're always the same, and their conversations remain stubbornly circular. She watches little Emma as she listens. Emma worries her. She isn't noticing things the way she should, and she sits far too still. The pediatrician said to give it a few more weeks before running tests but—

'Yes, I'm still here. Perhaps he needs a break, you know, a little space. No, he won't leave you for good. He'll probably just be glad of a—'

Her mobile goes. It's set to Vibrate And Ring, and the resonance sends it skittering along the counter so that she only just manages to catch it before it falls. 'Lucy, let me call you back. Five minutes, I promise. Make yourself some tea. Put a spoonful of Manuka honey in it.' As she switches phones she looks beneath the sink. Water is pouring from the white plastic U-bend all over the detergent boxes.

'Mummy.' Melanie points to her nose. It has pine needles sticking out of it.

'How did you do that?'

'I looked inside the tree. What can I do now?'

'You're supposed to be changed, both of you.' But the childminder's not here yet, so she relents. 'All right, you can help me wipe down,' she hands Melanie a sponge and returns her attention to the phone.

'Mrs Reeves?'

'Who is this?'

'Mrs Angela Reeves?'

'Yes, who is this?'

'I was with your husband, John.'

'Oh.' Her voice shrinks. She waits for more while she watches Melanie setting about her task with great seriousness.

'Dying in the line of duty like that, it's a noble thing.'

'He was chasing a car thief. The guy stood his ground. He had an iron bar.' Fifteen months ago. Can it already have been that long?

'I bet he left you short of money.'

Suddenly the call bothers her. 'What did you say your name was?'

'I'm the man your husband arrested.'

The house phone rings sharply, making her jump. She can't take the call right now. It's either Lucy or the plumber, and she can call the plumber back. She looks to the sink, where Melanie has just finished carefully wiping his mobile number away.

'Oh Mel! Look what you did!' The number has gone. Lucy called on the house phone since, so she can't hit Redial. The house phone stops ringing.

'What did you say?' she asks her mobile.

'He arrested me, and I hit him.'

'How did you get this number?'

'I hit him and he just went over. But you know that. You were in court the whole time. I watched you.'

Startled, she shuts off the mobile and throws it down onto the counter. Emma is launching herself across the floor in that strange way babies have of running with their arms held high, staring delightedly down as though balancing on the brow of a hill. Angie scoops her up because she's heading for the wet patch beside the washing machine, and there's catfood everywhere. The cat is threading its way between them all, trying to lick the floor. Victoria is cutting star shapes from a large sheet of coloured paper, but she's not allowed scissors, so what is she using?

'Vicki, show me your other hand.'

The house phone rings, and Angie slips it under her ear as she advances on her oldest daughter. 'One double eight five. What? You're speaking to her. Wait.' The voice goes on in her ear, reading something from a card. She can tell instantly that it's a cold-call.

'Wait, this is a cold-call, isn't it? Look, I realise you're just doing your job but it's an invasion of my privacy, so I'm putting the phone down now to save us both time.' The moment she does, it rings again.

'Lucy, I said I'd call you back.' She pulls an adjustable spanner from the toolbox beneath the sink and fixes it around the base of the tap, trying not to drop the phone into the water. Upstairs, the hammering doubles in intensity. 'Things are difficult right now, that's all.' An understatement; she's supposed to be at work. Christmas Eve will be busy but the child-minder hasn't turned up. Angie is already an hour late. She is careful not to mention the call she received on her mobile. Like many people on the police force, John had enemies. It was part of the job. 'No, I'm sure he didn't mean it. Men can be very cruel in the heat of the moment. I don't suppose he really wants to break up.'

She wishes she believed her own words. John had always been wonderful. Lucy's boyfriend has been with her for ten months, and wants to get the hell out. There's no use telling her. It's like pointing out a bright red pattern to someone who's colour-blind. Her sister is crying again, great hacking sobs of self-pity. Angie can see her now, sitting on the edge of a pink bedspread surrounded by the kind of large cuddly toys that give men the creeps.

'Lucy, I really have to go.' As she listens, she urges Victoria to give up her cutting instrument. Where the hell did she get scissors from? The sewing basket in the lounge, but that means she must have smuggled them into the kitchen, the little – Angie needs to take them from her. Her right hand is still pushing against the spanner. It slips against the serrated base of the tap and bruises her knuckles. A horrendous screaming noise comes from the radio, following by the guffaws of the DJ, who says; 'Isn't that the worst noise you ever heard?'

She gives the spanner a thump with the heel of her hand and the nut shears, freeing the tap from its mooring on the sink-top. A fierce two-foot plume of water rises out of the hole and spatters everything. Behind her, the two older girls scream in delighted horror. Even Emma looks up and grins. The mobile rings and Angie grabs it, praying to hear the plumber's voice.

'Don't hang up on me again.' It's her husband's attacker. She's supposed to call a direct number at the station if she ever hears from him – what did she do with the piece of paper? The children are dancing under spraying water while the radio DJ tries out other annoying noises.

'I've been away for nearly two years. I only hit him.'

'I remember. I was in court.' John's arm had been broken but the suddenness of the assault had caused him to slip over in the rain-slick alley. According to the coroner, he'd ruptured a vertebral vein at the level of C2 in his cervical cord. It was the fall that killed him. They discovered he'd been drinking. A few beers with his mates, somebody's birthday. Alcohol renders you more susceptible to rupture. The thief got off lightly. His mother slapped Angie's face outside the courtroom. The shame was transferred to John's family. In their eyes, drinking on duty caused his death, not some nutter with an iron bar.

'You were pregnant. I remember the look on your face when I was sentenced.'

'I remember you, too.' With the phone under her chin, she tries to pull Melanie out of the water's path. 'You'd better get off the phone before I hang up again.' Grabbing a frying pan from beneath the sink, she inverts it over the fountain, wedging the handle under the tap. The girls moan with disappointment.

'I'm near your block of flats. What a crappy area. He didn't leave you much of a pension, did he? I'm calling by to pay my respects.'

'You stay away from here!' she shouts.

'I've paid my debt. I'm a decent citizen, not like this lot in your high street. I'll be there in a minute.'

Angie throws down the mobile and tries to smack Melanie across the back of the legs, but the girl darts out of the way. Now that the drama at the sink has subsided Victoria is back at the table, scissors in hand. Melanie starts to grab at the back of her sister's chair.

Angie sees the accident coming before it happens, but she's still powerless to prevent it; the chair tips back taking Victoria with it, and there's a scream of pain, matched by Angie's scream as she reaches out for them. The cat leaps away with a yowl. She pulls the girls apart looking for the scissors. The points have jabbed Victoria's forearm. The cut isn't deep but both girls are shocked into silence by crimson droplets on white skin.

'First aid box, over there, get it.' For once, Melanie does as she's told. Victoria starts to whimper. Angie wipes the cut dry and is just putting a plaster on when the house phone rings.

'No, I didn't hang up on you, Lucy, I dropped the phone. Listen, do me a favour – the child-minder hasn't turned up, could you ring her for me? Because I've got three hungry kids here and Vicki's just cut herself and – it's not "my fault" for having kids, as you put it, all I'm asking is for you to make one lousy phonecall. God, I listen to you all the time without complaining—' She's talking to a dead line. Lucy has rung off in anger. She thinks everyone's actions are deliberately planned to cause her anguish.

The water isn't draining from the sink. Now it has reached the top and is flowing over the edge of the counter onto the floor, where Emma is sitting.

'Oh, shit.'

She roughly hikes the child up, but is too late to stop her from getting wet. The radio DJ says 'Tony from Croydon has just sent us this annoying sound.' The tip of a knife skids across a china plate, magnified a thousand times. Melanie is unwinding a length of sticking plaster around Victoria's arm, which is turning blue. The cat is licking the water creeping across the floor tiles.

'You'll cut off her blood supply doing that!' snaps Angie. 'Unwind it at once, and do it slowly. Victoria, don't just sit there like a lump, stop your sister.' She has always been the unflappable one. She does not like public displays of emotion. She didn't cry at the funeral because she was too busy trying to organise the seating plan for the cars. She still hasn't cried. This, in her parents' eyes, makes her hard-hearted. She is not hard-hearted, she just copes instead of falling apart.

'What did I tell you about touching the scissors? You've just seen how sharp they are.' She snatches them from Melanie and throws them across the room.

Behind her, the frying pan slides off the tap stump and the geyser resumes at a higher pressure. Angie grabs the pan as water splashes up on one of the lights under the kitchen cabinets, exploding it with a pop and scattering tiny shards of broken glass everywhere.

'Nobody move,' warns Angie grimly, frying pan outstretched.

The house phone starts to ring again. The DJ on the radio plays the number one annoying noise in the country. Emma starts to cry. The doorbell rings. The hammering upstairs gets even louder.

Angie reaches the front door in three strides. She yanks it open.

A well-fed man with a familiar tattoo on his neck stands before her. 'So how are you coping all alone?' he says, taking an arrogant step into the lounge.

'I am dealing with the situation,' she explains through bared teeth, glancing back at the children. Emma is under the table squeezing the cat. Melanie is winding the plaster around Victoria's face, pulling up her nose.

'I think it's payback time.' He looks past her to the children, infecting them with his stare. He bounces on the tips of his trainers, withdrawing something from his pocket. Almost without thinking, Angie swings the heavy frying pan with both hands. The pan makes a cartoonish gonging sound as it connects with his face. Wide-eyed and open-mouthed, he falls backwards into the corridor and collapses against the wall.

'*I said I'm dealing with it,*' she shouts as he lies there in the rain. She kicks his feet out of her doorway and slams the door shut.

'Victoria, get the cat away from Emma,' she says with determination, 'put the plaster roll back in the first aid box, and go and get changed.' A list appears in her head, each item supporting a tick-box. Cancel the child-minder, call the plumber, dress the children, call her sister, phone work and tell them she's spending Christmas Eve with her girls instead.

Angie looks past the dripping curtains, out of the kitchen window to the man lying on the balcony, and shakily adds one more item to the bottom of the list.

The pale, still body is cleansed by the hard rain. In the back pocket of its jeans is the cheque made out in Angie's name that no one will ever cash. It is the evidence that can prove the policeman's wife was not attacked, and the start of another situation she will have to deal with. Angie can do it now. She can do anything.

THE GREEN MAN

Josh Machen told himself that jealousy was as much part of being in love as all the other demonstrable gestures, like twiddling your partner's hair across a dinner table and giving her knowing glances on crowded tube trains, that it simply proved how much you cared. Kate teased him about it. 'By your reckoning, Othello was a regular guy acting pretty much within his rights,' she suggested. Being jealous meant that someone was always on your mind, which was desirable, so the subject remained a joke between them.

It stopped being a joke after Josh followed her to a hen night and accused a male stripper of touching her thighs. As they argued about the exact height of the young man's teasing hands, Kate's amused smile faded. After that, he questioned her movements, checked her mobile phone for unrecognisable addresses and her e-mail box for mysterious correspondents. Usually he apologised afterwards, but that didn't make it better.

'It's living in London,' Josh told her over a conciliatory dinner in his favourite Camden restaurant, the Cypriot joint he always used for making announcements. 'Eight million people all on the make, lots of men looking at you with an eye on the main chance, it's no wonder relationships don't last in this city.'

'Are you telling me this is why we never eat anywhere fashionable?' she asked, only half teasing. The one-eyed owner slipped beadily between his patrons, making them uneasy.

'How different could our lives be if we were living somewhere else? Somewhere warm and dry, where the streets aren't covered in trash and every other shop isn't a fried chicken outlet? London's dying, it doesn't have residents now, it has inmates. There's more crime here than in New York, it's got a Third World transport system, there are just too many people. I look at old photographs of half-deserted streets and think *that's the city I want back.'*

'You can't stop the world, Josh. You have to keep pace with it.'

'Maybe, but you can find a place that suits you better.'

'You really think it would make a difference to us living somewhere else?'

'Yes, I do.'

'Do you have a place in mind?'

'If I came up with an idea, would you at least consider it?'

'I suppose so,' she agreed vaguely. 'This isn't anything to do with getting me all to yourself on some island, is it?'

'Of course not. I think it would be good for both of us to see a little more of the planet. I never took a gap year like you.'

She wondered whether it was the city he longed to run away from, or the fact that he could not trust himself to trust her here.

For a long time, Kate refused to get married. She had seen how marriage had crushed the life from her parents, and had no desire to follow in their carpet-slippered footsteps. Why else was it called wedlock? She finally relented because she thought it would answer the question of trust that hung between them once and for all. Josh centred his world too much around hers. He got under her feet. With the mutual trust engendered by their marriage vows, he might become free to find himself.

After a grimly nondescript civil ceremony which her parents boycotted, she moved in with him, shoving an extra bed into his tiny flat near Victoria Park. The wedding contract held an implicit promise, that Josh would learn to behave more like a husband. She wondered what had happened in his past to make him so scared of losing her.

She worried at first that life together in Victoria Park would become claustrophobic, but as they worked flexi-time in different parts of the city – she was a research scientist at the King's Cross College of Tropical Medicine, he worked as an in-house designer for an ailing record company in Kensington – they didn't see as much of each other as she had imagined. They were both Londoners, both had too many old friends, too many birthdays to celebrate, too many arrangements to squeeze into their free hours. There was never enough time.

Then Josh lost his job, and suddenly there were too many hours in the day.

After three months spent sitting around the flat waiting for companies to call back, he was becoming morose and frustrated. Cutbacks, retrenchment, the music business faring poorly, the same excuses were trotted out time and again. They were looking for cheap labour, and that meant buying young staff. Josh was thirty-one, and as a designer working to attract teenage sales, employers feared he was past his sell-by date. He maintained his old contacts and managed to keep some occasional freelance work, but it wasn't enough to pay the bills. Kate often went out in the evenings with colleagues from her department. Josh had nothing in common with these intense biologists, and stayed at home, but always waited up so that he could discreetly question her when she returned.

It didn't take either of them long to see how the strain of their new circumstances was damaging their relationship. Something, they knew, would have to be done. They loved each other very much, but too many things were getting in the way.

It was Kate who heard about the offer from a Malaysian lady who had recently joined the department.

'You're talking about a pretty severe change of lifestyle,' said Josh, after she explained what the move would entail.

'You said you wanted to get out of London,' she reminded him, anxiously unfolding the map across the table.

'London, yes, but giving up the whole western hemisphere seems a bit extreme.'

'It would be perfect for my thesis. Look, Malaysia's divided into two separate chunks, the west peninsula, and the north-west section of Borneo. Taman's supposed to be somewhere off the west coast of the peninsular.' Her finger traced the line of the sea. 'Here it is. You have to look carefully.'

'I thought she said it was tiny.'

'You're looking at Langkowi. Taman Island is a little further to the north. See?'

'It's a speck. What's the scale of this thing?'

'Flights go to Kuala Lumpur, then it's an internal hop to Langkowi and finally there's a short ferry ride.'

'Dear God, that's a long way off the map.' They examined the emerald droplet together. The island was so small that there were no towns marked on it. Kate checked the map again, looking for something positive to remark upon.

'It looks nearer to the coast of Malaysia than Langkowi Island. It's just not been opened to tourism as much. The ferry only goes twice a week at the moment, but they'll expand the service if more visitors come.' She pressed her hand across his. 'Think about it. One of the most futuristic cities on the planet will be just a few hundred miles away. From that point of view, it's no more remote than, say, the Isle of Man.'

He ran his hand down through his hair, pressing a frown into place. 'Exactly,' he said gloomily.

After two meetings with the proprietors of the new hotel on Taman, Josh remained unconvinced that they should take the posting. They would be required to act as caretakers for a minimum period of four months, while the builders were finishing the rooms in the hotel's main building. The owners were a pair of Swiss bankers, and wanted someone to keep an eye on the place until they were ready to open for business in the first summer season. The money they were willing to pay for a European couple to take the job was substantial. A suite had already been furnished in the hotel's residential section, and the bankers were prepared to provide them with anything they wanted. Kate would be able to realise a cherished dream of writing up her toxicology research, something she could never find time to do in London. Josh would be able to reconsider his options, and maybe get around to the photographic career he had always wanted to pursue. But as their deadline for making a decision approached, he still refused to commit.

Then Kate ran into an old boyfriend who announced that he was single again and wished he had never broken up with her. He offered to take her to the Gordon Ramsey restaurant at Claridges for dinner on Saturday night, and try to make amends for what had once passed between them. While she was deciding whether to go or not, Josh announced that they were leaving for Malaysia.

They signed the papers, locked up the flat and transferred through Kuala Lumpur with a single large suitcase between them. Backpackers, package tourists and businessmen crowded the shuttle to Langkowi, but only a handful of locals continued on with them to the port. It was late October, a month before the start of the island's rainy season, and the first guests on Taman were to be expected at the end of March. The sleek white ferry was more modern than anything Josh had travelled on in Britain. They cut through a smooth green sea that filled with a delicate aquamarine light where the sun hit it, and felt at once that they had made the right decision to leave behind the grey dome of London sky. All around them, improbably steep plugs of jungle rose from the glittering jade water.

At Taman's jetty they were met by the works foreman, a smiling freckled Australian named Aaron Tunn, who pumped their hands hard and insisted on carrying their suitcase, hefting it onto his shoulder as though it weighed nothing. The hotel proved to be a drive away in a juddery jeep that threatened to tip over as it climbed the slippery red tyre ditches in the unlaid roads.

'This area around you is ancient rainforest,' Aaron explained, pointing to the white-legged eagles that dipped into rocky outcrops behind the greenery. A streak of orange as wide as the world was settling over the jungle, pointing to the close of day.

'How old do you think it is?' asked Kate, enchanted.

'About three hundred million years, although much of it has been cut down recently. The government hasn't got a very good environmental record, but this time they're trying to get the balance right. We're dry-walling with reclaimed stone, and barely touching the forest canopy except to bury pipes. The cut paths will have completely grown over by the end of the rainy season. You can expect a downpour every day soon, but plenty of hot sun, too.'

Josh clung to the side of the jeep and focussed his eyes on the green shadows of the forest. Dusty lianas looped between the trees like the arcs of a suspension bridge. Parasitic plants grew with the same thickness and strength as the trees they clung to. Something was jumping between bushy branches, shaking whole trunks and violently rustling treetops.

'What about poisonous insects?' he shouted to Aaron. 'Is there anything we have to look out for?'

'There are one or two bugs they don't tell the tourists about,' Aaron called over his shoulder, 'and a very mean breed of jellyfish that turns up in lagoons when it rains hard, but generally speaking, the fauna's safer here than it is back home in Perth. We've got about sixty men working on the site, a mix of locals and experts from Far East territories. They won't talk to you much, they just get on with their work and go home when the bell rings. Me and three of the lads are on site overnight, but we go to the mainland at weekends. That's the only time you'll be alone here.' Aaron laughed. 'You'll probably be glad of the peace and quiet by then.'

For a brief moment Josh wondered if he was entering a hell

of his own making. Sixty sweat-stained men slyly watching the fragrant white woman who walked past them to her bedroom, smirking at the skinny London lad who couldn't keep her satisfied. *You've been watching too many old movies*, he told himself.

The track led down toward the sun, and Josh realised they had reached the far northern tip of the island. The hotel was so well concealed in the undergrowth that he could not see it at first. As they drew nearer, angled stone walls could be glimpsed between the trees. It looked like an Incan city in miniature, a central block built low to the ground in natural materials that blended harmoniously with the dense olive landscape surrounding it. Set away from the main body of the building, a series of wooden-roofed villas could be discerned beneath the feathered leaves of the jungle's primary growth.

'It's a beaut, isn't it?' said Aaron, with the pride of a man who knew he had achieved something special. He stopped the jeep and jumped out, pulling back the seats. 'We had you marked down for a suite in the main building, but it got flooded, so we built you a villa. We only finished it this morning, so you may find some of the wood seals a bit sticky, but apart from that it's ready to live in. They'll be a dozen of them when we open.'

It was clear that the work whistle had just blown, because men were returning from the hotel's staff room in white short-sleeved shirts and jeans, carrying holdalls. They nodded politely at Aaron as they passed, but barely seemed to notice the new arrivals.

'They won't bother you,' Aaron explained. 'They're industrious and religious, only interested in getting paid and getting home. They don't speak much English, only Malay, but they're good men and won't get in your way. You'll enjoy it here. All you have to do is keep the site safe.'

'Safe from what?' asked Josh, his eyes searching the

undergrowth for leaping shapes. 'Are there any dangerous locals hanging about?'

'Oh, nothing like that,' Aaron replied airily, 'it's just a condition of the building's insurance contract. But there are small problems. There's been some stealing. Tools, clothes, stuff left lying around.'

'You think it's your workmen?'

'No, they value their jobs too highly to touch anything.'

'Then who do you suspect?'

'We all know who the thieves are.' Aaron set the case down on the step of their villa. 'We'll talk more when you've unpacked and had a chance to freshen up.'

'This will be so good for us,' said Kate, folding her legs beneath the silk kimono that had been left, folded, on the bed. 'Look at this place, it's incredible.' The villa's teak legs had been punched into the angled, loamy floor of the forest. The suite was basically one large polished hardwood room, divided by alcoves that extended into a pair of private bathrooms. White linen drapes hung in swathes across the shuttered windows. There was no glass in the villa; the seasonal winds were likely to draw them out.

'I thought it would be quiet, but listen to all that noise outside.' Josh looked uneasily at the swaying vegetation beyond the veranda. A long yellow stick suddenly sprouted legs and moved, running along the railing to jump into the bushes. The wildness of the forest would take some getting used to. Strange birds squealed like electric saws in the tops of the trees, while crickets and toads provided a low rolling trill that had begun the moment shadows fell on the leaves. Something hooted angrily near the shore, its upturned call answered by a mate or an enemy. The canopy of the forest was so close around them that it touched the roof of the villa.

'I thought it would be quieter,' repeated Josh, as he tipped the blinds shut.

Aaron's helpers had set up a meal in the partially finished dining room. They sat on fat silk cushions sorting through dishes of chicken, banana-leaf wrapped rice and a splayed fried fish with hundred of small bones.

'Two monsoons a year, nine major airstreams, a rainfall of a hundred inches, eighty-five per cent humidity, it's a fantastic ecosystem for breeding unique plant species,' said Aaron, crunching the fishbones in strong white teeth. 'Birds, too. We've got hornbills, parrots, swifts, eagles. I can watch 'em for hours. The island used to deal palm-oil with the mainland, but the government protected the trees. The locals weren't too happy until organic tourism came along.'

'What about animals?' asked Kate, nipping a chunk of tender chicken from its green bamboo splinter.

'Mainland's got the lot, elephants, tigers, the eastern half even has a few rhinos left. We've got pelandok, that's kind of a small deer, dusky leaf monkeys, some small crocs, monitor lizards, and you have to keep an eye out for snakes, mostly cobras. Good news is that the mozzies are malaria-free, but you'll still get bitten to buggery around the swamps. You get the best of both worlds here. Taman has its own natural selection patterns and its own micro-climate. The animals and plants grow up differently, behave differently. You won't see stuff like this any-where else. Zoological teams from all over the world come here. Kate tells me you're into photography, Josh. You want to take pictures, this is the place to do it.'

'I used to be good at it.' Josh eyed the carcass of the bony fried fish with suspicion. 'I don't know whether I've brought the right equipment.'

'No problem, mate. The ferry will bring in anything you order from the internet.'

It crossed Josh's mind that Kate might find this plain-speaking blonde southerner attractive. 'Doesn't your wife miss you out here?' he asked casually as Kate shot him a look.

'I'm not a married man, Josh, not in that sense.' He popped

open beers and slid them across the table. 'I'm afraid I had to put the wine stock on hold because we haven't been able to drain the cellar yet. No, to answer your question, Josh, I've got a partner back on the mainland, but she runs a gardening centre and can't get away often.' Kate's follow-up look to Josh warned him. *Satisfied?*

'You were going to tell us about your thief,' reminded Josh, anxious to move away from his clumsy display of insecurity.

'Thieves, actually. We've got a troupe of macaques on the island, big green-haired bastards with muzzles like baboons, you can't miss 'em. That howling noise? They head for the beach around sunset. They dig up crabs and eat 'em. The Malays train them to pick coconuts. They'll take the washing from the lines, and won't give it back until you feed 'em. They're smart, but they're mean-spirited fuckers. They'll try to get you to join in with their games, but it's best not to interfere. You really don't want to get involved, believe me. So we let 'em steal a little, just not too much.'

The next morning, Josh saw the macaques, ten or twelve of them looping through the trees on long, muscular arms. As casually as waltzing around a maypole, their leader swung on his liana and dropped to the ground near the villa. Leaning on his forepaws, he raised a doglike whiskery head and sniffed the air through broad flat nostrils. After a few minutes, he scooted toward the verandah. The others held back, as if waiting for their leader to pass judgement. Josh realised that he was much larger than the rest, almost as big as a man. He had to weigh well over twenty kilos. His shaggy coat was, as Aaron had pointed out, a curious shade of brownish-green, his head framed by a centre-parted lion's mane of straight, swept-back hair. Implacable silk-brown eyes stared at Josh. No, not at him – past him. He turned and followed the macaque's gaze. Kate was standing in the doorway of the bedroom, pulling a white T-shirt above her breasts, over her head.

'Don't move,' Josh warned her.

'What is it?' She snapped off the shirt.

'One of the macaques.'

'Where? Oh. My God, he's enormous. Much bigger than I imagined.'

'Stay where you are.'

'It's all right, he's more scared of you than you are of him.' Kate smiled and turned. 'Would you put some sun-block on my back?'

'Don't let him see you like that.'

'Like what?'

'Without your top on.'

'He's an animal, Josh.'

'That's not the point.'

'He doesn't look at me in the same way.'

'How do you know?' Josh took a step forward. The macaque released a startling wide-mouthed howl and bounded off, followed by the rest of the troupe.

'All right, you showed him who the man was,' said Kate. 'Come on, Alpha Male, put some cream on me, then let's check out the beach.'

It was the perfect place to build a hotel; a crescent of cadmium yellow beach surrounded by heavy underbrush, the sand striped with stream outlets from the hills behind. Low rolling waves indicated the shallow slope of the bay, ideal for safe swimming. White birds fell from the sky, streamlining as they hit the water, to emerge with wagging fish in their beaks. Josh held Kate's hand as they walked. In the distance he could hear Aaron's men knocking hammers on posts. They had started at six that morning, and would continue until darkness.

Aaron took them on a tour of the property boundaries. Most of the hotel was finished. Only the rest of the outlying villas remained to be built. Gangs of Malays were digging out the foundations, but water filled the ditches as quickly as the earth was shovelled out. 'It'll be worse when the rains come,' warned

Aaron cheerfully. 'Look, there's Sinno.' He pointed to the burly leader macaque they had seen near the verandah earlier. He was seated in a clearing near the water's edge, cracking a large crab out of its shell by carefully prising apart its exoskeleton. The creature's disembodied legs were still waving as he levered them into his pouting mouth. The other members of the troupe foraged for smaller pickings on the banks of a stream.

'How did he get his name?' asked Kate as they passed.

'From his genus, Celebes "Cynomacaca". He's a moor macaque, a crab-eater, although they'll eat anything in a push. He's the most intelligent one I've ever seen, but fuckin' bad tempered. I've a book on them if you're interested.'

'Yes, I'd like to see that,' said Kate. 'Josh, you could take pictures of them.'

'Just don't get too close,' Aaron warned. 'He's capable of pulling your arms out of their sockets, although his shout is mostly for show.'

'Listen to this.' Kate flattened out the page and marked a passage. 'They're arboreal, diurnal, and love the company of others. They're fast swimmers, climbers and runners. Some were used in studies that led to the development of the polio vaccine. Macaques provide the models for the Buddhist saying, "See No Evil, Hear No Evil, Speak No Evil". Some people believe that they are human insofar as they embody the worst traits of man.'

'He's sitting outside right now,' said Josh, who was shaving in the bathroom.

'Who is?'

'Sinno. The leader. Sitting in the branch of a tree. I can see him from the window.'

'He's probably getting used to having new neighbours.'

'He's sniffing the air like he did this morning.'

'I bet he can smell my perfume. After all, no one else here wears any.'

Josh shaved bristles and foam from beneath his nose, but he

could see the macaque in his mirror. The damned thing was sitting on its haunches calmly watching his wife. He studied the monkey's face too intently; the razor slipped and the blade nicked him just below the nose.

After supper that evening Josh kept watch from the verandah, but the vast, slim trees were still and silent. The forest's nocturnal residents crept silently through the undergrowth while, somewhere far above them, Taman's troupe of monkeys dreamed away the star-filled night.

The next three weeks passed easily. As their lives decelerated into an elegance of relaxed motion, boredom became inconceivable. To hurry was to sweat and grow tired. During the mornings, Josh busied himself more than was strictly necessary with administrative chores around the hotel, where the floor tiles were being polished and relays of electric wiring were being discreetly added. Kate helped out in the main building, but spent most of the day working at her computer, mapping out a thesis on primate toxicology that remained incomprehensible and private to everyone but her. Late afternoons were passed in makeshift hammocks as the site lost its human sounds and all activity ceased. Shadows deepened, eye-searing yellows faded to cool greens, and small animals could be heard snuffling on the forest floor. Kate took languid baths while Josh lay face down on the bed reading.

When the tide turned, the macaques would return from the beach where they had been digging out crabs, led by Sinno, who would lope past the villa, pausing to check the verandah. Josh knew that he took small items of Kate's from the deck, hairbrushes, hand-mirrors, combs, but never saw him do it. One day, the monkey left a neat pile of bulbous green fruit on Kate's sunchair. The fleshy split pericarps were crimson and yellow, and oozed sweet-smelling juice onto the teak deck until Josh cleared it away.

'He hangs around here like a lovesick suitor,' Josh complained as they walked through the compound to the dining room. 'And you're doing nothing to discourage him. You hardly ever wear clothes in the villa. The way he looks at you, it's not the way an animal looks at a person.'

'Then how is it?'

'The way a man looks at a woman.'

Kate laughed off the idea. 'It's too hot in the afternoon. What do you want me to do, dress as if I was in London? I'm just someone new to him, and I smell different. Besides, it helps me that he comes so close. So much of my writing is purely theoretical, he reminds me that the subjects are flesh and blood. But they don't think like humans. For years scientists tried to teach primates the American Sign Language system, but they discovered their so-called "trained" monkeys used exactly the same signs in the wild. People have this idea of the noble savage. Everyone from Swift to Huxley has suggested that we can learn sensitivity from the apes, but the species simply don't correspond at a sociological level.' She touched his arm. 'I thought you were going to concentrate on your photography. You haven't taken any shots in days.'

'I haven't been in the mood. Besides, Aaron's kept me busy with the inventory.'

'You know he's going to the mainland at the end of the week. You'd better make a list if you want him to pick up any supplies for you.'

Aaron knew that with the coming of the rains their drainage problems would increase, and was hoping to return with the spare parts he needed to keep his pumps working.

The next morning, Josh rose earlier than usual, and sat on the verandah leafing through a catalogue of photographic materials as Sinno's troupe hooted and hollered through the branches on their way back from the beach. He tried to concentrate on the pages of sleek software options, but found his attention sliding to the shapes in the trees. Behind the hulking form of their leader he could see the troupe's females. They had never come this close before. Josh slowly reached for the small digital camera he had left on the table. He quietly switched it on and studied the LCD monitor. Several of the females nursed small babies against their breasts, but one turned away whenever Josh focussed his camera on her. The other females seemed to shun her. Once or twice he caught her in the display panel, but by the time the light had adjusted to a level his equipment could read, she had sensed his attention and turned aside.

When the troupe passed in the evening, he called Kate out to the verandah. She tiptoed beside him and studied the females.

'Her baby's dead,' she pointed out. Looking more closely, Josh could see now that the mother was nursing a dry furry corpse. The dessicated body was curled against a dark nipple. 'She won't let it go because she wants to be like the other mothers, but she knows you know that it's dead, and she's ashamed to let you see.'

'You really think they can play those sorts of games?' asked Josh, surprised.

'They're not games,' said Kate, 'it's human nature. Shame is a natural instinct.'

'I bet he's the father.' Josh glared at Sinno, who had wedged himself into his usual position overlooking the villa's bedroom. 'He's waiting for you to undress again.'

Kate gave an angry sigh and went indoors.

By the end of the first month, both Kate and Josh looked physically different; leaner, blonder, shoulders as shiny as leather from working outside. Kate, at least, was more relaxed. Aaron offered to take them to the mainland, but they decided to wait until a desire for the noise and chaos of cities had returned to some degree.

The rains arrived in a deafening display of ferocity. Aaron's men splashed through the building hauling portable pumps, hunting down floods and leaks in the first real test of the building's durability. Sluices of rainwater appeared in dry alleys. Kate and Josh were increasingly confined to the villa, as getting to the main building involved crossing treacherous torrential slides. Between storms the sun blazed hard, filling the forest with steam. The air was laden with the smell of rotting vegetation. Kate worked, Josh read, and they got on each other's nerves.

'I've been watching the macaques,' said Kate one morning in December. 'The females are getting thinner. They don't look well. Their fur – it's changing, losing its gloss. I don't know a great deal about their social behaviour patterns, but it looks as if they don't forage, and the males provide for them. But lately the males have stopped.'

Josh knew why. Sinno was taking their supplies and daily dumping piles of fruit at the villa as some kind of votive offering. The monkey clambered into place on his branch and waited for her to appear, but raced off when Josh appeared. Every morning he cleared the verandah, throwing it all back into the jungle before Kate came out.

The next day Josh opened the door to find an enormous injured crab lying on its back, grasping at the air. Sinno sat motionless in the tree in the falling rain, his fur dripping over his implacable eyes. 'I'm not going to play your game,' Josh muttered, gingerly raising the crab by a waving leg and hurling it into the bushes. 'You're going to play mine.'

The next morning, he waited until the troupe had passed, then climbed out into the forest with the linen bag he had filled with scraps from the kitchen. The macaques were omnivores, and the females were clearly being starved. They kept to a secondary route behind the males, so this was where Josh laid the trail of food. He was still shaking the last scraps of fish from the bag when he heard the troupe returning. His heart thumped in his chest as Sinno and the other males passed within feet of him. The females followed, guiltily stopping at the trail of food and shoveling the delicacies into their cheek pouches. Sinno screamed at them and slapped at their heads as they passed, then caught sight of Josh. His inexpressive face, striped in leaf-stencilled sunlight, betrayed no emotion. He continued to stare for a full ten minutes, then swung sharply up into the trees as if scampering up a set of ladders.

Josh was frightened, but excited. He had shown the monkey who was really the boss. He had undermined Sinno's command. Over the next few days, the piles of pungent fruit left on the balcony dwindled, but Sinno soon returned to his usual place, watching Kate.

When the refrigeration units arrived on Friday morning, Aaron needed help with the stock-orders and Josh rose early to help him, leaving Kate asleep in bed. He was more concerned about missing the troupe's morning patrol.

'We need the inventory pad,' said Aaron, searching under the workbenches in the new wine cellar. 'You didn't take it with you last night?'

'It's my fault, you're right,' Josh admitted, 'I took it back to the room. I shouldn't have had that last bottle.' They had been celebrating the arrival of the French wines by working their way through a crate of breakages. 'I'll get it.' He picked his way back across the muddy paths, passing through scorched strips of sunlight. Ahead of him a battalion of centipedes, pillarbox red and each longer than a man's hand, undulated over the dead wet leaves. He could hear water running as he approached the villa. Kate was using the outside shower, a slatted hardwood box on the verandah with a broad copper spray head. She had her back to him, and was soaping her thighs, her tanned stomach. White foam drifted down the channel of her back to her buttocks. She was humming as she washed, a song they had used to sing together as they drove across London to the apartments of friends, now a distant world away. High in the dark tree to the rear, Simmo sat in position watching her, his blank brown eyes unmoving, his arms hanging below the branch, the exposed tip of his penis like a furled scarlet orchid.

Bellowing, Josh ran at the tree with a rock in his hand and threw it as hard as he could. The rock hit Simmo squarely in the face. The macaque released a howl of pain and defiance, and vanished. Kate screamed. Josh's eyes were wild. 'You knew he was there!' he yelled. 'You saw him! What the hell did you think you were doing, leading him on?'

'Are you insane?' Kate shouted back, frightened by his sudden outburst. 'I had no idea he was there. I never even thought to look. What kind of sick person do you think I am? What on earth is wrong with you?'

'Remember what Aaron said, you play games with them, they'll play games with you,' said Josh, fighting to regain his breath in the heat-saturated air. 'He's the leader, your alpha male, the others will follow him anywhere, do whatever he tells them to.'

'Whatever he *tells* them?' Kate shut off the shower and grabbed a towel. '*My* alpha male? Listen to yourself. You did this in London, and you're doing it again, when there aren't even any humans around. These are animals you're talking about, Josh, *animals!* You don't even know you're doing it any more, do you?'

Josh suddenly felt lost. He tried to take Kate in his arms, but she moved beyond reach. 'Forgive me, Kate,' he whispered, 'it's the way he looks at you, I know he wants you. I know it's grotesque but you must see that you're in danger. He studies you. He leaves gifts for you. He waits for me to leave so that he can spy on you alone. You once said some men have the souls of animals. Couldn't an animal have the soul of a man?'

'Not on a biological level, no.'

'Perhaps this isn't about biology but something deeper than blood and tissue. So much here comes from a time before there were demarcations between man and beast. How can we hope to understand? There are human needs, you said so yourself, and where there's need there's always deception. I love you, darling, I just don't want you to get hurt.'

'When we get back I think you need to get some professional help.' Kate stomped back inside the villa and slammed the door in his face.

Josh knew it was beyond anything either of them could understand. They were far from their own social circle, away from the rules that controlled them. When he was a child, visiting the Regent's Park Zoo, animals were something to be seen pacing behind bars, half-demented by their incarceration. Back then there had been little understanding and less respect for animal psychology; chimpanzees were dressed as humans and given tea parties each afternoon, as if their clumsy etiquette was intended to remind children of man's superiority as a species. The very word 'ape' evoked mimickry of human action. But here, he and the primates were on equal footing, simply moving in different spheres.

He returned to work, but all day long his fear and anger grew.

On Saturday morning, Aaron caught the ferry to the mainland, promising to return that night, but in the afternoon rising monsoon winds put paid to any chance of his return. A storm-sky as grey and unbroken as the concrete walls Aaron's men had built raced overhead. In the distance they heard the tumble of thunder. The air was so oppressively hot that it caught in Kate's mouth and blocked her sinuses. Numb with headache, she lay on the bed in her underwear, listening to the colliding treetops, waiting for the storm to break and lower the temperature.

Josh prowled the main building with his camera, taking close-up test shots of butterflies drying their wings, as large as the pages of paperbacks. A sense of unease had settled on him in a suffocating caul. The thought of being away from his wife disturbed him, but he knew that she would be angry if she suspected that he was guarding her.

That was when he realised. He had not heard from the macaques all afternoon. He found himself at the far side of the compound. From here it was a twenty-minute walk back to the villa. He went to Aaron's locker and took the keys to the jeep, the only motorised vehicle on the island.

The fat green Jeep was parked out front on the half-gravelled drive. He climbed in and tried the ignition, but the engine would not turn over. Leaning from his seat, he lowered his head over the side and followed the trail of petrol back to the external tank. He could see from here that the petrol canister had been punctured. Kneeling beside it, he touched the indentations left by rows of wide-set teeth. The acrid contents had drained away into the earth. Could a macaque do that, even one as large as Sinno? Could he somehow have evolved more quickly than his relatives? Josh studied the teethmarks again and felt a lurch of fear.

Aaron kept a loaded 12-gauge slide action shotgun in his locker. He had told Josh about it the first week he was here, had even shown him how to pump and fire the damned thing in case of an unspecified emergency. Josh ran toward the locker now, dragging it out by the stock and throwing it across his arm as he ran back into the forest.

The rain began just as he was within sight of the villa. He stopped for a moment to catch his breath, and heard lightning split a branch somewhere above him. The deluge fell in large hard pellets of water, hammering the leathery leaves around him, instantly churning the ground to mud. The noise was incredible. Suddenly he could no longer see the villa.

But he could see the macaques. They were pushing their way toward the verandah in a broad semi-circle, and at the centre rose the great green back of a single primate, twice as big as any of the others. He slipped on the muddy slope, his leg collapsing under him, and rolled into the undergrowth. Thick thorns jammed themselves into his arms and legs, tearing gouts of flesh as he hauled himself upright. In a fold of the rain he could see the macaques moving in.

'Come on, you fuckers,' he shouted, pumping the gun and firing it into the air, igniting a cacophony of bird screams around him. The kickback wrenched his shoulder, but he stumbled on toward the scattering monkeys, bearing down as the beast headed away toward the beach. This time he stopped and steadied the gun against a tree before he fired. There was an explosion of terrified parrots, flashes of red and blue in the downpour, a mad tumble of feathers and leaves, as he smashed his way through the thinning undergrowth toward the sea.

He wondered if he had managed to wound it, because the great monkey was moving more slowly now, so that the rest of the troupe quickly overtook their leader. The macaque was dragging his left leg. The forest cleared to rain-pocked sand and rock as Josh entered the farthest end of the beach, where the streams formed treacherous deep-sided pools. The rain was blinding him, making it hard to keep his eyes open, but he closed the distance.

'Who's got the balls now?' he shouted through the downpour, closing in on the limping macaque. He needed to steady himself in order to take aim, and searched for a suitable rock. Sinno was trapped. All that stood ahead of him was a broad water pit filled by the rain-flattened sea. Still the creature had its back to him, as if unwilling to admit defeat. It hobbled to the far side of the pool and squatted heavily on the wet sand. Josh turned, searching for something stable on which to rest the shotgun.

It was then that he saw the others. Alarmingly close, they had drawn into a ring about him, and were moving quickly forward. He felt the sand softening beneath his feet and realised that he was sliding forward into the sand pool as the rain-soaked bank shifted with his weight. He tried to steady himself, but the weight of the gun overbalanced him.

On the other side, the great macaque slowly turned – or rather, he split in two, not one great primate at all but a pair of the troupe's younger males, one spread across the other's shoulders, their coarse green hair ratted together. They jumped apart and found their places in the circle, turning their calm brown eyes to him.

Josh sank swiftly into the pool. There was something odd about the water, a viscous texture he had seen before when it rained hard. As the first sting penetrated his shirt like an electric shock, he remembered Aaron's warning about swimming in heavy rain; it was when the most dangerous jellyfish surfaced. The pool was alive with them, hundreds washed in by the tide and now rising like clear plastic bags as the rain drummed the surface of the water. Their purple stings trailed and wrapped about his limbs, sticking to his waist, his back, his neck, jolts flashing through his disrupted nervous system, ten, fifty, a hundred. He tore at the strips but they stuck to his flesh, needles burrowing like thorns. Paralysed by the strobing pain, the endless jabbing injections of venom, he thrashed and stilled, sinking into the deep green darkness, watched by the motionless members of the loyal troupe. The rain pattered and the monkeys watched, their souls ranged beyond human emotional response, their hearts obeying only the patterns of their communal life.

On the roof of the villa, Sinno scratched himself and waited until silence returned once more to the forest. Then he slid down onto the verandah and peered in through the window slats, to the bedroom where Kate lay uneasily sleeping. As quietly as Josh had ever moved, the great macaque opened the bedroom door and slipped inside, closing it ever so gently behind him.

BREAKING HEART

'The man situation is starting to get a bit desperate,' said Emma, clearing a patch on the steam-fogged window and peering out into the rainy street. 'I must say I'm beginning to wonder about the Keatsian ideal of true romance. It doesn't seem very relevant to anyone living in the Hammersmith area.' She unfocussed her eyes and tried to remember the words.

She took me to her elfin grot,
And there she wept and sighed full sore;
And there I shut her wild, wild eyes
With kisses four.

'We did that at school. Round here it's all elfin grot and not many wild kisses.'

'Quite a lot of stabbings, though.'

'Remember they found that girl's body in pieces under the flyover? They've caught the guy who did it. The police said it was a romance that went wrong. I'll say.' Emma sipped distastefully at her coffee. She had asked for a cappuccino with no froth but the waitress said the machine couldn't do it. 'What do you think this is, a Starbucks?' the waitress had asked, a reasonable question considering Emma and her best friend Marisa were in a public house called the Skinner's Arms. Emma had settled for instant with an unopenable plastic pot of non-dairy creamer. She was still just under age, and had decided to break precedence with her peers by waiting to be legal before getting drunk. Marisa was managing a pint of cider. She'd been drinking for years, and was faintly disgusted by Emma's sobriety. The pair of them were balanced on very high stools scouring the St Valentine's Day message pages in a music paper. Emma set great store by the saints.

'My mum's clairvoyant says that in the course of a single evening two people can make enough mistakes to last a lifetime,' Marisa explained.

'How do you mean?'

'I don't know. I suppose she means disease. Like *Ghosts*.'

'What, Patrick Swayze?'

'No, the other one. Ibsen.' Emma and Marisa were out for a drink and a laugh, two young girls too smart for their own good, one currently appearing as Cinderella in a production touring old people's homes and mental institutions, the other working behind a poultry counter, both hoping for something better, both dateless and footloose for one London night only, thanks to a workman drilling through the old folk's home's power cable. It had put him in hospital, and had got Emma the evening off.

'Don't you get depressed doing panto for people who don't know you're there?' asked Marisa.

'Some of them know. One old lady came up during the inter-mission and touched my dress, and said "You're Cinderella, aren't you?" and I said "Yes, I am." And she said "Cinderella, can I ask you something?" I said "Yes, of course." She said "Cinderella, where the *hell* am I?" When I look out from the stage I see a row of zimmer frames parked down the side of the hall. Last night one old lady stood up in the middle of Buttons' solo number and shouted "Help me!" No fairy tale endings there, I'm telling you.'

'I love checking out the personal ads in this paper,' said Marisa. 'Talk about looking for love in all the wrong places.'

Emma read over her shoulder and tutted. 'You can't plan

something that's meant to be special. It is, isn't it, special? Real love, I mean. And you can mess it up right from the start if you're not careful, like sticking your fork into a perfectly iced cake and smooshing it all around, you can never get it back as it was.'

'I'm not sure I care for your analogy. Of course it has to be special. The people who resort to advertising themselves can't see that. You can give me any classified description and I'll tell you what it really means.'

'All right.' Emma folded the newspaper back. 'Let's see. Older gentleman.'

'Gentleman's the giveaway, no one under forty would call themselves that. Older means ancient, mummified, something out of H. Rider Haggard.'

'Here's one. Fun loving.'

'Practical joker, scary laugh.'

'Youthful.'

'Stopped getting taller at eleven.'

'Open-minded.'

'Wants you to shag his friends.'

'Keen clubber.'

'Drugs. Shouts in your ear all evening and spends the whole of Sunday in bed.'

'Hmm.' Emma narrowed her eyes at her friend and turned the page. 'I think you're being over-cynical.'

'Trust me,' said Marisa. 'Men have got to be special or they're not worth it. You find your prince every night, it's all right for you.'

'Yeah, but he's five foot two and has phenomenal body odour. Okay.' She searched further down the page. 'Free spirit.'

'Backpacker.'

'Professional.'

'Works in a shoe shop.'

'Ordinary-looking.'

'Really ugly. Belongs on a cathedral spouting water.'

'Lonely.'

'Desperate.'

'Quiet type.'

'Harold Shipman.'

'Shame for Primrose. Do you think she knew more than she was letting on?'

'I imagine so. She must be a size eighteen.'

'Domesticated.'

'Bedridden. Possibly into humiliation. Could be a code for medical sex. Enemas, colonic irrigation, stuff like that.'

'Eugh.' Emma grimaced. 'Family man.'

'He got custody of the kids and needs a maid.'

'Artistic.'

'Hasn't come out yet.'

'Sporty.'

'Thinning ginger hair, sweaty red face, fat legs, wears rugby shirts.'

'Happy go lucky.'

'Out of work.'

'Spontaneous.'

'Turns up on your doorstep in the middle of the night. God, I hate men. I really hate them. I *really* hate them.'

'No, you don't. Here, try the women's ads. Here's one. Lovely lady, pert and petite.'

'That's easy. She'll be microscopically small, with a face like a weasel.'

'Vivacious.'

'Stick-thin, borderline hysteric.'

'Pleasingly plump. This one's included a picture.'

'Show me. My god, she looks like the Hindenberg. I didn't know Henney's made tops that big. She should have guy-ropes hanging off her. Don't show me any more, it's too depressing.'

Emma held up the back of the paper and point to an advert. 'He's nice.'

'He's a model. It's all he has to think about. You're wasting your time. Straight men don't moisturise.' She watched through the rain-distorted window as a passing housewife got her heel caught in a drain and fell onto the pavement, white plastic shopping bags haemorrhaging meat and fruit. No one stopped to help her. 'I read somewhere that a single woman over thirty-five has more chance of being kidnapped by terrorists than getting married.'

'That can't be right.' Emma dug in her bag for an illicit cigarette. 'Louise's mum got married at forty.'

'Wasn't she in an airplane hijack once?'

'Oh, yes.'

Marisa looked around the nicotine-tinged walls and sniffed disapprovingly. 'I can't drink more than two pints on an empty stomach. Do you fancy a Mexican?'

'No, I'm not eating anywhere where the toilets are labelled *Senoritas*. You can get syphilis from bar mints.'

'Anyone in here you like the look of?'

'What, a man?'

'No, a sperm whale. Of course a man.'

'I don't really know.'

'Behind you. Don't turn around. He looks like a doctor. That's a neck you can hang a stethoscope on.'

Emma twisted on her stool and smiled knowingly. He had short dark hair and pale fine features. He was slowly turning the pages of a newspaper, starting from the sports section. 'His neck could do with a shave. The backs of his hands are as hairy as a monkey. And his arms are too long. I'm surprised he's not eating a banana.' She always found fault with admirable men. They were too perfect otherwise. She breathed softly through her nose as she watched him skim the pages.

'Go and get some sugar, and talk to him on the way back.'

'I can't. I'm on sweeteners. You go.'

'He's very cute, don't you think?'

'You haven't got your lenses in.'

'Shit, he's leaving. Let's follow him.'

'What for?'

'See where he's going. Where's your sense of adventure?'

'I don't call traipsing through the rain behind strangers adventurous. I thought we were going to eat.' He was slipping into a scuffed leather jacket and heading for the door.

'Come on, quick, we'll lose him.' Marisa led the way. She always had, since they were nine and seven. Marisa, in trouble for breaking the door of the china cabinet, Emma, the shy one at the back of the choir. Marisa, charging across traffic-tensed roads, Emma stranded imploringly on the centre island. Marisa with a smile that opened like an accordian, Emma waiting with clenched lips and downcast eyes. Marisa playing terrible games, Emma being terribly honest. Marisa with the lies of a demon, Emma with the heart of an angel.

They followed him at seven paces, spinning away as he stopped before the window of a gift shop, then following his broad back inside.

'All these pink cupids and pastel teddy bears are so depressing.' Marisa picked a ribboned rubber heart from the shelf and squeezed it, making its voicebox release the sound of a smashing window. 'What on earth's the point of this?'

'It's a breaking heart,' whispered Emma. 'A joke.'

'How pathetic. Look, look, look. Check out the doctor.'

He loomed at the counter, making a purchase. The girl giftwrapped a teddy bear in squares of pink paper and placed it in a carrier bag. He chose a card, a glittery crimson heart speared with an arrow, borrowed a pen and thoughtfully wrote inside it.

'He's already got a hot date tonight. So much for your theory.'

'He's watching me,' said Marisa, peering out from behind a pile of stuffed unicorns.

'What are you talking about? He just bought something for his wife.' Emma felt ashamed of their behaviour. Marisa always pushed her where she didn't want to go. Marisa raised a finger to the convex mirror in the corner of the ceiling. The doctor's eyes fleetingly turned in her direction.

'He probably thinks you're mad, peering at him through the plush. You've not got a stage whisper.'

As he left, he smiled at Marisa.

'You home-wrecker,' hissed Emma.

Marisa hopped behind him, through the closing door. 'Come on, cowardy cat.'

They followed along a rain-gritted high street of puddle-greys and browns, darting beneath the yellow lamps that were just coming on. Past the barbers, the bookmakers, the dingy sauna, the poulterers where Marisa wrapped chicken breasts in butcher's paper, into the alleyway that cut to the residential street behind.

'He's got long legs, hasn't he?'

'And hairy hands. Enough's enough, Mari. I thought we were going to eat. I'm getting wet.'

'Oh, Emma, are you a man or a mouse? Squeak up. Don't you want to see where he's going?'

'Honestly? No. He must be fifteen years older than you. He was just looking because – that's what they do.' It was what they always did to Marisa. Their eyes slid past her, Emma. She was embarrassed. Marisa was brave. Men liked Marisa. In the high street someone screamed, but the scream turned into shrieking laughter and faded with the surge of traffic.

He stopped at the steps of a terraced block inexpertly finished in grey stone, dim and ugly rainstreaked flats that would wither the superlatives in any estate agent's mouth. *It's the wrong place for him*, thought Emma. *Shiny shoes, expensive coat and here he is among the drug dealers. This can't be where he lives. It's not good enough.*

He pushed open a door of steel-meshed glass and slowly climbed the stairs to the first floor, reappearing on the dripping balcony, a set of keys in his right hand. Somewhere water fell from a height, a blocked overflow spattering as mournfully as a memorial. The apartment doors were matched in fierce council colours. He stopped before the first one and bent over the lock. A click, a rattle and he was gone. Marisa stood facing the flats, staring up into the rain.

'Marisa, come on, this is creepy and stupid.'

'He'll be back out.'

'He won't.'

'He will. Watch. He's just switching on the lights.'

And suddenly Emma knew. She knew that Marisa had done this before. They were witnessing part of a secret routine. She studied Marisa's sly brown eyes and saw something, an expectancy she had never seen before. 'You know him,' she said stupidly. 'He really is a doctor, isn't he?'

'Of course I know him. He's married, but she's out tonight, it's Thursday. Big bucks at bingo.' Marisa couldn't remove her gaze from the balcony. 'He's checking to see that the coast is clear.'

A few seconds later he reappeared at the concrete parapet and stood motionless, calmly looking down at her. Emma knew then that they were lovers, Marisa and the hairy man, and with the knowledge some private part of their friendship was damaged forever.

'I'm going up.'

'Don't be a slut, Marisa. He could be a psycho.'

'He's just a man. His name's John. He used to be my mum's GP.' She pushed her hair back into her hood and set off for the steel-meshed door that had been left ajar for her.

Emma hovered at the entrance of the alley, unable to leave, but hating herself for staying. She heard Marisa's shoes on the concrete steps, steady and rising. She looked up at the balcony and heard the flat latch click softly. After that, the door stayed shut and the lights stayed off.

'How could you,' she shouted to the rain-shimmered darkness. 'It's St Valentine's Day. How could you.'

The card had fallen from his bag and lay in the gutter,

glittering under dirty water. She gingerly raised it and looked inside. 'With all my love, John.' The letters were blurring. It could have been written to anyone.

'I thought you said it had to be special. We agreed on it.'

Emma stood alone in the deep shadows. For the rest of the night, the rain fell in silvery arrows that pierced her through the heart.

WHERE THEY WENT WRONG

SCOTT MILLER: THE EARLY YEARS

Scott Miller was unnaturally tidy for a twenty-two-year-old. There were no unfolded clothes in his bedroom, not even any dust under the bed. He regularly cleaned the side of his toothbrush where crusts of paste gathered, and wiped the glass shelf below the mirror in the bathroom so that it was free of smears. His parents were not responsible for breeding these habits in him; rather, they were vaguely disturbed by his quest for perfection. His books and CDs were arranged according to unfathomable rules, as though a private catalogue existed in his mind, and had to be adhered to at all times.

As a child he was intimidated by any change in routine. He found reasons to stay home while schoolfriends travelled. He was not one for adventures. An imposition of order was more important to him than the excitement of sudden upset. He seemed happy, but remained guarded in his conversation, and never allowed his parents to see inside his mind.

Scott's father particularly noticed this careful veiling of his son's true nature. He entertained the usual suspicions about the boy: a problem with drugs, or perhaps his sexuality. But Scott seemed quite ordinary. He had no desire to get drunk, swallow tablets or have sex with lots of strangers. He showed no allegiance to any political party, or any specific religion. He held no extreme views of any kind. He was more than normal, too normal, in fact, except that he had no close friends. No one came up to the exacting standards that Scott set himself. Not that he considered himself to be someone special, even though he was.

Scott was a statistician. He worked for a large insurance company in Holborn, quantifying risk and analysing safety data for shipping companies. He appeared to enjoy the job, if only because he never complained about it. He still lived at home, in his parents' run-down flat in the scruffy, dangerous end of the borough of Lewisham. His mother suffered with her nerves, and hardly ever went out. His father worked for an ailing stationery company, and earned less with each passing year. The family held together through impecunious circumstances, and there was 'always food on the table', as his father put it, but very little else.

Scott's parents looked older than they were, and were later to age rapidly when public attention turned to them. A lack of luxury had worn them out and left them bloodless. They were too frightened and tired to take pleasure from the small grace-notes of life anymore. They loved their son; they were careful to tell the newspapers that. But Scott worried them. Consequently, even when he was just a schoolboy, the three of them behaved as though everything was fine, when in fact everything was far from fine. A lot went undiscussed; there are families where you just don't mention problems.

SCOTT MILLER: A STUDY IN ANGUISH

As Scott walks down the street on his way to buy a sandwich at lunchtime, he entertains thoughts of violence. In his head he is so extremely violent that he can barely bring himself to pay the appallingly rude girl who shoves his sandwich in a bag and slings it over the counter at him. He is offended by her off-hand attitude, and he wants to place a hand over her mouth as he tears open her striped shirt, biting her shoulders until his teeth meet through the flesh, yanking off her pants and thrusting away at her sex until there is nothing left of her but raw unidentifiable meat.

Everywhere he looks he finds rudeness, slipping standards, creeping lassitude. England, he has decided, is filled with disgusting people, and London is home to the worst offenders. He finds the behaviour of almost everyone with whom he comes into contact vulgar, childish, rude, sluttish, cretinous, pathetic. He entertains thoughts of killing them all.

He sees money swilling around the city, usually in the hands of those who are too stupid to even notice that it is there, or too venal to ever consider that there are others without. He watches the vulgar white stretch limos disgorging bottle-waving office workers, blank-faced drug dealers barging a path along the sticky, trash-filled pavements of Tottenham Court Road, whorishly dressed girls screaming at each other on the tube as if it is the most normal way in the world to behave. In summer the city is bursting to the seams, violence is palpable, sex takes place in public, criminals operate on every main thoroughfare, and nothing is done. Even the police laugh and turn a blind eye. This is not the world he was promised.

Back in his bedroom, Scott watches an old black and white film, one of his father's tapes, and finds it impossible to imagine the place it portrays. In the film, a beautiful blonde girl in a mini-skirt walks along an elegant Kensington High Street devoid of cars and almost as devoid of people. It is as though everyone else has been tidied away. The streets are clean and smart, and even a girl serving in a shop is polite, speaking with an impossibly clear-cut accent. It is odd that Scott should crave a world he has never experienced, a time before mass-transit and global warming and junk food that now only exists on the ageing, increasingly spackled videotapes in his father's collection.

Scott is thin and tall, with the slight stoop that often develops in such men from politely listening to shorter people. He has cropped fair hair, a high forehead and a thin beaky nose, a look that he feels points him out as a particularly English type, of the sort that started to disappear after the war, as nutrition improved.

Scott's life weighs heavily on him. He is becoming a paradox; an angel drifting into darkness. He considers himself the last bastion of decency, not the prudish, narrow definition expounded by home county Tories, but the kind of decent man who holds a door open for a girl, who smiles and says 'Good morning', who listens patiently to the troubles of others. The force of tolerance makes him tired. He knows he cannot afford to lower his guard, even for a second. As each passing day brings the city closer to chaos, it also takes him closer to a breakdown. He is a ticking bomb, a gun with the safety trigger off. Scott is aware of this time-limit on his rational self. He understands a primary truth about the capital city; that a man can make a violent mark on the populace, only to see the wound heal and fade within a single day, scuffed away by the continuous shuffle of people.

The only thing that protects the city from Scott is his own self-control. He knows that if he hits his tipping-point and goes berserk he will have proved himself no better than any of the scum around him. He'll join their ranks. He will cease to be special.

So he bites his tongue and turns his cheek, and contents himself with the peculiar huffs, sighs, glares and grimaces that an Englishman makes when he hates strangers for performing acts of minor slight.

Scott gets the elbow from his job. He is told about staff cutbacks, retrenchment, restructuring, but the real reason he is fired is because he's not fun to be with. He makes his colleagues uneasy. Terrified of unemployment, terrified by the thought of any change at all, Scott takes the first work he sees on offer. Given his parlous state of mind, it is probably not a good idea for him to take a position in customer relations, dealing with the public, working for a chain of supermarkets, but he does. And soon he comes to see it as his salvation.

SUSAN GARRET: THE CHILDHOOD FEARS

Every day Susan Garret gets more scared. She thought the feeling would go away once she grew up, but it just keeps accumulating. When she was a skinny kid of six, with a pageboy haircut and the knock knees of a Disney foal, the dark at the top of the stairs was frightening. She had to beat the flush on the toilet and get down to the kitchen before it stopped, or something unspeakable would rush out of the gloom and kill her. When she was nine, the lounge ceiling fell in while she and her mother were out visiting the doctor. Her mother said they were lucky not to have been killed. It was an old house, and the war had left a lot of buildings cracked. Susan became convinced that her bedroom ceiling would fall next, and nightly cowered with her head under the damp, musty blankets.

Her parents fought constantly. Susan's mother was still shocked about marrying the wrong man. Sometimes she stared at him across the breakfast table, shaking her head slightly at the memory of her seduction, as if to wonder whether she had been mad. Susan's father had once failed to take a chance that might lead them to a better future, and blamed his wife and child for holding him back. He made noises to himself, growling, hissing and groaning with such frequency that it became an uncontrollable tic.

Susan was sure that her father would one day kill all of them, her mother and anyone else unfortunate enough to be visiting the house that day. She became scared, not of her father's temper, but of what would happen if he killed her mother. How would she survive?

Susan's ancient Aunt Mary lived with them. She wasn't a real aunt but her grandmother's spinster companion, drafted in to stop a family war. She hid tins of food in a suitcase under the bed in case of another real war, and on the occasions when she smiled she looked like a skull, the shape of her mouth forming a cruel rictus far more frightening than any scowl. Susan hated her. At the age of eleven, she was alone in the house with her aunt when the old lady had some kind of a fit and collapsed. She slowly tipped over on a dining chair and landed in the fireplace, banging her head on the brass surround. Susan tried to get help from her neighbours but they wouldn't open their doors, even to a little girl. Aunt Mary died a few days later.

Susan became convinced that she too would die soon after because she had seen how easily it could happen.

She was a lonely child, and rarely played with other children, because a classmate's father had gone to jail for interfering with his daughters, and stories of their alleged complicity had made the children in her class suspicious of one another. A few years later Susan discovered masturbation, and was sure that it had given her a venereal disease. She searched the family's medical dictionary for proof that she was infected, and passed another year of torture, locked in her bedroom with a hand mirror. The first time she kissed a boy, she was sure she had failed him in some way, because he didn't seem very happy afterwards and never called her again, so sex became a source of fear for her.

Susan was so desperate to please that she irritated people.

She was not a practical girl. She loved books, and hated anything mechanical. Her father tinkered with motorbikes and dismantled them inside the house. He left oily patches in the hall that her mother found hard to remove. He made his daughter help him because he had wanted a boy, and bullied her when she dropped something. He told her that if she did not know how to wire a fuse by the time she grew up she would have to sit in total darkness, and everyone would laugh at her.

She became scared of growing up.

The family was broke all the time. Her mother had two jobs, and for a while three. Her father said that without hard work they would starve, that hard work made them decent. She became scared of poverty.

SUSAN GARRET: AN ESSAY IN ANXIETY

Fear is a great goader. Susan passed all her school exams because she was scared of failing. Her friends never analysed their futures. Susan foresaw the whole grim scenario: failure of exams, failure to get a decent job, failure to make alliances, failure to love someone kind. She saw herself forced into begging on the streets, she saw humiliation, degradation, starvation. She made little slashes up and down her arms with a penknife, or bits of wire – even paperclips worked – because she was angered by her lack of fortitude.

Susan worked hard, harder, harder still, but couldn't even order in a restaurant without feeling embarrassed. She tried to form romantic relationships, but couldn't make any last. She watched her parents grow furious and confused by the raw deal life had brought them. She landed a good job and became moderately successful, but the higher she climbed the scarier it got. The pressure not to fail became intense. Once you get used to the good things of life, it's hard to imagine doing without them.

At twenty-two, Susan tried a radical change of lifestyle, and moved to California to be with a young man she had met on holiday. It was here that her worst fears were crystallised into something horrifyingly concrete. All around her, bright young people were being snubbed and made fun of until they fell by the wayside and became mad or ill. They died unmourned and ignored, like dogs on the highway. It seemed to her as though the entire state was suffering from some kind of collective stupidity. Her boyfriend behaved in an increasingly grotesque fashion, until she feared for her life. She finished with him, and stopped believing in love.

Susan left Los Angeles because she was tired of being

intimidated by huge portions of food, tired of being lied to, tired of being told how to look and what to think, tired of hearing people talk rubbish, tired of their pervasive obsession with youth, tired of egos, tired of pretending everything was just great.

She thought it would be safer and less boring to live in England. But the place had changed. She returned to find old friends becoming soured by possessions and sharpened by under-achievement. Robbed by time of the little charm she possessed, she allowed herself to become overweight. She noticed some of her colleagues beginning to sicken and die, one or two in horribly unkind and undignified ways. She became scared of dying unloved and unremembered.

One thing, though, began to scare her above all others. The senselessness of her peers. They lied and stole and carried on the way thoughtless people do, but they did it with such little purpose that it was clear they were insane. With each passing day the world around her made less and less sense, until she reached a point where nothing she heard people say or do made any sense at all. All she could see were frightening, greedy, selfish, narrow-minded animals craving little beyond sensation, people who did not even bother to question their fate as they fell, chattering away into the abyss.

Susan vowed never to become like that. But what could she do to stop herself from being scared? When she reached her thirties, she realised that her generation had watched the world poison itself. What hurt most was that she remembered there had once been a better place. All too soon, it would be her turn to die, leaving the world incrementally worse off. She and the other people of her age would pass unrespected and unmissed, kicked into their graves by the selfish young. Now she was scared of getting old.

Susan realised that there was only one thing that did not scare her, and that was death. When you stop questioning the actions of the world, you lose the ability to consider suicide.

Once you accept death, you can do anything. She became invulnerable to the terrifying screaming panic inside her head.

SUSAN AND SCOTT: MADE FOR EACH OTHER

Susan realised that nothing could be worse than being alive. So she rented a shabby hotel room on the outskirts of Manchester, near where she had been born, and lay down on the bed, and neatly cut the fat blue veins in her wrists with a razor blade, and waited to enter the kingdom of perpetual night.

As she watched the blood pump from her hot openings into the bedspread, she felt happier with each passing second. Her worries fell away, and for the first time she clearly saw how foolishly she had behaved, and how it was possible to live a peaceful, unfrightened existence. She saw with tremendous clarity – like looking at the sea just before it rains – how she had been completely wrong about the world and its people, how misled she had been by the shadow of her childhood, and how she could simply put everything right. By then, of course, her epiphany had arrived almost too late.

It took dying to make her see the opportunities in life. She wanted to make the process stop. But she could not move, and dying began to hurt. A small, terrible voice scratched inside her brain.

It said: 'This is the secret that is only revealed at the end of your being. You could have had a happy time on earth, Susan, simply by not being scared. But you have chosen to leave behind a world of joy and laughter, and venture into the numb darkness, which is just like the darkness you feared as a child, only this time there really is something to be afraid of. The fear of everlasting nothingness.'

And as her panicked eyes began to close, everything she had ever feared rushed from the beyond to greet her.

If it had not been for the hotel chambermaid entering the

room at that moment, she would have fallen and become lost in that damned penumbra.

Rushed to hospital and healed on the outside, she began the painful process of healing inner wounds. She moved back to London with a new sense of purpose. She got a new job, working for a chain of supermarkets. In one of the branches she met a man who was so like her that they could have been brother and sister. He was nothing much to look at; his beaky nose and prominent Adam's apple reminded her of old photographs, the way men used to be.

Scott and Susan were quickly married. Together they felt strong enough to survive. They made each other complete.

They rented a modest basement flat in Finsbury Park, and started to see the world through fresh new eyes, as a couple who were always together, and who would support one another through every crisis of faith, no matter how unbearable things became for them. They were at exactly the same point in their lives, and thanked God each day that their paths had crossed.

SUSAN AND SCOTT: PEACE AT LAST

Seven years later, after they were both dead (he hanged himself in prison, she took an overdose of Epinephrine), after the naked bodies in their bricked-up cellar had been reassembled to give the police a rough idea of numbers, after questions had been asked about how so many people could go missing without remark, after the house had been pulled down to deter ghoulish onlookers, after the incomplete remains of their victims had been reburied amid public displays of grief and bouquets left in plastic wrappers, after everyone had sold their stories to the *News of the World*, after the social workers had been castigated, and after politicians had explained why it could never happen again, the newspapers still shared a common verdict:

NOT SINCE FRED AND ROSEMARY WEST

Or Ian Brady and Myra Hindley. Or Dr Harold Shipman. Or

Ian and Mary Carr. Or whoever else had broken the national record for inexplicable atrocities. Scott and Susan Miller were nothing like any of them, of course, they were quite unique, but the press was at a loss to come up with anything more original. Their lives were analysed, their relatives interviewed, their motives dissected, their biographies recorded, but no one was any the wiser for having every detail to hand. And no one had the power to stop it from happening again.

Besides, by then the newspapers were already searching for fresh scandals to spread across their pages, and new fingers of blame to point that would grab the attention of their distracted, disillusioned readers.

The past lives of Susan and Scott became as clouded and mysterious as the layers of police polythene that protected the scored dead flesh of those they had befriended. Their motives were so stratified with secret pain that they remained impervious to analysis. As teenagers, they would have been horrified to see what they would become. Eventually, though, the monstrosity of their actions overshadowed their normality, removing them to a realm of remembrance reserved for the few who had discovered the power to touch the world.

Scott and Susan. Their names became linked forever. In death, they became an example of unforgettable evil. But as children, watchful and serious, downcast in photographs, frowning in sunlight, all they had sought was a fair way to live their lives, in the quiet, forgotten way that explains what it means to be English.

IN SAFE HANDS

Simon Woolf's mother knew a lot of crazy people.

That's to say, she would listen carefully to complete strangers and give consideration to their problems, no matter how peculiar they eventually turned out to be. She did it because she cared, because she was bored, because no one else could be bothered.

Simon and his older brother Harry found her behaviour embarrassing. They would stand by, desperately pretending not to know her while she engaged people who were barely more than tramps in conversation. Later they grew used to her habits, but it made them no easier to understand; how could she invite these virtual strangers – some of them Gentiles – in to share the family's *Shobbas* dinner? The boys would sulk and barely speak before these interlopers, no matter how hard their mother tried to make conversation.

Father went along with it because he loved her, even though he preferred privacy. Simon and Harry feared that the town would think them fools. Instead, they were surprised to discover that this willingness to befriend the unfavoured made their mother liked, even admired, and improved her social standing. It was, perhaps, the gratitude of others who recognised no such charitability in themselves.

Inevitably, there were those in the town who also disapproved. They watched suspiciously as Hannah sat beside dispossessed folk on seaside benches, listening to their stories.

What was she up to? What was she after? Why couldn't she behave like normal people? It was when Simon saw their pinched faces looking down on Hannah as they passed that he rallied to her side, to be rewarded with a grateful smile from his mother.

As he grew into his teens, he became accustomed to Hannah's dinner guests, few of whom had ever told their stories, although they had suffered greatly in their lives. Their families had fled from Russia, Poland, Germany, France, the great diaspora surviving the devastation of pogroms and the subtler destruction of sly prejudice, to settle down in quiet obscurity in the temperate seaside town. Their families had died, leaving a son here, a daughter there, usually middle-aged and unmarried, often befuddled by the changing world in which they found themselves. And Hannah would invite them to Sabbath supper, something she continued to do until the very week she died of pancreatic cancer.

By this time, Harry had moved up to London, where he had married and set up a company that manufactured shirts. Simon stayed on the Sussex coast with his ailing father, who refused to sort through his wife's belongings, leaving the job to his son. Simon dutifully carted away the clothes and sold the books that no one wanted. Harry had married a *shiksa*, and rarely made the journey down on Friday nights, but called, at least, to check on his father. Soon *Shobbas* dinner had become a quiet affair between Simon and the old man, and they realised that they missed some, if not all, of Hannah's guests, but it was too late to do anything about that. There were no addresses for most of these people, although occasionally Simon would see them wrapped in thick coats on the seafront, or walking in the town's high street, looking a little lost.

Simon had been expecting the call from the family lawyer, summoning them to a meeting at which they would discuss the dispersal of Hannah's finances. They were expecting no surprises; the Woolf family was hardworking, but far from wealthy.

They had rented their apartment and lived meagrely ever since Simon's father declared himself bankrupt. His father was too ill and upset to visit the lawyer's office, and Harry was detained in London on business, so the younger son went alone. He was surprised, however, to find that the subject was not his mother.

'You've been left a substantial property,' explained Mr Rosen, the firm's senior partner. 'Mr Howard Silverstein was a friend of your mother's, I believe. He died of a heart attack just under two weeks ago, and we found ourselves instructed to dispose of his estate.'

Simon tried to recall the man shown to him by Mr Rosen in a photograph dating back some thirty years. The younger Silverstein was pictured with his staff standing outside the cluttered windows of a drapers' shop, in the manner of photographs from a much earlier era. Simon mentally added the lapsed time to Silverstein's features, extra weight and less hair, and came up with one of his mother's most frequent dinner guests, even though the old man had appeared less regularly in the last few years. He recalled Silverstein's intense political discussions with his mother. It was presumably one of the reasons why she invited him, for her husband could never be drawn on subjects of topical interest.

Simon was puzzled. 'Did he have no dependants to whom he could leave his property?'

'His wife died ten years ago, but there is a son. For some reason, Mr Silverstein chose not to leave his only heir the family house, although he has arranged a healthy annual income to be paid to the boy in perpetuity. He's a little younger than you, twenty-one or two.'

'Are you familiar with the property?' asked Simon, amazed and somewhat ashamed of his good fortune, which surely belonged to a direct descendant.

'Unfortunately not. My partner usually handles Mr Silverstein's affairs, but is away on leave. I have all the details here. All I require from you is a signature on the necessary documents.'

Mr Rosen passed Simon a thick envelope containing the deeds, the plans of the house and all the related documentation he would require. Simon studied the address. It was in the older part of town, where the houses were large and in want of upkeep, relics from a wealthier time.

'Mr Silverstein thought very highly of your mother. Decency isn't a word one hears very often nowadays . . .' Mr Rosen was uncomfortable with reminiscence of the departed, and busied himself with the keys, which he handed to Simon on a large brass ring. 'Sometimes it's hard to understand why our clients choose to reward or ignore their friends and relatives,' he said. 'All we can do is carry out their wishes. I'm sure there was a special reason why Mr Silverstein wanted you to have the property.'

'Do you know what that was?' asked Simon.

Mr Rosen shrugged. 'Perhaps he had fond memories of you from your mother's dinners. He told my partner that you would know what to do.'

As Simon thanked the lawyer and left, he wondered if he would discover what this meant.

He found the property, a red-brick Victorian end-house, at the corner of a road leading from the seafront. There were sixteen keys in the bunch Mr Rosen had presented to him. Inside, the dark lincrusta-coated hallway reeked of damp. None of the furniture had been removed, and the rooms were clean, but there appeared to be no electricity. Ancient brass-hooked gas mantles still jutted from the sepia walls. Simon worked his way through the gloomy house room by room, unlocking each of the doors, as though finding his way into a labyrinth. When the sun vanished behind rainclouds it robbed the building of any remaining light, and he was unable to see at all. He had no torch, but there were candles and matches to be found in the kitchen. Lighting them threw the house further back into the past. Simon knew it would take a small fortune to renovate the property. It was money he didn't have.

On the top floor he discovered a door that could not be opened. None of the keys fitted its lock; they all appeared to be too small. According to the floor plans, the entrance led to a series of large connecting rooms that ran the full length of the house. Simon tried to force the door, but it was too well-built, and easily withstood his shoulder. He was still trying each of the keys in the lock again when he heard a thump come from inside. It was too heavy to be a rat, or even a dog.

Simon set down the candle. 'Is there anyone in there?' he called, but there came no answer. He could sense someone moving away on the other side of the door. 'Would you let me in?' he asked, but now the movement stopped altogether.

Simon returned downstairs to puzzle out the problem. He had a feeling that there was someone still living in the house – could the old man have neglected to mention a sitting tenant? He made himself a cup of tea and sat with his feet up on the small kitchen work-table, trying to decide what to do next when he saw the brass key, larger than any of the ones on the ring, hanging above the butler sink.

This time the handle twisted and the door opened. The room revealed to him was ramshackle and lived-in. An opposite door led to further rooms. 'Hello?' called Simon, nervously venturing in with the candle raised. A rain-laden breeze blew in through a cracked window in the kitchen. Dirty plates were stacked in the sink. A dishcloth hung across a cupboard door was dripping water on the bare floor. Simon stepped into the next room, a dingy brown lounge overfilled with moulting Victorian furniture. 'Hello, is there anyone here?' he called again.

He sensed the movement rather than saw it, a faint tremor in the floorboards, a displacement in the air. Someone was hiding in the bedroom, behind the remaining closed door. As he turned the handle, he heard a whimpering sound. Beside the old brass bed, huddled so tightly in the corner that he seemed barely human, was a cowering man. His shoes scuffed against the rug as Simon approached, and he raised his hands above his head as if fearful of being punished.

Simon sat on the end of the bed. The room smelled stale, lived in for too long. 'You have nothing to be frightened of, I'm not going to hurt you,' he said, 'but I'm not going to leave until you tell me who you are.' They sat together in silence. Slowly, the frightened figure unbent and sat up.

Simon was shocked to realise that the young man had been expecting to be hurt or dragged from the room. 'I'm Simon.' He held out his hand. 'Do you know Mr Silverstein?'

'I'm Mr Silverstein,' said the young man quietly.

'Well, I don't see how that's possible. Howard Silverstein has passed on, so who are you?'

'I'm – Marcus.'

'Well, I'm pleased to meet you, Marcus.' His first thought was that Marcus had gained access to the empty house to shelter from bad weather, or perhaps was a sitting tenant. Then he saw the startling resemblance to the man in the photograph Mr Rosen had shown him. 'You're Howard's son,' he said, surprised.

They sat beside each other in the kitchen. Marcus cupped his hands around the tea mug. 'I haven't been down to this floor sinced my father died. I've been sitting *shiva*.'

'By yourself? He died over ten days ago,' said Simon. 'What have you been doing for meals?'

'There's a year's supply of food in the freezer,' Marcus explained. 'But the gas was cut off, so I had to eat everything raw. We always kept stocks high – just in case.'

'In case of what?' He waited as the pale young man knotted his hands in his lap, but there came no reply. He tried another tack. 'Have you always lived here?'

'No, we moved around when my mother was alive.' Marcus smiled at the memory. His blue eyes were remarkable when they came to life. His skin was as pale as paper. 'We were happier then. But she became ill, so we had to stay in one place. Someone had poisoned her.'

'Why would anyone want to do that?'

Another silence as Marcus sipped his hot tea.

'How do you know she was poisoned?'

'My father told me.'

'Was your father proved correct?'

'The family doctor told me she died of natural causes. He asked my father to attend counselling, but he only went a couple of times. I had been through a bad patch at school, I'd been bullied a lot, so I left early to stay at home with my father.'

Simon looked at the young man and saw no happiness within him, only the burdens that come with later life. He was upset to imagine the anguish of such an existence.

'And you've been here ever since.'

'Yes.'

'Then you must come and eat with us.'

While Marcus changed his clothes, Simon waited in his bedroom. On the walls were magazine pictures of the Arizona desert, sweeping vistas of sand and stars. Marcus came in buckling his trousers. 'I collected them from my father's *National Geographic* magazines,' he explained, reaching up to touch a favourite scene. 'So beautiful. How could you not feel free in a place so open to the sky?'

Simon watched Becky as she placed the sliced roast chicken in the centre of the table. He had been due to have dinner with his fiancée that evening, and had brought Marcus along with him, although it had been a struggle to get him to leave the house. 'I'd forgotten that Howard had a son,' he said. 'I didn't mean to startle you this afternoon.'

'I'm sorry for my behaviour,' Marcus replied, eagerly helping himself to a plate of potatoes. 'I thought – I thought you were someone else.'

Becky was clearly confused by the young man. Marcus was

thin and white, his thick black hair cropped in an old-fashioned short-back-and-sides cut. It was as though he came from another time, a bystander in an old monochrome newsreel.

'Please warn me if I'm being insensitive,' Simon apologised, 'but I'm trying to understand. Where exactly did your father die?'

'In the house,' said Marcus. 'He was watching television when he had his heart attack. *Family Fortunes*. May I have some chicken?'

'Of course. You must treat our home as yours,' said Simon, who keenly felt himself in the embarrassing situation of inheriting a property that should not rightfully be his.

'That must have been awful for you.' Becky caught Simon's eye and held it, as if to ask *what is this guy about?* 'What did you do?'

'He wore a hospital alarm around his neck, so I pressed it and an ambulance came, but by that time he had died. I went back up to my room and stayed there until everyone had gone.'

'You didn't make yourself known to the doctor? Why not?'

'My father always told me not to speak to strangers. He said it wasn't safe.'

'What do you mean?'

Marcus gave her a knowing look. 'I'm glad you came when you did,' he said. 'I was having trouble unfreezing the food.' *He's not all there*, Simon thought. *The old man kept him at home rather than have him put away somewhere. That's why he didn't leave him the house.*

'You mean you stayed in the house all that time? You haven't been out?'

'My father bought all our basic necessities. He didn't like me to go out into the street by myself. He knew people, he could move freely through the town without being arrested.'

'What do you mean?' Simon asked. 'There's nothing dangerous in town.'

'It's dangerous everywhere,' said Marcus through a mouthful of food. 'You must know that, everyone knows that.'

Simon was starting to lose his patience. 'I promise you, Marcus, I have no idea what you're talking about.'

Becky laid a placating hand on his arm. 'Marcus,' she said gently, 'suppose you explain to us what you think the problem is with going outside.'

'You must be aware of what's happening.' Marcus looked to each of them in turn with the wide eyes of an innocent. 'I mean, you are practising Jews?'

'Well, we don't keep strict kosher,' Becky pointed out. 'My mother used two sets of crockery, and I still won't drink milk straight after a meal, but we're not exactly – what are you getting at?'

Simon and Becky lowered their knives and forks as they waited for a reply.

'He believes that a great anti-Semitic conspiracy still exists,' Simon told the lawyer Rosen over lunch. 'Apparently the guy has had a history of mental illness since his mother died, nothing so serious that he has to be confined, but enough to keep him out of regular employment. His father taught him a lot of weird stuff, and he seems to have bought all of it.'

'What sort of weird stuff?'

'Okay.' Simon took a deep breath. 'He doesn't believe that Germany really lost the war. The old man told him the Nazis continued to spread until they infiltrated every government on the planet. He convinced his son that the Jewish people are being lulled into a false sense of security, so that they can eventually be rounded up in one grand cull. Marcus wouldn't step outside the house after his father died. He flatly refuses to believe in the state of Israel. I explained that it was made an independent state in 1948. I've read him books and newspaper articles, I've taken him onto the internet, but I can see that he still doesn't believe a word I tell him. He didn't have a television, so I showed him footage on TV, but he just dismisses it as propaganda. Of course, the newsreels of the Palestinian bombings didn't do much to convince him of his safety. How do you convince a person when they've set their mind at something?'

'I've been doing some checking for you,' said Mr Rosen, pouring wine. 'Marcus Silverstein's grandfather was a concentration camp survivor. And his own father developed some extreme views as he grew older. He was banned from some places in town for causing arguments, like the library and the Rotarians Club. People eventually kept away from him, which was why he appreciated your mother's hospitality so much. Do you think he's solely responsible for poisoning his son against the new world, or did Marcus partly come to these opinions by himself?'

'I don't know,' Simon admitted. 'This isn't a matter of faith, it's a more primal fear of persecution. Hell, we all have a few irrational beliefs tucked away in the dark corners of our minds. I mean, I think of myself as an enlightened non-practising Jew but I still become deeply uncomfortable when I read in the local papers about synagogues being desecrated. The past surfaces. I tell myself they're stupid kids, that it's a cyclical thing and that it'll blow over, but I'm not sure I completely believe it.'

'Have you come to a decision about the house?'

Simon sighed. 'I said he could stay there as long as he wanted. What else could I do? Becky has this plan. She wants to draw Marcus out of his shell, get him to attend the local synagogue and listen to the rabbi. He'll assure him that he's safe.'

'Well,' said Mr Rosen, raising his glass. 'I admire what you're trying to do. You're good people. Marcus is lucky he met you both. *L'chaim.*'

They toasted. 'Perhaps that was the idea,' said Simon. 'His father knew us. Maybe he was searching for a pair of safe hands before he died, someone whom he could trust to take care of his son.'

'But to fill his head with such terrors – what kind of man would do such a cruel thing?'

'One who believed it himself.' Simon set down his glass. 'He'd suffered in his own life, and was heartsick at what he saw in the world. As I see it, my job isn't to strengthen Marcus's faith in God, but to give him faith in ordinary people.'

'Come on, you can do it.' Becky coaxed her reluctant charge forward. She and Simon stood with Marcus between them on the station platform. 'I think he's agoraphobic, Simon.'

'Come on, Marcus, the first time will be the worst,' urged Simon, but he wasn't sure if Marcus would manage to move. He was staring at the crowds ahead in horror. 'What's the matter?'

Marcus began to shake his head violently. 'The crowds.'

'It's a busy city. No one is even looking. They're not going to hurt you.' He had been expecting this reaction. It was Marcus's first time in London, a day trip to see the sights.

'But there are men in the crowd – dangerous men.'

'Can you see these dangerous men? Can you point them out?'

'Yes. There and there, and there.' He pointed to several dark-suited commuters weaving their way to the tube entrance. The tannoy boomed above them, making Marcus flinch.

'They're just ordinary businessmen, pal. They're going to work. Watch.' Simon darted over to one of the men Marcus had singled out and asked him the time. The man checked his watch, replied and hurried on.

'See? They're not after you, they're not Nazis, they don't hate anyone, they're just ordinary, regular people late for work.'

'But my father—'

'I know it's difficult for you to understand, Marcus, but not everything your father told you was strictly true,' began Becky. 'Bad things happened in his lifetime, and worse in his father's lifetime, but much of that terrible suffering is past now. Yes, ethnic groups are still persecuted. The Croatians in former

Yugoslavia suffered in much the same way as the Jewish people did during the war. In Africa, tribes still attempt to wipe each other out, each claiming superiority over the other. But your father raised you here in the west, where there are systems in place to make sure that it's harder for such things to happen anymore.'

'It's easy for you to say that,' said Marcus doubtfully, but Becky could tell that he was starting to trust them.

As they exited from Waterloo Station, through backpackers and elderly couples and Chinese tourists, through the arch filled with the etched names of the glorious dead and out onto the broad grey steps, a look of amazement grew on Marcus's face until it became uncontained excitement. He had never been to London. They walked him to the centre of the new bridge connecting St Pauls to Borough, and shared his delight as the wind swept beneath their arms so strongly that for a moment it felt as though it might carry them all away.

They walked along the Embankment until they were facing the Houses of Parliament, then returned to have lunch at Somerset House. Despite Becky's protestations about putting Marcus through too much on his first day out in the world, Simon marched them on to Trafalgar Square and the National Gallery, where he was rewarded by a look of thrilled incredulity on Marcus's face. The sun shone with rare fierceness, sharpening shadows and turning the interior of the museum into cool cloisters. They seated themselves beneath a row of vast allegorical religious paintings; the point was not lost on their new friend.

'So much beauty,' he murmured, looking from one great canvas to the next, 'so many ways of telling a single story.'

'It's a story that has survived the devastation of centuries,' replied Simon, 'and though we now recognise these scenes as illustrated lessons rather than historical episodes, they continue to inspire generations to believe in the innate goodness of mankind.'

'But they're full of vengeance,' said Marcus doubtfully. 'Look over there – thunderbolts and storms, idolators attacked, temples destroyed, sinners condemned. This is a God that has no trust in the people he has created. They have to be constantly punished in order to be kept on the path to salvation.'

'He's not going to be won over in a day,' Becky whispered to Simon with a smile. 'You have to give him time.'

They made the London trips a regular feature of their days together. It was the very least Simon could do for accepting the house. He had discussed the old man's legacy with Marcus, who was entirely happy with the new arrangement. Howard had left him enough to live comfortably without the pressure of employment, and he did not want the worry of looking after such a large property. Simon would work with Marcus on the renovation. When the house was fit to be sold, they would come to some arrangement that would ensure Marcus gained financially and would always have somewhere to live.

But it was clear to Becky that their new friend was not well. On one of their trips to London they passed a group of men in military uniform, and Marcus began to shake so violently that they were forced to get him off the street.

'They come for you in the night, as they did for my grand-parents,' he said, accepting a glass of water and bringing it to his chattering lips. 'They watch from the corners of their eyes because they hate us.'

'They have no reason to hate us anymore,' Simon insisted. 'The man who made them do so is dead. I showed you the television programme about him, remember?'

'But there is always another to take his place, and another after him.'

'There is no country in the world like Germany in the 1930s,' said Becky.

'What about America? The most powerful country of all, yet its corporations are corrupt, its people are economically enslaved and its politicians make the threat of war the keystone of their foreign policy. Why has so little been learned from the past?'

'Even I can't answer that one,' Simon admitted. 'Sometimes even democracies aren't perfect. The world has improved, but it hasn't entirely changed.'

'I'd just like to point out, Marcus, that all of the wars in the world have been waged by men,' said Becky.

'Not true. Margaret Thatcher, the Falklands, "Sink The Belgrano".' Simon raised an eyebrow at her behind Marcus's back. They were feeling comfortable enough to argue in front of him, even on his frightened days.

'But what about when you meet a nice girl?' asked Simon. They were on the last hole of the Crazy Golf course. Simon took his shot and the ball rattled inside a green wood windmill. 'You may want somewhere to live together and raise children. Maybe you should think about keeping the house. You do a lot of things for yourself now.' He potted the ball.

Becky thought the remark was tactless, seeing that Marcus still had trouble going about by himself, but Michael, their rabbi, disagreed. 'What he needs is a nice Jewish woman to take control, someone who just wants to be a wife and mother, and maybe a bookkeeper. All right, all right.' He thrashed at his ball and bounced it over the concrete divide. 'It's an old-fashioned idea, I know, but believe me, there are plenty of girls around who just want to do that.'

'Do I get a say in this?' asked Marcus.

'No,' everyone agreed.

'I think you just talked yourself into the job, rabbi,' said Simon.

'What job?'

'You can introduce Marcus to someone for us. Think of it as long-term insurance for improving the size of your congregation.'

'The things I do to keep a full house under God's roof,' said Michael, resettling his ball for another go. 'It's a deal. But I want at least four kids out of it.'

'A good rabbi should always be prepared to cut a deal,' said Simon. 'It shows you're in the right profession. Let's face it, you'd never make a professional golfer.'

Michael was as good as his word. The girl's name was Sarah. She was three years Marcus's senior, the remaining unmarried daughter of a Reform family who owned a linen company in the next town. She was small and graceful, with shiny dark hair that fell to the middle of her back and a stubborn streak that ran through her like a bracing joist. Michael introduced them at synogogue, and then invited them over for coffee. In a short time she and Marcus had fallen very much in love.

Sarah knew what she was getting into. The Silverstein family doctor had discussed Marcus's delicate mental condition frankly and without any offerings of false hope. He warned her that although the conditioning had been put in place by his father, Marcus's own disturbed mindset had done little to improve matters, and would certainly deteriorate in time unless carefully counteracted by those he trusted.

It was Marcus who proved more doubtful about proposing marriage. He had never needed anyone apart from his father, and this new idea was a while taking root. Realising that he was urging someone else into marriage without making a commitment of his own, Simon finally proposed to Becky.

Both couples were married in Michael's synagogue. At the wedding of Marcus and Sarah, only Simon and Becky attended on the groom's side. Afterwards, at the reception, they unveiled their wedding gift.

'We're paying for your honeymoon,' Simon explained. 'It was Becky's idea.' She nudged him. 'Well, partly mine as well. I remembered the pictures of the great orange desert you used to keep on your bedroom wall from the *National Geographic*, what you said about feeling safe under such an open sky. So I thought, Arizona.'

Marcus shifted uncomfortably. 'That's very kind of you,' he said quietly, glancing down at his shoes, 'but you shouldn't have. I don't even have a passport.'

'We know that, dummy, so we filled out all the forms. We just need a snapshot and your signature and you'll have it in twenty-four hours. It's all been arranged.'

'It's a wonderful present, but I couldn't.'

'You know what he means,' warned Sarah, taking them to one side. 'He's never flown before. The idea of crossing borders makes him nervous. All that stuff his father drummed into him still surfaces once in a while.'

'Simon already thought of that,' said Becky. 'We don't want it to be stressful for Marcus in any way, so we're going with you. It'll be our honeymoon as well. Simon's been there several times, and knows his way around. Between the three of us, we should be able to keep Marcus from suffering any panic attacks. You watch, he'll soon come around to the idea.'

Becky was right. Marcus grew more excited as Simon outlined their itinerary, showing him photographs of the places they would visit together. 'We're going to a ranch where you can sleep outside in the desert, right under the stars, just as you always wanted,' he told his friend. Marcus didn't reply. He didn't have to; the look in his grateful eyes said it all. Simon felt as if he was doing more than just burying the old man's legacy of fear and suspicion. It felt like he was completing his mother's work.

The four of them left rainy England behind as the white skyliner coasted high above the earth. Marcus found it impossible to tear himself from the view, even when dinner arrived. 'I had no idea the tops of the clouds were so beautiful,' he told Simon. 'It's how I imagine Heaven to be.'

'Don't worry,' Simon grinned, 'they'll still be there when you finish eating. It's a long flight.'

They drank a toast to each other's marriages in plastic cups. 'Sometimes it's like being with a child,' Sarah told Becky. 'He sees the world in such a different way that I fear for him.'

'Oh, you'll soon knock him into shape.' Becky finished her glass. 'I hear you've got him a job lined up.'

'We'll see. It depends if he's prepared to work for my father. I wouldn't want him to be turned into everyone else.'

'I don't think there's much danger of that,' Becky replied as she watched Marcus twisting his head at the window, trying to see beneath the plane.

The immigration queue at LAX was controlled chaos. Ahead, a harassed heavy-set black woman in a gold-braided uniform ushered arrivals into different lines. Simon and Becky tried to stay together with Marcus and Sarah, but the officer broke them up. Simon looked back, concerned, as the queues diverged to different ends of the hall. The arriving passengers snaked back and forth between the makeshift barriers, shuffling forward with their hand luggage.

'He won't be enjoying this part,' Simon worried. 'You know what they're like with rules and regulations here. They'll only have to shout "Stay behind the line" at him and he'll freak.'

'Will you stop fretting?' Becky pushed her bag forward with her foot. 'Sarah's with him.'

But when they reached the white line in front of the immigration officer's desk, Simon looked over to see Sarah standing alone. 'Where is he?' he mouthed across to her. She pointed to the area behind the inspector's booth, where two officials were leading Marcus away. 'What's wrong?' he gestured, only to receive a shrugged reply.

'I knew it,' he told Becky, 'there's some kind of screw-up with his passport. They've taken him off for interrogation.'

'I checked his passport, Simon, it was fine. Perhaps there's something undesirable in the files about his father. Did Howard ever have trouble getting into the States?'

'How should I know?'

'Maybe there's some kind of black mark against his name. They probably just want to verify he's who he says he is.'

'He's going to think it's a conspiracy after all, isn't he?' said Simon, growing more agitated by the second. 'He'll think we lied to him all along. Sat in a room being asked questions by blokes in uniforms.'

'Don't be silly, he's a grown man, even he doesn't—'

'No, he's not, that's the point. Everything is new to him. He sees it all with the eyes of a child. Jesus, I should have known this wasn't the right place to bring him.'

'Will you lighten up?' asked Becky. 'We're in America, not Russia.'

'Does it make a difference? You have to bribe everyone with tips here to get anything done. Where are they taking him?'

But Marcus was already lost from sight.

Becky went through first. The immigration officer seemed annoyingly slow, but, she supposed, had been required to perform his job more thoroughly since September 11th. As soon as she was stamped she ran ahead, checking the interview rooms set to one side of the hall, but many of the doors were closed.

'Where is he?' asked Simon as he came through and caught up with her. 'Have you seen him?'

'Not yet. It can take a while. I was stuck waiting for my dad for over an hour once. Here comes Sarah.'

'What happened?' they asked her.

'I don't know,' Sarah admitted. 'He was called out of the line even before he got to the booth. These two guys were doing spot-checks on passports. They read through his and asked him to come with them. They were polite, but they wouldn't let me accompany him. Is he still being interviewed?'

'We guess so, we don't know,' Simon admitted.

'Well, what if he came out while you were answering the

immigration officer's questions?' asked Becky. 'He'd have already been through the barrier.'

'Maybe he looked for us and just followed everyone else to the baggage hall when he couldn't see us. Why don't I go ahead to the hall? Becky can wait here with you.'

Simon pushed on through the crowd and found the black ribbon of the baggage carousel. He searched the vague faces, people caught in the temporal stasis of travel. Recognising one of the passengers from the flight, he asked about Marcus, but the man recalled nothing and seemed in a daze. The heat was unpleasantly oppressive. Everyone here appeared mesmerised, as if they were victims of shock, or perhaps they were merely bored, waiting to be herded from one pen to another by someone in charge.

Simon stood on the edge of the carousel and studied the sea of faces. Marcus might be an innocent with strange ideas, but he wasn't stupid; he would know to wait here for them and not head for customs or leave the terminal building. The place was so crowded with passengers carrying everything from golf clubs to carpets that he couldn't see . . . but then he heard.

He heard Marcus shouting as one of the men pulled at his arm. They weren't airport officials, even from here Simon could see that their khaki uniforms were military, their peaked caps pulled low more to avoid recognition than to command respect. Marcus was tightly held between the pair, who walked him briskly between the customs officials toward the exit. He knew he would lose sight of them the moment he jumped down from the carousel, but he had no choice.

By the time he reached the doors, they had vanished into the world outside.

Simon ran across the road where taxis stuttered and slammed between their fares. He run through the plexiglass walkway connecting the car parks, scanning the vehicles on either side, sweat soaking his shirt collar, then moved out across the car park, hard sun in his eyes. Here in the land of the automobile, cars hooted angrily, warning him him to keep out of their way. He had no idea what he was looking for, only a vague sense of the threat that Marcus had been taught to feel.

He entered another walkway, hard to see out through the scarred plastic, but suddenly he saw it – a grey steel high-security truck with window slits along the side. Marcus spotted him across the vortex of the rush-hour car park, his hands held high, shouting to him, *stay back, stay back, they only want me*, and then the khaki-clad men threw arms around his chest, hauling him back by his armpits and upward into the wagon, slamming the steel doors shut behind him. Simon caught a final brief glimpse of his face through the truck window. He looked less frightened than resigned to this mysterious fate.

Simon bellowed for help, desperately searching for a way through the plexiglass barrier to the car park beyond. He slammed his fists against the windows, but could only watch as the unmarked van pulled away into the traffic, to be lost in the humid haze of the LA afternoon.

The airport authorities were less than helpful. They were vaguely annoyed that the airline's passenger figures registered a discrepancy with the tally of their immigration forms and baggage receipts, but acknowledged that it happened from time to time, and there was nothing they could do about it. The movement of such vast numbers meant that their job was more about damage limitation than providing a service. Soon they weren't prepared to discuss the matter any more, and went so far as to suggest that Simon was in the wrong. They found it suspicious that his friend had no credit cards, no financial history of any kind, not even a registered home address, and implied that he had arranged to meet someone without telling his new wife, or his best friends. The state decided that Marcus Silverstein didn't exist, at least on their soil, and closed its doors against him.

Officials at the British embassy proved impotent. There were no leads, no suspects, although an assistant at the embassy said he had heard of something similar before, but couldn't remember when or where. Had Mr Woolf considered the idea that his friend might have wanted to disappear? Everyone wanted to come to America; what they did when they arrived was their affair.

Back in England a website was set up, but elicited no response.

Simon sat in the attic of the Silverstein house and listened to the rain falling on the roof tiles just above his head. Here were stored all of the books that Howard Silverstein had left for his son, over a hundred volumes on the rise of Nazism and right-wing ideology throughout world history. In a battered copy of *Mein Kampf* he found one famous passage translated and heavily underscored: 'The broad mass of a nation will more easily fall victim to a big lie than a small one.'

As Simon looked down into the streets of people he no longer knew or trusted, he cried for his friend, and wondered if the credulity of a nation had finally, secretly grown to encompass the entire world.

SEVEN FEET

Cleethorpes was a crap mouser. She would hide underneath the sink if a rodent, a squirrel or a neighbour's cat even came near the open back door. Clearly, sleeping sixteen hours a day drained her reserves of nervous energy, and she was forced to play dead if her territory was threatened. She was good at a couple of things; batting moths about until they expired with their wings in dusty tatters, and staring at a spot on the wall three feet above the top of Edward's head. What could cats see, he wondered, that humans couldn't?

Cleethorpes was his only companion now that Sam was dead and Gill had gone. He'd bought her because everyone else had bought one. That was the month the price of cats sky-rocketed. Hell, every cat's home in the country sold out in days, and pretty soon the mangiest strays were changing hands for incredible prices. It was the weirdest form of panic-buying Edward ever saw.

He'd lived in Camden Town for years, and had been thinking of getting out even before he met Gill; the area was being compared to Moscow and Johannesburg after eight murders on its streets in as many weeks earned the area a new nickname: 'Murder Mile'. There were 700 police operating in the borough, which badly needed over a thousand. It was strange, then, to think that the real threat to their lives eventually came not from muggers, but from fast-food outlets.

Edward lived in a flat in Eversholt Street, one of the most

peculiar roads in the neighbourhood. In one stretch of a few hundred yards there was a Roman Catholic church, a sports centre, a legendary rock pub, council flats, a bingo hall, a juvenile detention centre, an Italian café, a Victorian men's hostel for transients and an audacious green glass development of million-pound loft apartments. Edward was on the ground floor of the council block, a bad place to be as it turned out. The Regent's Canal ran nearby, and most of the road's drains emptied into it. The council eventually rivetted steel grilles over the pipe covers, but by then it was too late.

Edward glanced over at Gill's photograph, pinned on the cork noticeboard beside the cooker. Once her eyes had been the colour of cyanothus blossom, her hair saturated in sunlight, but now the picture appeared to be fading, as if it was determined to remove her from the world. He missed Gill more than he missed Sam, because nothing he could do would ever bring Sam back, but Gill was still around, living in Hackney with her two brothers. He knew he was unlikely to ever see her again. He missed her to the point where he would say her name aloud at odd moments for no reason at all. In those last days after Sam's death, she had grown so thin and pale that it seemed she was being erased from her surroundings. He watched helplessly as her bones appeared beneath her flesh, her clothes began hanging loosely on her thin arms. Gill's jaw-length blonde hair draped forward over her face as she endlessly scoured and bleached the kitchen counters. She stopped voicing her thoughts, becoming barely more visible than the water stains on the walls behind her. She would hush him with a raised finger, straining to listen for the scurrying scratch of claws in the walls, under the cupboards, across the rafters.

Rats. Some people's worst nightmare, but the thought of them no longer troubled him. What had happened to their family had happened to people all over the city. '*Rats!*' thought Edward as he welded the back door shut, '*they fought the dogs and killed the cats, and bit the babies in the cradles . . .*' He couldn't remember the rest of Robert Browning's poem. It hadn't been quite like that, because Camden Town was hardly Hamelin, but London could have done with a pied piper. Instead, all they'd got was a distracted mayor and his dithering officials, hopelessly failing to cope with a crisis.

He pulled the goggles to the top of his head and examined his handiwork. The steel plates only ran across to the middle of the door, but were better than nothing. Now he could sort out the chewed gap underneath. It wasn't more than two inches deep, but a cat-sized rat was capable of folding its ribs flat enough to slide through with ease. He remembered watching thousands of them one evening as they rippled in a brown tapestry through the back gardens. There had been nights when he'd sat in the darkened lounge with his feet lifted off the floor and a cricket bat across his knees, listening to the scampering conspiracy passing over the roofs, feet pattering in the kitchen, under the beds, under his chair. He'd watched as one plump brown rat with eyes like drops of black resin had fidgeted its way between books on a shelf, daring him into a display of pitifully slow reactions.

The best solution would be to rivet a steel bar across the space under the door, but the only one he had left was too short. He thought about risking a trip to the shops, but most of the ones in the high street had closed for good, and all the hardware stores had sold out of stock weeks ago. It was hard to imagine how much a city of eight million people could change in just four months. So many had left. The tubes were a no-go zone, of course, and it was dangerous to move around in the open at night. The rats were no longer frightened by people.

He was still deciding what to do when his mobile buzzed its way across the work counter.

'Is that Edward?' asked a cultured, unfamiliar voice.

'Yeah, who's that?'

'I don't suppose you'll remember me. We only met once, at a party. I'm Damon, Gillian's brother.' The line fell warily silent.

Damon, sanctimonious religious nut, Gill's older brother, what was the name of the other one? Matthew. Fuck. *Fuck*.

'Are you still there?'

'Yeah, sorry, you caught me a bit by surprise.'

'I guess it's a bit of a bolt from the blue. Are you still living in Camden?'

'One of the last to leave the epicentre. The streets are pretty quiet around here now.'

'I saw it on the news, didn't recognise the place. Not that I ever really knew it to begin with. Our family's from Hampshire, but I expect you remember that.'

Stop being so damned chatty and tell me what the hell you want, thought Edward. His next thought hit hard: *Gill's condition has deteriorated, she's made him call me*.

'It's about Gillian, isn't it?'

'I'm afraid – she's been a lot worse lately. We've had a tough time looking after her. She had the problem, you know, with dirt and germs—'

Spermophobia, thought Edward, *Mysophobia*. A lot of people had developed such phobias since the rats came.

'Now there are these other things, she's become terrified of disease.'

Nephophobia, Pathophobia. Once arcane medical terms, now almost everyday parlance. They were closely connected, not so surprising when you remembered what she'd been through.

'It's been making life very difficult for us.'

'I can imagine.' Everything had to be cleaned over and over again. Floors scrubbed, handles and counters sprayed with disinfectant, the air kept refridgerated. All her foodstuffs had to be washed and vacuum-sealed in plastic before she would consider eating them. Edward had watched the roots of fear digging deeper within her day by day, until she could barely function and he could no longer cope.

'She's lost so much weight. She's become frightened of the bacteria in her own body. She was living on the top floor of the house, refused to take any visitors except us, and now she's gone missing.'

'What do you mean?'

'It doesn't seem possible, but it's true. We thought you should know.'

'Do you have any idea where she might have gone?'

'She couldn't have gone anywhere, that's the incredible part of it. We very badly need your help. Can you come over tonight?' *This is a turnaround*, Edward thought. *Her family spent a year trying to get me to clear off, and now they need me.*

'I suppose I can come. Both of you are still okay?'

'We're fine. We take a lot of precautions.'

'Has the family been vaccinated?'

'No, Matthew and our father feel that The Lord protects us. Do you remember the address?'

'Of course. I can be there in around an hour.'

He was surprised they had found the nerve to call at all. The brothers had him pegged as a man of science, a member of the tribe that had helped to bring about the present crisis. People like him had warmed the planet and genetically modified its harvests, bringing abundance and pestilence. Their religion sought to exclude, and their faith was vindictive. Men who sought to accuse were men to be avoided. But he owed it to Gill to go to them.

He used the short steel bar to block the gap in the door, and covered the shortfall by welding a biscuit-tin lid over it. Not an ideal solution, but one that would have to do for now. The sun would soon be setting. The red neon sign above the Kentucky Fried Chicken outlet opposite had flickered on. It was the only part of the store that was still intact. Rioters had smashed up most of the junk-food joints in the area, looking for someone to blame.

Pest controllers had put the massive rise in the number of rats down to three causes: the wetter, warmer winters caused

flooding that lengthened the rats' breeding periods and drove
them above ground. Councils had reduced their spending on
street cleaning. Most disastrously of all, takeaway litter left
the street-bins overflowing with chicken bones and burger buns.
The rat population rose by thirty per cent in a single year. They
thrived in London's Victorian drainage system, in the sewers
and canal outlets, in the tube lines and railway cuttings. Beneath
the city was a maze of interconnected pipework with openings
into almost every street. They moved into the gardens and then
the houses, colonising and spreading as each property became
vacant.

One much-cited statistic suggested that a single pair of rats
could spawn a maximum number of nearly a hundred billion
rats in just five years. It was a sign of the burgeoning rodent
population that they began to be spotted during the day; starvation drove them out into the light, and into densely populated
areas. They no longer knew fear. Worse, they sensed that others
were afraid of them.

Edward had always known about the dangers of disease. As a
young biology student he had been required to study pathogenic
microbes. London had not seen a case of plague in almost a
century. The Black Death of the Middle Ages had wiped out
a third of the European population. The bacterium *Yersinia
pestis* had finally been eradicated by fire in London in 1666.
Plague had returned to consume ten million Indians early in the
twentieth century, and had killed 200 as recently as 1994. Now
it was back in a virulent new strain, and rampant. It had arrived
via infected rat fleas, in a ship's container from the East, or
perhaps from a poorly fumigated cargo plane, no one was
sure, and everyone was anxious to assign blame. Rats brought
leptospirosis, hantavirus and rat bite fever, and they were only
the fatal diseases.

Edward drove through the empty streets of King's Cross
with the windows of the Peugeot tightly closed and the air-
conditioning set to an icy temperature. Lying in the road outside

McDonalds, a bloated, blackened corpse had been partially covered by a cardboard standee for Caramel McFlurrys. The gesture, presumably intended to provide some privacy in death, had only created further indignity. It was the first time he'd seen a body on the street, and the sight shocked him. It was a sign that the services could no longer cope, or that people were starting not to care. Most of the infected crept away into private corners to die, even though there were no red crosses to keep them in their houses this time.

The plague bacillus had evolved in terms of lethality. It no longer swelled the lymph-glands of the neck, armpits and groin. It went straight to the lungs and caused catastrophic internal haemorrhaging. Death came fast as the lungs filled with septic-aemic pus and fluid. There was a preventative vaccine, but it proved useless once the outbreak began. Tetracycline and streptomycin, once seen as effective antibiotics against plague, also failed against the emerging drug-resistant strains. All you could do was burn and disinfect; the city air stank of both, but it was preferable to the smell of death. It had been a hot summer, and the still afternoons were filled with the stench of rotting flesh.

Edward had been vaccinated at the college. Gill had blamed him for failing to vaccinate their son in time. Sam had been four months old when he died. His cradle had been left near an open window. They could only assume that a rat had entered the room foraging for food, and came close enough for his fleas to jump to fresh breeding grounds. The child's pale skin blackened with necrosis before the overworked doctors of University College Hospital could get around to seeing him. Gill quickly developed a phobic reaction to germs, and was collected by her brothers a few weeks after.

Edward dropped out of college. In theory it would have been a good time to stay, because biology students were being drafted in the race to find more powerful weapons against the disease, but he couldn't bear to immerse himself in the subject, having so recently watched his child die in the very same building.

He wondered why he hadn't fled to the countryside like so many others. It was safer there, but no one was entirely immune. He found it hard to consider leaving the city where he had been born, and was fascinated by this slow decanting of the population. An eerie calm had descended on even the most populous districts. There were no tourists; nobody wanted to fly into Britain. People had become terrified of human contact, and kept their outside journeys to a minimum. *Mad cow disease was a comparative picnic*, he thought with a grim chuckle.

The little car bounced across the end of Upper Street, heading toward Shoreditch. The shadows were long on the gold-sheened tarmac. A blizzard of newspapers rolled across the City Road, adding to the sense of desolation. Edward spun the wheel, watching for pedestrians. He had started to think of them as survivors. There were hardly any cars on the road, although he was surprised to pass a bus in service. At Old Street and Pitfield Street, a shifting amoeba-shape fluctuated around the doorway of a closed supermarket. The glossy black rats scattered in every direction as he drove past. You could never drive over them, however fast you went.

There were now more rats than humans, approximately three for every man, woman and child, and the odds kept growing in their favour. They grew bolder each day, and had become quite brazen about their battle for occupancy. It had been said that in a city as crowded as London you were never more than fifteen feet away from a rat. Scientists warned that when the distance between rodent and human lowered to just seven feet, conditions would be perfect for the return of the plague. The flea, *Xenopsylla cheopis*, sucked up diseased rat blood and transported it to humans with shocking efficiency.

A great black patch shimmered across the road like a boiling oil slick, splitting and vanishing between the buildings. Without realising it, he found himself gripping the sweat-slick wheel so tightly that his nails were digging into his palms.

Rattus rattus. No one knew where the black rat had originated, so their Latin name was suitably unrevealing. The brown ones – the English ones, *Rattus norvegicus* – lived in burrows and came from China. They grew to nearly a foot and a half, and ate anything at all. They could chew their way through brick and concrete; they had to keep chewing to stop their incisors from growing back into their skulls. The black ones were smaller, with larger ears, and lived off the ground in round nests. Edward had woken in the middle of the night two weeks ago and found a dozen of them in his kitchen, feeding from a wastebin. He had run at them with a broom, but they had simply skittered up the curtains and through a hole they had made in the ceiling to the drainpipes outside. The black ones were acrobats; they loved heights. Although they were less aggressive, they seemed to be outnumbering their brown cousins. At least, he saw more of them each day.

He fumigated the furniture and carpets for ticks and fleas, but still developed clusters of painful red welts on his ankles, his arms, his back. He was glad Gill was no longer here, but missed her terribly. She had slipped away from him, her mind distracted by a future she could not imagine or tolerate.

Damon and Matthew lived with their father above offices in Hoxton, having bought the building at the height of the area's property boom. These had once been the homes of well-to-do Edwardian families, but more than half a century of neglect had followed, until the district had been rediscovered by newly wealthy artists. That bubble had burst too, and now the houses were in fast decline as thousands of rats scampered into the basements.

As he climbed the steps, spotlights clicked on. He could hear movement all around him. He looked up and saw the old man through a haze of white light. Gill's father was silently watching him from an open upstairs window.

There was no bell. Edward slapped his hand against the front door glass and waited. Matthew answered the door. What was it about the over-religious that made them keep their hair so neat? Matthew's blonde fringe formed a perfect wave above his smooth scrubbed face. He smiled and shook Edward's hand.

'I'm glad you could make it,' he said, as though he'd invited Edward to dinner. 'We don't get many visitors.' He led the way upstairs, then along a bare white hall into an undecorated space that served as their living quarters. There were no personal effects of any kind on display. A stripped oak table and four chairs stood in the centre of the bright room. Damon rose to shake his hand. Edward had forgotten how alike the brothers were. They had the eyes of zealots, bright and black and dead. They spoke with great intensity, weighing their words, watching him as they spoke.

'Tell me what happened,' Edward instructed, seating himself. He didn't want to be here any longer than was strictly necessary.

'Father can't get around any more, so we moved him from his quarters at the top of the house and cleaned it out for Gillian. We thought if we couldn't cure her we should at least make her feel secure, so we put her up there. But the black rats . . .'

'They're good climbers.'

'That's right. They came up the drainpipes and burrowed in through the attic, so we had to move her. The only place we could think where she'd be safe was within our congregation.' *Ah yes*, thought Edward, *the Church Of Latter Day Nutters. I remember all too well.* Gill had fallen out with her father over religion. He had raised his sons in a far-right Christian offshoot that came with more rules than the Highway Code. Quite how he had fetched up in this biblical backwater was a mystery, but Gill was having none of it. Her brothers had proven more susceptible, and when the plague rats moved in adopted an insufferably smug attitude that drove the children further apart. Matthew was the father of three immaculately coiffed children whom Edward had christened 'the Midwich Cuckoos'. Damon's wife was the whitest woman he had ever met, someone who encouraged knitting as stress-therapy at Christian coffee mornings. He didn't like them, their politics or their religion, but was forced to admit that they had at least been helpful to his wife. He doubted their motives, however, suspecting that they were more concerned with restoring the family to a complete unit and turning Gill back into a surrogate mother.

'We took her to our church,' Matthew explained. 'It was built in 1860. The walls are three feet thick. There are no electrical cables, no drainpipes, nothing the smallest rat could wriggle its way into. The vestry doors are wooden, and some of the stained-glass windows are shaky, but it's always been a place of safety.'

Edward had to admit it was a smart idea. Gill's condition was untreatable without access to a psychiatrist and medication, and right now the hospitals were nightmarish no-go areas where rats went to feast on the helpless sick.

Matthew seated himself opposite. 'Gillian settled into the church, and we hoped she was starting to find some comfort in the protection of the Lord. Then some members of our congregation started spending their nights there, and she began to worry that they were bringing in plague fleas, even though we fumigated them before entering. We couldn't bear to see her suffer so we built her a special room, right there in the middle of the apse—'

'—we made her as comfortable as we could,' Damon interrupted. 'Ten feet by twelve. Four walls, a ceiling, a floor, a lockable door and a ventilation grille constructed from strong fine mesh.' He looked as sheepish as a schoolboy describing a woodwork project. 'Father directed the operation because he'd had some experience in carpentry. We moved her bed in there, and her books, and she was finally able to get some sleep. She even stopped taking the sleeping pills you used to give her.' *The pills to which she had become addicted when we lived together,* thought Edward bitterly. *The habit I was blamed for creating.*

'I don't understand,' he said aloud. 'What happened?'

'I think we'd better go over to the church,' said Matthew gently.

It was less than a thousand yards from the house, smaller than he'd imagined, slim and plain, without buttresses or arches, very little tracery. The former Welsh presbytery was sandwiched between two taller glass buildings, commerce dominating religion, darkening the streets with the inevitability of London rain.

Outside its single door sat a barrel-chested black man who would have passed for a night club bouncer if it wasn't for the cricket pads strapped on his legs. He lumbered aside as Damon and Matthew approached. The small church was afire with the light of a thousand coloured candles looted from luxury stores. Many were shaped like popular cartoon characters: Batman, Pokemon and Daffy Duck burned irreverently along the altar and apse. The pews had been removed and stacked against a wall. In the centre of the aisle stood an oblong wooden box bolted into the stone floor and propped with planks, like the back of a film set. A small door was inset in a wall of the cube, and that was guarded by an elderly woman who sat reading in a high-backed armchair. In the nave, a dozen family friends were talking quietly on orange plastic chairs that surrounded a low oak table. They fell silent with suspicion as Edward passed them. Matthew withdrew a key from his jacket and unlocked the door of the box, pushing it open and clicking on a light.

'We rigged a bulb to a car battery because she wouldn't sleep in the dark,' Damon explained, passing a manicured hand around the room, which was bare but for an unfurled white futon, an Indian rug and a stack of dog-eared religious books. The box smelled of fresh paint and incense.

'You built it of wood,' said Edward, thumping the thin wall

with his fist. 'That makes no sense, Damon. A rat would be through this in a minute.'

'What else could we do? It made her feel safer, and that was all that counted. We wanted to take away her pain. Can you imagine what it was like to see someone in your own family suffer so much? Our father worshipped her.'

Edward detected an undercurrent of resentment in Damon's voice. He and Gill had chosen not to marry. In the eyes of her brothers, it was a sin that prevented Edward from ever being treated as a member of the family. 'You're not telling me she disappeared from inside?' he asked. 'How could she have got out?'

'That's what we thought you might be able to explain to us,' snapped Matthew. 'Why do you think we asked you here?'

'I don't understand. You locked her in each night?'

'We did it for her own good.'

'How could it be good to lock a frightened woman inside a room?'

'She'd been getting panic attacks, growing confused, running into the street. Her aunt Alice has been sitting outside every night since this thing began. Anything Gillian's needed she's always been given.'

'When did she go missing?'

'The night before last. We thought she'd come back.'

'You didn't see her leave?' he asked the old lady.

'No,' replied Alice, daring him to defy her. 'I was here all night.'

'And she didn't pass you. Are you sure you never left your chair?'

'Not once. And I didn't fall asleep, either. I don't sleep at night with those things crawling all over the roof.'

'Did you let anyone else into the room?'

'Of course not,' she said indignantly. 'Only family and regular worshippers are allowed into the church. We don't want other people in here.' *Of course not*, thought Edward, *what's the point of organised religion if you can't exclude disbelievers?*

'And no one except Gillian used the room,' Damon added. 'That was the point. That was why we asked you to come.'

Edward studied the two brothers. He could just about understand Damon, squeaky clean and neatly groomed in a blazer and a pressed white shirt that provided him with an aura of faith made visible, but Matthew seemed in a state of perpetual anger, a church warrior who had no patience with the unconverted. He remained a mystery.

'Why me?' Edward asked. 'What made you call me?'

Momentarily stumped, the brothers looked at each other awkwardly. 'Well – you slept with her.' Presumably they thought he must know her better for having done so.

'I knew her until our son died, but then – well, when someone changes that much, it becomes impossible to understand how they think anymore.' Edward hoped they would appreciate his point of view. He wanted to make contact with them just once. 'Let me take a look around, I'll see what I can do.'

The brothers stepped back, cognisant of their ineffectuality, their hands awkwardly at their sides. Behind them, the church door opened and the congregation slowly streamed in. The men and women who arranged themselves at the rear of the church looked grey and beaten. Faith was all they had left.

'I'm sorry, it's time for our evening service to begin,' Damon explained.

'Do what you have to do.' Edward accepted the red plastic torch Matthew was offering him. 'I'll call you if I find anything.'

A series of narrow alleys ran beside the church. If Gill had managed to slip past the old lady, she would have had to enter them. Edward looked up at the dimming blue strip of evening sky. Along the gutters sat fat nests constructed of branches and binbags, the black plastic shredded into malleable strips. As he watched, one bulged and disgorged a family of coal-eyed rats. They clung to the drainpipes, staring into his torchbeam before suddenly spiralling down at him. He moved hastily aside as they scurried over his shoes and down the corridor of dirt-encrusted brick.

The end of the alley opened out into a small litter-strewn square. He hardly knew where to begin his search. If the family had failed to find her, how would he succeed? On the steps of a boarded-up block of flats sat an elderly man in a dirty green sleeping bag. The man stared wildly at him, as if he had just awoken from a nightmare.

'All right?' asked Edward, nodding curtly. The old man beckoned him. Edward tried to stay beyond range of his pungent stale aroma, but was summoned nearer. 'What is it?' he asked, wondering how anyone dared to sleep rough in the city now. The old man pulled back the top of his sleeping bag as if shyly revealing a treasure, and allowed him to look in on the hundred or so hairless baby rats that wriggled over his bare stomach like maggots, pink and blind.

Perhaps that was the only way you could survive the streets now, thought Edward, riven with disgust, you had to take their side. He wondered if, as a host for their offspring, the old man had been made an honorary member of their species, and was therefore allowed to continue unharmed, although perhaps the truth was less fanciful; rats sensed the safety of their surroundings through the movement of their own bodies. Their spatial perception was highly attuned to the width of drains, the cracks in walls, the fearful humans who moved away in great haste. Gill might have been panicked into flight, but she was weak and would not have been able to run for long. She must have stopped somewhere to regain her breath, but where?

He searched the dark square. The wind had risen to disturb the tops of the plane trees, replacing the city's ever-present bass-line of traffic with natural sussurance. It was the only sound he could now hear. Lights shone above a corner shop. Slumped on the windowsill, two Indian children stared down into the square, their eyes half-closed by rat-bites.

He returned to the church, slipping in behind the ragged congregation, and watched Matthew in the dimly illuminated pulpit.

'For this is not the end but the beginning,' said Matthew, clearly preaching a worn-in sermon of fire and redemption. 'Those whom the Lord has chosen to keep in good health will be free to remake the land in His way.' It was the kind of lecture to which Edward had been subjected as a child, unfocussed in its promises, peppered with pompous rhetoric, vaguely threatening. 'Each and every one of us must make a sacrifice, without which there can be no admittance to the kingdom of Heaven, and he who has not surrendered his heart to Our Lady will be left outside, denied the power of reformation.'

It seemed to Edward that congregations always required the imposition of rules for their salvation, and desperate times had forced them to assume that these zealous brothers would be capable of setting them. He moved quietly to the unguarded door of the wooden box and stepped inside, shutting himself in.

The sense of claustrophobia was immediate. A locked room, guarded from outside. Where the hell had she gone? He sat on the futon, idly kicking at the rug, and listened to the muffled litany of the congregation. A draught was coming into the room, but not through the door. He lowered his hand down into darkness, and felt chill air prickle his fingers. At first he failed to see the corner of the hatch, but as he focussed the torch more tightly, he realised what he was looking at; a section of flooring, about three feet by two, that had been sawn into the wooden deck beside the bed. The floor was plywood, easy to lift. The hatch covered the spiral stairwell to the crypt. A black-painted Victorian iron banister curved away beneath his feet. Outside, Matthew was leading a catechism that sounded more like a rallying call.

Edward dipped the light and stepped onto the fretwork wedges. Clearly Gill had been kept in the wooden room against her will, but how had she discovered the staircase to the chamber beneath her prison? Perhaps its existence was common knowledge, but it had not occurred to anyone that she might be able to gain access to it. The temperature of the air was dropping fast now; could this have been its appeal, the thought that germs would not be able to survive in such a chill environment?

He reached the bottom of the steps. His torchbeam reflected a fracturing moon of light; the flagstones were hand-deep in icy water. A series of low stone arches led through the tunnelled crypt ahead of him. He waded forward and found himself beneath the ribbed vault of the main chamber. The splash of water boomed in the silent crypt.

With freezing legs and visible breath, he stood motionless, waiting for the ripples to subside. Something was wrong. Gillian might have lost her reason, but she would surely not have ventured down here alone. She knew that rats were good swimmers. It didn't make sense. Something was wrong.

Above his head in the church, the steeple bell began to ring, cracked and flat. The change in the congregation was extraordinary. They dropped to their knees unmindful of injury, staring toward the tattered crimson reredos that shielded the choir stall. Damon and Matthew had reappeared in sharp white surplices, pushing back the choir screen as their flock began to murmur in anticipation. The dais they revealed had been swathed in shining gold brocade, discovered in bolts at a Brick Lane saree shop. Atop stood the enshrined figure, a mockery of Catholicism, its naked flesh dulled down with talcum powder until it resembled worn alabaster, its legs overgrown with plastic vines.

The wheels of the wooden dais creaked as Damon and Matthew pushed the wobbling tableau toward the altar. The voices of the crowd rose in adulation. The figure on the dais was transfixed in hysterical ecstasy, posed against a painted tree with her knees together and her palms turned out, a single rose stem lying across the right hand, a crown of dead roses placed far back on her shaved head, her eyes rolled to a glorious invisible heaven. Gillian no longer heard the desperate exultation of her worshippers; she existed in a higher place, a vessel for her brothers' piety, floating far above the filthy, blighted earth, in a holy place of such grace and purity that nothing dirty or harmful would ever touch her again.

Edward looked up. Somewhere above him the bell was still ringing, the single dull note repeated over and over. He cocked his head at the ribs of the vault and listened. First the trees, then the church bell, and now this, as though the forgotten order of nature was reasserting itself. He heard it again, the sound he had come to know and dread, growing steadily all around him. Raising the torch, he saw them scurrying over the fine green nylon webbing that had been stretched across the vault ceiling, thousands of them, far more than he had ever seen in one place before, black rats, quite small, their bodies shifting transversely, almost comically, as they weighed and judged distances.

They had been summoned to dinner.

They gathered in the roof of the main chamber, directly beneath the ringing bell, until they were piling on top of each other, some slipping and swinging by a single pink paw, and then they fell, twisting expertly so that they landed on him and not in the water, their needle claws digging into the flesh of his shoulders to gain purchase, to hang on at all costs. Edward hunched himself instinctively, but this exposed a broader area for the rats to drop onto, and now they were releasing themselves from the mesh and falling in ever-greater numbers, more and more, until the sheer weight of their solid, sleek bodies pushed him down into the filthy water. This was their cue to attack, their indication that the prey was defeatable, and they bit down hard, pushing their heads between each other to bury thin yellow teeth into his soft skin. He felt himself bleeding from a hundred different places at once, the wriggling mass of rat bodies first warm, then hot, now searing on his back until they made their way through his hair, heading for the tender prize of his eyes.

He was determined not to scream, not to open his mouth and admit their poisonous furred bodies. He did the only thing he could, and pushed his head deep under the water, drawing great draughts into his throat and down into his lungs, defeating them in the only way left to him, cheating them of live prey.

Gill, I love you, was his final prayer, *I only ever loved you, and wherever you are I hope you are happy*. Death etched the thought into his bones and preserved it forever.

In the little East End church, a mood of satiated harmony fell upon the congregation, and Matthew smiled at Damon as they covered the tableau once more, content that his revered sister was at peace. For now the enemy was assuaged, the commitment had been made, the congregation appeased.

Science had held sway for long enough. Now it was time for the harsh old gods to smile down once more.

AMERICAN WAITRESS

The woman on Table 4 has a laugh like a hen getting sucked into a jet engine. She's been sitting there for hours fooling around with a tuna melt that's gone grey on her. Clearly she has nothing better to do than sit there taking up a whole booth, filling in time between the carwash and the nail bar, yakking with her friends about what one woman said to another, and how the husband is fooling around on both of them. It never ceases to amaze Molly how small the talk can get toward the tail-end of the afternoon, when the orange light is low and fierce behind the restaurant blinds.

She's managed to keep the four 'til twelve shift at the restaurant so she can work with Sal, who has more years on her and won't work after midnight, because she has a little girl with a twisted spine who won't let anyone else put her to bed. Sal lives in an EconoLodge near Junction 17N which is filled with frat boys throwing parties and looking to get laid, but it's safe enough for the kid, who feels safer where there's noise. Sal is a classic; she washes her hair in bleach and keeps it filled with pins and pencils in case any guy has a mind to run his fingers through it. Molly likes her; no Ps and Qs but no airs and graces either, so they help each other in the two hours that their shifts overlap.

Molly likes her job, and she's good at it. Her mother was a waitress in those chrome-fitted fifties roadside diners that have mostly been demolished now, except in states like Missouri and

Florida, where they've been preserved with a kind of airquote-irony she doesn't take to. As a kid, Molly passed her life in diners and family restaurants waiting for her mother to come off duty. She never got bored. She read the books diners left behind, or watched the cook orbiting elliptically between the counter and the grill. Her mother yelled the old diner slang – Adam 'n' Eve on a raft, murphy in the alley, shingles with a shimmy, burn the British, hounds on an island – nobody uses that stuff anymore.

Now her mother is gone, and Molly has been a waitress long enough to type any customer within seconds of him coming through the door. That's how she knows the guy on Table 7 is going to be trouble. True, he doesn't have any of the usual tell-tale signs, he doesn't look angry or drunk or both, but there's something about him she doesn't want to get too close to. For a start he looks like he has too much money to be eating in a place like this, forget that crap about family restaurants being great social levellers, you don't eat here unless you're watching the pennies more than the carbs. He's in a blazer, tie and cotton twill slacks, high-top boots and some kind of fancy silver watch peeking out from his sleeve, and it just doesn't feel right. Still, he's in her section so she has no choice.

Molly's worked everywhere, Eat 'N' Park, Chili's, Hooters, Village Inn, Denny's, Red Lobster, Tony Roma's, Chi Chi's, Houlihan's, Applebee's, Red Onion, Lone Star, IHOPs, TGI Friday's, but she prefers the little family places away from the highway, where the regular trade consists of couples who've been coming for years, local workers and lonely widowers who won't cook for themselves. Plus, you get people passing through who are just looking for a place to eat where the arrival of their eggs won't interfere with their reading of the newspaper.

In some places the work is seasonal, so it requires her to move across state. Molly doesn't mind; she has no kids to worry about uprooting, so she follows the job. But the mom and pop joints are disappearing as more people eat on the run. The chain takeouts are carefully situated to cater for office crowds. What they serve is less important than where they're based. The chains purchase tactical real estate, and keep throughput high by avoiding the comfortable familiarity of diners. They expand ruthlessly, encroaching on each other's territory so much that Molly has to look harder than ever to find the places she likes to work. Eventually she'd shifted all the way from Arizona to Florida. She likes warm weather and doesn't want to head upstate, but knows she might eventually have to in order to find a place where she can more easily afford to live.

Molly side-glances the loner as she grabs the coffee pot and swings by his table, dropping the menu in front of him. He's staring at her strangely. *Okay, I've got a weird one*, she thinks, unfazed. Some eateries attract nothing but crazies, they're situated too close to the bus station, but this place isn't one of those, even though they make you wear pink nylon uniforms that gather more static than thunderheads. She glances at Sal, with her hair like a ball of unravelled blonde wool, stuck through with pens, and wonders how she does it. Sal has five full plates and a coffee pot in her hands. Like Molly, she's on an eight-hour shift making $2.70 an hour plus tips, and she never stops smiling. 'Honey, I can outsmile anyone if I have to,' she tells Molly, 'some days it feels like I have a clothes hanger in my mouth.' She can handle eight tables at a time, no problem, more if she has to. There are seventeen tables in Mickey's, so the girls take turns to pick up the overlap. She'll give refills on coffee and water but not soda (although her offer to top 'em up gets noticably slower after three trips) and she takes no shit from anyone.

Molly stands beside the guy at Table 7 and offers: 'Hi, what'll it be?' because he's closed his menu.

'What's the special?' he asks, making eye contact and holding the look too long, too deep. He knows damn well what the special is because it's on the board right over the cook's hatch. He's late twenties but going to seed young, too tanned, watery brown eyes, expensive clothes that fit a little too snug. He looks like he doesn't get laid too often.

'Meatloaf, mashed potatoes, onion gravy.' Molly stands with her pen poised.

'You have a really pretty face, you could try smiling like your friend over there,' he tells her in a refined, not-from-around-here voice.

'I'll smile when I finish my shift. You want the special?'

'No, I'll have the hash and an egg-white omelette.'

'We finish breakfast at midday. I can do you the hash as a side.' He sighs and reopens the menu, taking a while to choose, finally settling for chicken-fried steak. Molly checks out his waistline and thinks maybe he shouldn't be opting for the most calory-laden dish on the planet, but keeps the thought to herself.

'Coffee?'

He nods and she goes to pour when his hand flashes out and grabs her wrist, twisting it hard until she's forced to drop the coffee pot, which bounces on the formica-topped table and cascades scalding liquid into his lap, soaking his crotch and thighs. He doesn't flinch or make a sound. Weirder still, he looks like he wanted this to happen. Then the flicker of a smile vanishes and he explodes, jumping up and batting at his wet pants in mock-horror.

'She goddamned scalded me!' he shouts so that everyone turns. 'Jeezus!'

'Sal,' Molly calls, 'some help here.'

Sal slides her plates down and shoots over to the table, but so does Larry, the assistant manager, who makes things worse by taking the customer's side without even checking to see what happened.

'I'm burning here, Christ,' yells the scalded guy, hopping around, 'your waitresses don't even know how to pour coffee, I'm gonna sue you for every fucking penny you've got and put you out of business, man. I have the best lawyers in town, you are *so* history.' Sal drops a wad of napkins on the table and throws the scalded guy another wad, saying, 'You knocked that out of her hand, mister, I saw you do it, you lowlife, you can clear your own damn mess up,' and with that all hell breaks loose, with customers taking sides and Larry fighting both of them, standing in front of the scalded guy like a shield. And that's when Molly knows this job is gone, because the customer won't let it go and the management has already decided who's right.

But she can't allow the incident to bug her. You let one mis-step like this throw you off and you're sunk. Money runs so tight that it only takes a small miscalculation to drop you into a whole world of ugly-ass debt, and once you fall down you never get back up. So Molly checks in her uniform and says goodbye to Sal, who ruefully promises to stay in touch. Then she begins circling the wanted ads, and the next place she can find that's hiring is called Winnie's Home Cookin', a dozen blocks further to travel from her apartment, twenty-eight tables split three ways, red plastic banquette seats and no tourists, because they stay uptown where there are no burned-out build-ings or mean-faced homeboys sitting on the backs of bus benches.

She chooses the place because of the menus, which at Winnie's are bonded carriage trade leather with linings, not sponge-cushioned PVC, and a sign that the place once saw better times. It's as good a way as any to pick a job when one restaurant is so much like another. A few years back, raffia-covered menus became popular, but customers picked the corners off and one pat of butter would ruin them. The public doesn't realise how much of a server's job is side work, clearing and cleaning and replenishing, and one mushed butter-pat can really throw you off. Molly waits tables in places that have cooks, not chefs, where the portions are big and hot, the salads still sweat ice from cold storage, the pie cream comes in a spray can and every other condiment from dressing to creamer is in a fluted plastic pot. She's given a two-to-ten shift with a half-hour break and an unflattering licorice-red uniform with a name-tag she has to get printed herself. The busboy is Indian and speaks better English than her co-workers, Marla and Jeanette, both of whom have allowed their everyday conversation to elide into short-hand order-speak.

The place is really busy tonight, and the table configuration is a bitch to get used to, but she's good at realigning herself to any environment, a homœostatic impulse that serves her well as she moves from job to job across America. Molly knows the secret of staying on top of the work is to be on good terms with the cook, because if he takes against you, your whole shift can go to hell. Unfortunately she got off on the wrong foot with Jomac by accidentally parking in his space. The heavy-set cook looks so uncomfortable in his sweat-sheened body that she half expects to see him step out of it like a discarded jumpsuit.

She's keeping busy in a quiet patch, folding cutlery into paper serviettes, thinking about the loss of her last job with some annoyance, when the guy from Table 7 walks right in, bold as a rooster. She recognises him instantly, because you never forget the face that got you fired, but she's careful to act like she's never seen him before, even when he arranges to be seated in her section. Her first thought is; how the hell did he find me? The only other person who knows where she's moved is Sal, and she would never tell.

This time he's wearing a blue double-breasted blazer with gold buttons and has blonde-frosted hair, a low-rent version of a high roller, like he has money and wants folk to think he's someone special but doesn't have the taste to pull it off. Molly makes sure she keeps the coffee pot well clear of him, and her hand is steady as she pours. He never takes his eyes off her, but she won't be drawn, because if she catches that look he'll know that she recognises him. Her rent is overdue because of the days she lost switching jobs, and she can't afford to screw this one up. She tries to sound casual as she takes his order, which he changes and fools with, trying all the while to connect with her, but she's steel inside, never once letting down her guard.

Placing the order at the hatch, she grabs a glimpse at the table and is shocked to see that he's still staring after her. She wishes Sal was here to back her up. She can't confide in Marla or Jeanette, who share a rented trailer together with Jeanette's boyfriend, so they obviously have no secrets and no time for anyone else's. She'll have to deal with it alone, but forewarned is forearmed, and this time she's not coming anywhere near his reach. When the meal arrives she slips the plate across from the far side of the table, smoothly withdrawing her hand before he can get near her, although he makes no attempt to do so.

She comes back from the table, serves the couple on 12 with lurid emerald slices of key lime pie, and is refilling their plastic water glasses when she hears the cry. She instantly knows where it's coming from, and looks over. He's sitting there clutching his mouth with both hands, and there's a thin trickle of blood coming out of the corner between his fingers. She tries to ignore him but knows he is calling to Marla, who's just passing his table. Her world slows down, because it has suddenly been rendered fragile.

She wonders what could be wrong. He couldn't have burned himself on the plate or found a piece of glass in his potatoes – Jomac is so meticulous in his preparation of the food that the servers are constantly hassled by impatient diners. Her mind flashes back over the service she provided – nothing she's done could have caused him injury; she's in the clear. He's yelling like crazy now, and if she pays no attention it'll look like she has something to hide, so she goes over and stands beside Marla, watching the performance.

The restaurant moves in a strange half-time as she watches Marla trying to convince the man to take his hands from his mouth. He tips the crimson-stained palms away and parts his bloody teeth as Marla probes. Molly sets down the water jug and realises, as she looks down at her uniform, that she is no longer wearing her name badge. She washed the outfit last night, as she does most nights, and ironed it before she left the room, pinning the badge in place as she walked down to her sideswiped Nissan, but sometime between then and now it has disappeared, and she has a terrible feeling that it is in his mouth.

Sure enough, the pin is hooked into his gum, but Marla's strong fingers pull it free, she just reaches in there without thinking, not worrying about germs or anything, she used to be a nurse at the city hospital, and he retches and spits onto the tabletop, the little red badge skittering out in front of him. Molly snatches the thing up, wiping blood from the raised letters to reveal her name. The pin has been jammed in his mouth so hard that it's almost bent double. Marla's trying to wipe him down with a wadded cloth but he's still yelling blue murder, and now the temporary manager, an ineffectual, almost ghostly Texan kid who goes by the wholly appropriate name of Sketch, is calling her over with a look of anger on his face that's the first genuine emotion she's seen him show.

It's raining hard, the first time in over a month, and it's falling too fast for her wipers to clear, pelting through the smashed window and soaking her shoulder, so she pulls over beside a phonebox. She no longer has her mobile – that was one of the first expenses to go. She's lucky – Sal is just leaving to start her shift.

'How he could even convince people he'd accidentally eaten it, for God's sake, it's a nametag, he said it had been deliberately pushed into the mashed potato where he couldn't see it, I mean, what is this guy's fucking problem?' She listens to Sal, who's a mix of common sense and Southern toughness, a woman who once went back on a double shift within hours of an abortion in order to pay the doctor.

'No, I didn't report the car window because what's the point? He obviously recognised the vehicle in the restaurant lot, looked in and saw my badge on the seat or the floor. Well, it seems pretty obvious to me that's what happened, 'cause I sure as hell didn't come near enough for him to rip it off me in the restaurant.' She listens some more. The rain is steaming off the car hood like mountain mist.

'The same as before. Won't press charges if they let me go, yadda yadda, they couldn't get me out of the door fast enough, everyone's so shit-scared of lawsuits. Marla with blood all over her, unbelievable. God, no, I don't want to track him down, I just want to stay the hell out of his path. I wouldn't even be able to give the police a clear description, he looked kind of different this time. Sure, I recognise him, but that's because of his manner, you know how you do in this job, complainers stay with you. But I'm going to change the car, that has to be how he found me. I have to anyway, I can't afford to get the window fixed, although what's gonna be cheaper than this heap of junk I don't know. No, I have no idea what car he drives. No, Sal, it's celebrities who get stalkers, I'm just a waitress, but I'd like to know what the fuck he thinks he's doing.' She scans the straight wet street as she listens. The sky is darker than the buildings. 'Sure, I'll be in touch just as soon as I get something.'

After hanging up she goes into the convenience store on the corner and collects the freesheets. She needs to start looking for hirers right now. She can sell the Nissan and go to Rent-A-Wreck until she's back on her feet, the cash will tide her over between jobs, but doesn't know how she'll ever cover the gap and save for another car.

Back in her room at the motel – she swore she'd never rent like Sal, the margin for financial error is just too slight, but there's no alternative now that she's moving around again – she looks at her face in the bathroom mirror, and knows that some restaurants will rule her out. She was always pretty, but the look is getting hard. She's not as light-hearted about the job as she used to be, and it's starting to show. The management want their 'girls' looking fresh, not troubled. She's always been good at hiding her worries behind a smile, has no problem with being on her feet all day and knows the work better than any of the younger ones, her customers always tell her that. If she'd been an executive she'd have risen through the ranks by now, but when you're a waitress there's nothing to be except another waitress, and the older you get the more management start thinking you'll want to use their health plans.

The tips at Winnie's were solid, she needs another place like that. For a while she toys with the idea of taking a second job, just until she's out of this money-hole. She could do mornings in a mall, grab a couple of hours' sleep and keep her regular afternoon shift, or just work one restaurant and pull a double every three days or so, but first she has to find one job, let alone two, and the ads aren't promising.

The first interview she gets is a disaster, a dingy deep-red ribshack staffed by downtrodden-looking migrants with ESL and a scary supervisor called Ethel who warns her that they don't tolerate slackers. The next, which she passes on the spot, is in a diner set behind the grafitti-blitzed bus station, populated entirely by derelicts surviving on handouts of old coffee. Getting in and out of the building involves walking through shadowed no-go zones to an unlit car park; and with her stalker waiting out there somewhere, it's not worth the risk.

Finally she gets a decent slot at Amanda's, a dessert-heavy joint in an unsafe but thankfully well-lit downtown neighbour-hood where the kids hang out in chicken-wire basketball courts smoking, dealing and constantly shifting loyalties within their social groups. Amanda's desserts are a source of fascination for Molly. They sit in a tall glass cabinet lit spearmint-neon in the middle of the restaurant, and appear to have been manufactured from entirely alien ingredients. The jello is coloured in eye-watering shades that don't exist in or out of nature, the cream is so white that it looks like plastic paint, and the pumpkin pie appears to be made of orange sofa foam.

But hey, it's a job, and the other girls seem okay, if a little distant. They're scared, she can see that, scared of slowing in case they stop altogether, like wound-down clockwork toys. The bad news is she gets the late shift, which is until 2:00am with another half-hour of clearing away after that, but servers can't be choosers and at least night diners aren't so picky about their food.

The motel where she's staying smells of damp and fast sex. It has a filthy pool, a scared-looking Mexican cleaner and a weird reception clerk who concentrates on comic books as though they were Dickens novels. She gets back from Amanda's too tired to wash out her uniform, but it has to be done the night before or it won't be dry in time. The tips are lower because the desserts are cheaper, which is no surprise considering how they taste. Amanda was the original owner, but the place killed her and now it's working on the rest of the staff, who have the bad skin and downbeat demeanour of drug mules.

In the moments when the work eases off, and she looks out through the plate window at the windy, desolate street, Molly sometimes wonders how it's come to this. She has no real friends to speak of, no one to share private jokes with, no loyal lover who waits up to tell her things will all turn out fine. And on the bad evenings, when rain weighs down the red plastic canopy and the place is deserted, she asks herself how long she can go on pretending that everything is fine, how long it will be before her ready optimism and her hopeful smile crack and die with the weight of getting by.

But you think like that and you're already lost. So she covers the burns on her wrist caused by hoisting the coffee pot and shows the surliest diner that she cares, and works on autopilot until at the end of the week, one rainy Sunday night, she doesn't even notice that he's back, the stalker is back, and has slipped into a booth at the end of her section just before the restaurant's due to close.

The lights are dim over the crimson seats, so when she catches his face it's a shock. He looks terrible, like he hasn't slept for a

month. He looks like a serial killer haunted by his deeds. His
hair has grown out and he's added a moustache that ages him,
and she knows she can't ask Rosemary, the other waitress, to
take over because her section is empty and she's slipped into
the alley for a cigarette.

Ted, the cook, is nowhere in sight. No one can help her. She
drops the menu onto his table and beats it, checking that her
name-tag is in place as she goes. But she has to return to take
his order, because that's her job, it's what she does. And he
says, 'Molly, I've been looking for you everywhere. You're the
only one who can help me. Please, don't go, I won't do anything
bad.'

She wants to go but has to stop and ask. 'Why did you get
me fired?' She's holding the coffee pot high above him, ready
to throw it in his face if he moves an inch toward her.

'You're too special to be working in a diner,' he tells her,
watching her eyes. 'Such big blue eyes, like an angel. You're a
good woman, Molly. You know how much it hurt me to let
you go? The first time I saw you I knew you could save me
from myself, stop me from doing harm to others.'

'You're crazy, mister,' she tells him. 'I can't even save myself.'

'Molly—' He reaches out a hand.

'You don't use my name, and if you move one more muscle
I swear to God I'll pour boiling coffee over you,' she warns.
'Now you can either eat and leave or just plain leave, there's
no way I'm listening to your bullshit.' Her hand is shaking, and
she's not sure how much longer she can hold the steel pot aloft.

'Apple pie and coffee,' he tells her, as normal as any other
diner. 'I won't make any trouble in here.' She goes to the cabinet
and cuts the pie, slipping the knife into her apron pocket, but
he's as good as his word. He eats as meekly as a punished child,
and leaves a twenty dollar bill on the table without asking for
the check. He picks up his raincoat and goes so quickly that
she has no time to see which direction he's heading.

She's coming due off duty in five minutes, and there's no

more side work to do tonight because they cleared and reset as the restaurant emptied. Outside, it's raining fit to drown rats. There's a stippled yellow pool stretching across the road where the drains are backed up. No cars, no people, like a movie set waiting for its cue. She thinks of asking Ted to walk her to her car, but doesn't want anyone to think there's something wrong. So she offers to close up for the night, and waits as the others pull their jackets over their hair and head out into the downpour. She douses the lights and watches, but there's nothing happening outside. Finally the waiting gets on her nerves, so she digs out the keys and locks the front door behind her. From the canopy to the car park is a couple of hundred yards max, but she needs to plot the route because parts of the broken tarmac are flooded and her canvas trainers will get soaked.

She negotiates an isthmus through the water toward the Rent-A-Wreck Datsun and already has her keys out when she realises he's sitting in the car, and the headlights come on as he pulls around her, shoving open the passenger door and dropping across the seats to pull her in, but she's fast and lashes out at his face. She's not expecting the pad across her mouth, though, and the gasp of surprise she takes draws chloroform into her lungs. That's the trick, not to put it across the nose like they do in movies, and now it's too late because everything's pressing in on her, and she knows she's losing consciousness. He's going to kill her and leave her body in a ditch, she realises stupidly, and that's not at all what she had planned for herself.

But not before she's pushed her way back out of the car, and although she's disoriented by the rain and the bitter smell in her head, she knows she must breathe clean air fast or she'll go down, and he's slowed up by having to stop the car and come around from the other side. And man, either he's slow or she's fast because she's stumbling back at the door of Amanda's before he comes sliding around the corner toward her. If she can shut the door she'll have won, but his strong hand covers the jamb and pushes back, and all it takes is one clean sharp punch in the face to floor her cold.

'Nurses are strong, of course, but they care in an entirely different way, and they empathise way too much.'

She hears him before she sees him. Her right eye is sore and feels swollen shut. She has a fat lip, a metal taste in her mouth, a jackhammer headache, but at least she's upright in one of the darkened booths, so she can get her bearings.

'You, though—' He shakes a finger at her as he paces about, '—you're a real piece of work. I've watched a lot of waitresses, and you're a classic. A dying breed. Like those Newfoundland women who gut fish all day, nothing touches you. I like that. A true *enfant de malheur*.'

'I don't know what that means,' she says thickly. She needs a drink of water, something to stop her tongue sticking to the roof of her mouth.

'It means you've had a tough time, Molly. It shows in your face. It's what makes you strong.'

'Just tell me what the deal is here.' She can't see him clearly. Why the hell doesn't he stand still for a moment? 'What's your name?'

'Duane,' he says softly.

'Well, Duane, what is it you want?'

'I know you're alone. I know you're broke. Christ, I've seen where you live and I have *no idea* how you can stand it.' He angrily throws out his hands. 'What is it that keeps you going? You've nothing, nothing at all. But you don't have to be alone. You don't have to fight so hard. I could help you.'

'Do me a favour.' She points at the counter behind him. 'Flick that switch down.'

He looks around and sees the steel coffee pot. 'Right, sure,' he smiles and shakes his head and the orange light goes on, then turns back to her. 'I promise you, Molly, I didn't want to hurt you and never will again. But I had to get you to listen to me. All I want is for you to be happy, and if we can come to a deal that will make me happy too, well, hey, everybody wins.'

She tries to focus, to measure how far she is from the phone, the door, the kitchen knives. 'What did you have in mind, Duane?'

'Okay.' He perches on a corner of the orange leatherette seat and slaps his hands on his thighs, pleased with himself. 'I come from a pretty wealthy family. We owned half the car lots in this city. When my old man died he left me a shitload of money. I can give you whatever you want. You'll never need to worry about making ends meet again. This country favours the wealthy, Molly. If you haven't got it now, there's no way you're ever gonna get it. But I can take care of you.'

'You're not in love with me. I got no real education, I got no money, I wait tables and fetch people coffee, for God's sake.' She glances at the pot. The orange light has clicked off.

'You're strong, Molly. Nothing fazes you. That's what I need, a really strong woman.'

'I need caffeine while I think about this. Could you grab me some?'

He rises, then seems to change his mind. 'You fetch it. You said it's what you do.'

She wonders how nuts he is to let her go near the boiling coffee pot. Maybe it's a trust thing. Maybe he just likes her to wait on him.

That's when she realises the true nature of his proposition. He loves her strength so much that her wants her to use it against him. He wants her to fling the hot liquid in his face, to stab him, to punish him, to make him cry, to expose his helplessness before her. He's making her an offer. It's a fucked-up world, he's thinking, but there are worse deals going. She could be alone for the rest of her life.

She fills the thick white cups that hold less than they look. With a steady hand she carries them together with the pot to the shadowed table. His eyes never leave hers as she sets the cups down and raises the hot steel container level with his face.

He dares her. 'Do it, Molly. Do it, and I'll make sure you never have to work in a hellish place like this again. I'll never hurt you. I'll look after you like a princess. There's crazier men than me out there.' He licks his lips. 'Come on, baby, show me what you're made of.'

Molly considers the idea for a moment, then lowers the coffee pot. She absently touches her swollen mouth before she speaks. 'You have a hell of a nerve, presuming this is what I need, just because of what I do.'

'Everyone wants to feel needed.'

She could throw the boiling coffee in his eyes and run out, but then it will never end. Instead, she sets the pot down quietly and walks to the door. 'Let me tell you something. I wait at your table, I take your shit, but you can't get inside me. I'm not running across town from you anymore, Duane. You come after me again, I swear I'll end up going to jail for killing you.'

'You stupid bitch,' he shouts after her, and she realises he's saying that because torture and death at her hands is what he most desires. She wonders what happened to him as a little boy that placed him in the sexual thrall of strong women. 'What have you got here? You'll grow old and die serving shitty food to people who don't give a fuck about you. You've got nothing and you'll get nothing.'

'That's right, lover,' she smiles to herself beneath the rain-sparkled streetlight, 'This,' she throws her arms wide, 'this is what I do. But you only have to do one thing well to have a reason for getting out of bed every morning. And I'm a damn good waitress. What keeps you alive?'

Later, she'll sit in a bar, have a drink, maybe cry. But right now, as she walks away into the night rain, she's already thinking about the ad she saw for the Chicken Lodge downtown, a rundown family joint, good shifts, minimum wage plus tips.

Four months on, there's a two-line piece in the *Cleveland Plain Dealer* about some rich guy found stabbed to death in a quiet family diner. Police want to interview the woman who served his final meal.

ABOVE THE GLASS CEILING

She couldn't believe she had missed the alarm call. Alana Dutton had asked the telephonist to ring her at seven, and now it was ten to eight, which meant that Max would have a head start. Her first meeting was due to start in ten minutes, before which she had to shower, dress and do something about her hair. At least she could dispense with breakfast; the multi-course supper in the old town had not concluded until two that morning. On business trips she was used to making do with four hours' sleep. Clients expected elaborate meals, good wines, thick sauces, and the service in the crowded fish restaurant had been perversely slow, requiring a consolatory drinking session in the hotel bar afterwards. She made up while booting her laptop, downloaded the day's emails while donning her trouser suit and slipped into the Negresco's main conference room as soon as the break in the opening address allowed. Outside, through the opaque curtains, she could see tanned boys roller-skating in sunlight along the Boulevard des Anglaises as if they hadn't a care in the world.

'Where the hell have you been?' whispered Ross, her assistant, 'you missed the Hong Kong delegate.'

'Overslept.'

'So I can see.'

'You didn't call me.'

'You said you didn't want me to, remember?' Ross pulled her neckline straight at the back. Alana wondered how he always managed to appear so immaculate. Ross looked as though he spent the night in bubble-wrap, a treasured Ken-doll preserved by an obsessive collector. Some people handled corporate life so fluidly that they seemed to have no other existence. 'Max was here fifteen minutes early.'

'He always is.'

'Maybe he sabotaged your alarm call.'

'He wouldn't do something like that, he's a straight arrow.' Everyone needed a business rival to keep them on their toes, but no one needed a rival like Max. Always on time, always one step ahead, always completely honest with his customers, always – damn it – three years younger. Wherever Alana went, Max was there first, wide and bright, buttering up the clients and tying up the deals. It wasn't supposed to be an issue, but he was also a man, with the easy confidence of his sex, a former decathlon champion who still wanted to win at everything.

'Daniel says he needs you to go to Frankfurt for the Ang-loCom presentation,' whispered Ross.

'You're joking, I thought he was going to handle that himself. I've only just got here.' Alana had arrived in Nice the previous evening for a three-day event. 'Please, not Frankfurt again. I was there Tuesday.'

'I've got your tickets.' Ross handed her a thick white envelope. 'You're on the four o'clock.'

'Why so late?'

'You have to see Rafaella in Ventimiglia first. I've got you a ticket for the ten-twenty train.'

'This is horrible, Ross, do you realise I've done five countries in under a week?'

'It gets worse,' her assistant replied. 'Nice to Heathrow business class was full. You're in economy.' And Max would be in first class, no doubt. How did the son of a bitch do it?

Alana was evil-eyed by her client as she slipped back out of the room. Ross would check her out of the hotel, leaving her free to head for the station.

A thousand mobile phones bleeped with the same message as the packed Nice-Ventimiglia train passed across the Italian border and the networks changed. The meeting with Rafaella took twenty minutes – long enough to hear her late delivery complaints, long enough for her to tell Alana that she had signed a three-year deal with Max Harwood – and as she headed back toward the passenger-crazed station, Alana grew angry over her wasted journey. Max had obviously charmed the bitch so much that she could pull her territory-marking bullshit with Alana, and make her feel as if they were competing over a man.

On the boiling Ventimiglia platform she helped to hoist an old lady up the two-foot high step to the double-decked train. Behind them, lying against a wall, a young African woman was in labour. The police, used to standing around and singling out gypsies to check on their identification papers, had draped a red woollen blanket over her while they waited for transport to arrive.

Alana sank back into the seat and watched the stations flash by. The tiny resorts of Roquebrune, Cap d'Ail and Eze were separated by enticing bays of fierce sapphire sea. She longed to tear off her suit and join the bathers she saw floating far below in these still coves, but there was no time for such frivolities; there was never any time. The department refused to hire more staff because it had been a bad year; it was always a bad year. Her hours and workload had incrementally increased until she only managed to see her son every third weekend. Whenever she saw Dexter, she noticed that he was falling more and more under the influence of his newly-religious father. Dan had taken up Buddhism and was determined to share his enlightenment with anyone who would listen, but at least this time he was in the thrall of a user-friendly religion. She wondered how other people managed to keep it all together. What did they have that she didn't have? *Age on their side*, she thought bitterly. A certain freshness. Max talked to every client as if it was his first day on the job. He had the kind of disturbing honesty you almost never saw anymore. And there was, it had to be said, the matter of the glass ceiling. She'd been smart and sharp and had risen through the ranks, but the jump into management had proven elusive, so here she remained, on the shop floor.

The Nice–Heathrow flight was full of red-faced English couples in striped shirts and ridiculous straw hats wrangling with check-in crew about luggage allowances. She sat with the other executives in a shadowed corner of the sunlit lounge, where they could jealously eye each other's laptops, mobiles and Palm Pilots. She fought back a surge of jealousy as Max boarded ahead of the herd with a brushed-steel Vaio tucked beneath his arm. Tall and slim, wearing his suit as neatly as if he had been slotted into it, he was the kind of man who elicited responsive smiles from attendants. It was more than just good tailoring. Max drew attention without ever meaning to, just as Alana tried and failed. The eyes of hotel and airport staff slipped over her, writing her off as a faintly butch businesswoman with whom they wanted minimal contact. Lately, Max was becoming less of a rival, more of a nemesis.

The flight was shorter than the journey back from the airport. She would have loved to stay on in Nice, maybe drive along the coast to one of those permanently misty mountain villages surrounding Monaco, but the idea was inconceivable with so much work to catch up on. She had never found time to do it before; why did she think she'd be able to now? This wasn't living, it was working in your sleep.

She pit-stopped at the office to file her report in person, swung by the flat for clothes and headed back to the airport before realising that she had failed to call Dexter to wish him good luck with his brace-fitting. It was too late to make amends; her mobile was switched off because she was already about to board another flight.

Alana arranged licences for homewares, the items everyone could live without: the vanilla room sprays, matt cream vases, citron-scented candles, silver picture frames and embroidered napiery that cluttered expensive shops throughout the world. It sounded pointless when she explained it to outsiders, not that she often bothered to, but when you added in the fairs and exhibitions, the fluctuating territories, the fashionable crazes that turned inefficient little factories into panicked and robotic corporate suppliers, it was a very big deal, and each country could be persuaded to stock the other's goods. The urbanised Italians, French and Spanish had a flair for luxuries. The equivalent English items were artless and overpriced, cursed by generations of home-county conservatism and the loss of a manufacturing base. Alana was a vice-president of European territories, but the title meant little, and her opposite number was in the employ of her biggest competitor. Max was easily winning the battle for orders, sewing up each European territory as he passed through ahead of her.

It didn't seem as if it was possible, but the events of the week gained speed. In the departure lounge at Schiphol, Alana watched a man of roughly her own age undergoing what appeared to be a fatal heart attack. He slumped in his seat and slid sideways, and no one would have noticed if he hadn't dropped his drink on the floor. Whisky soaked into the man's socks as the business lounge hostess vainly tried to set his body upright for the sake of decorum. Later that evening, from a hotel window in Birmingham, she saw the couple in the room across the courtyard having a fight, which they resolved by noisily making love. It seemed in those twelve hours of fast-changing scenes she witnessed every form of human behaviour, yet none of it touched her. Travel had thrown open the world, but reduced it to nothing more than a series of distant tableaux.

She was pleased when the office called to redirect her once more; a new project would at least end this passive observation. Her itinerary was checked and locked. The destinations blurred; she displaced her thoughts and stared from the glittering black windows of departure lounges, holding bays for the executives who kept The Continent, as it was once called, competitive.

The night was stormy; she was in Cologne or Berlin, one or the other, waiting to board a delayed flight to Amsterdam, when the sky broke with a bang. Alana remembered thinking she had flown through the worst of it when the plane bucked and dropped after its rough climb into the flaring night; then there was nothing but grey dead air. The weightless sensation lasted for the remainder of the flight. She landed in Holland, dazed and unable to think of anything except putting one foot before the other, getting through the next ten seconds. With a buzzing head she attended a meeting about scatter cushions in Bruges, flew to Gatwick but missed her son, took off again, landed again, but now the sense of keeping up and coping had come undone, as though the rhythm had faltered between what she saw and what she was doing, like soldiers breaking step or an orchestra losing its way in a difficult musical passage.

She no longer recalled her journeys as a linear parade of events, but as underlit Polaroids of an indistinct life: shelves of room colognes, boardroom tables, drivers holding signs that bore her misspelled name, club lounge wet bars, cocktails and canapés, order books, pens, endless counters of smiling women checking tickets against computer screens, arguments over napkin rings and candlesticks – none of it made sense. She held a meeting about leather placemats as though her life depended on it. The tableaux raced past in a garish blur of sights, sounds and moods.

She even forgot about Max, despite his name continuing to crop up in emails and trade magazines. At least, she forgot until the night of the International Soft Furnishing Awards, when Max picked up a lucite plaque honouring him as salesman of the year. Even that wouldn't have been so bad, but Max had to stop by her table and smile condescendingly at her until she was forced to congratulate him.

She drank too much – she was angry, damn it – and found herself at the bar with other executives whose working lives had passed unrewarded and unhonoured that evening. Pretty soon a slanging match started, with Max Harwood as the object of pity and envy.

'He fucks all his female clients,' said Peter Olexa from the Milan office. 'Then as soon as he's got them to sign for three years, he's gone.'

'He never delegates, and he sets a pace no one else can keep up,' complained Simon Carter-Phillips, an overweight also-ran from the Chelsea Emporium who looked about eighteen months away from his first heart attack. 'He works so hard that he gives the rest of us a bad name.' As they knocked back their scotches in agreement, Alana found it hard to be bitter. Christ, the man was good at his job, and everything else was just jealous bullshit. She wondered if he had been married.

On her way back to her room she passed Max's door just as the man himself was entering. She wanted to say – actually, she wanted to ask Max how he had managed to top his personal best this season – but found herself becoming angry when he invited her in for a drink, because it wasn't playing by the rules.

Quite what happened in the next few seconds remained a mystery to her for several weeks. Certainly, there was a scuffle that tumbled them into the room, and Max seemed to trip over the edge of the bed. He whacked his head on the corner of the minibar and fell face down so hard that Alana heard his septum crack. The blood that pooled around his head was as black and glossy as tar. Alana gingerly checked his pulse and found there was nothing, not the faintest beat. The blood in Max's veins had simply stopped moving. They had all been drinking heavily – Alana had read somewhere that your blood vessels ruptured much more easily when there was alcohol in your system, so much so that a simple fall could kill you, and Max looked pretty much one hundred per cent dead.

She staggered back into the corridor, pulling the door shut behind her, but even in her confused state of mind was careful to wipe the handle clean of prints, just in case she'd touched it.

The corridor was empty – it was nearly midnight – as she headed to her room on tiptoe and showered the bitter sweat from her body.

As much as she was sure that someone would find out what had happened, Alana felt equally convinced that no one could directly link her to the death scene. After all, the guy had fallen over and died in his own room. There was nothing to connect the two of them. They hadn't shared a lift to the floor. There were no closed-circuit cameras in the hall. They hadn't spoken since the awards ceremony earlier, and then they were seen to be on good terms. It hadn't been her fault, for Christ's sake, he had grabbed at her.

Even so, she didn't sleep a wink all night.

Nobody noticed that Max had failed to appear for breakfast. He usually ate on the road and beat everyone to the airport. It took a few days for the rumours to start. At a conference in Berlin: 'Have you heard about Max Harwood? He suffered a stroke after the Soft Furnishing Awards and died.' In Paris: 'Max had a massive heart attack. Too many hotel dinners. They're looking for someone to take over his territories.' In Amsterdam: 'He'd been drinking, choked to death on something he ordered from room service. Just shows how the dumbest thing can bring a good man down.'

Alana applied for the position because it seemed stupid not to, and was so sure of not being granted an interview that she didn't even bother to check her emails. When she did, she discovered that she had been offered the job. They knew all about her; the interview was little more than a formality. A breezy heavy-set American in his fifties named Brent Kaye welcomed her to the fold, inviting her to a small gathering of company directors the following Friday. They had drinks at an underlit bar in a Holborn hotel, then Brent took her off for dinner, where they sat in a quiet alcove, behind sharp white linen. Brent drank quite a lot for an American, and handled it well.

'Glad to welcome you aboard,' he said, playfully punching Alana on the shoulder. His manner was corny but endearingly awkward. 'You've made it to the club. You're one of us now.' Alana assumed he was talking about the company, but Brent pointed to his lapel, and the small gold and black enamel pin stuck in his buttonhole. The badge formed a pair of entwined letter E's. 'Seen one of these before? Sure you have!'

Now that Alana thought about it, she had. Over the years she had noticed the discreet initials pinned to a number of ties and lapels. 'What does it stand for?' she asked.

'Executive Elite,' Brent explained. 'You mean you never heard of us?'

Alana wondered if it was something to do with the Elks. 'No, but it seems—' she waved a nail over the badge, '—I've seen that logo around a lot.'

'Hell, it's more than a logo. You've seen it because you travel in the same circles. You should be very proud of yourself. You're the first woman in our industry.' Brent drained his wineglass and refilled it. He dug in the top pocket of his jacket and produced a slim fold of brown leather, which he slipped across the tundra of tablecloth to Alana. 'Go ahead, little lady, we reckon you've earned it.'

Alana unfolded the little pouch and shook out the gold pin. 'I don't understand. What did I do to get this?'

'Come on, you don't need to be modest. I think you know very well what you did. You're gonna find that this little baby opens a lot of doors for you.' Brent watched while she clipped the badge to her lapel, but wouldn't be drawn further on the subject.

Throughout the next day's meetings, Alana took note of those executives who wore the badge – although they were from many different countries, they seemed to have something in common, a look, a manner, something she couldn't put her finger on. If other members noticed her pin, they didn't comment on it. At the weekend she spent time with Loic, a copyright lawyer she was seeing in Paris, and watched television while he was dressing, noting a number of officials at a televised UN meeting who appeared to be wearing the same pin. She was starting to get a bad feeling; the more she looked at the damned thing, the more it looked like a modern-day version of the SS insignia. And the ones who wore it – men only, it seemed – looked like the kind of people who denied having anything to do with military atrocities. At night she unclipped the pin and studied it carefully, tipping it into the lamplight.

E E.

Executive Elite, what the hell did that mean? Did you get Air Miles or something with every deal you clinched? She'd been promoted, but what was so elite about that, and why the secrecy? True, the senior executives with whom she dealt seemed to be treating her with a new respect, and sure enough, doors were opening more easily than they had in the past – that wasn't just her imagination, was it? But what had she really done to deserve the honour? What marked her out for special treatment from all the other executives?

She woke in the middle of the night sweating ice.

It was blindingly obvious. She wondered how she could have failed to spot it before. She had murdered a man – at least, they thought she had – and it had made her eligible to join some kind of club – a society for everyone who had managed to get away with it. She'd proved she had the right stuff to move to the inner business circle. They thought she had murdered Max to get ahead. Upright, honest Max, who was loved with a ferocious loyalty by his staff, and hated by everyone at the top for making it all look so damned easy.

Alana threw cold water on her face and stared at her red eyes in the bathroom mirror. She wasn't a murderer, she was a professional. Max had slipped. It was the kind of accident that happened to people all the time. She needed to talk to someone. She had to see Brent.

'Executive *Execution*?' hissed Brent, pantomiming horror.

'Jeez, Alana, this is not the place to talk about it.' They were standing in the overcrowded bar at Claridges, waiting to go into the richly carpeted dinner lounge that looked like an old cinema. 'Why don't we go through to the table before the others arrive?' It was twenty-five minutes past eight and the room was starting to fill up. The Americans ate early, the French ate late, and English businessmen only ever booked tables for eight-thirty or nine. Brent drank some water and licked his lips, looking a little nervous. 'Like I told you, it stands for Elite. Nobody ever – *ever* – says anything about execution. I always argued that we should explain more to our new members, but the board thinks it's better to let initiates work it out for themselves. Where did you get the idea about the initials?'

'I worked it out for myself. Maybe that isn't what you're called, but that's what you mean.'

'I always thought you were gonna be one of the bright ones,' laughed Brent. 'Well, you know now, so if you have any questions, it's the time to ask them.'

'What do I have to do?'

He looked at her blankly. 'Nothing. You don't "do" anything. You already earned the mark of respect. It'll get you anywhere you need to go. Take a look around, you'll meet other club members but no one will ever talk to you about it, because there's really no need. It's the ultimate club, Alana, one you don't have to ask to join, one that acknowledges you by one simple act that you've arrived at yourself. We have EE members in all walks of life. Insurance, banking, law, media – newspaper proprietors, we sure have a lot of those. What you've done is win yourself a gold pass card, honey. Think about it, you surrendered your life working your butt off to keep the pistons of commerce pumping. Your world is a waking dream filled with the art of the deal – that's true, isn't it?' He gave her a secret smile. 'Come on, look what you do: brokering, planning, forecasting, profit and loss, balancing figures, and all too soon it's over, but you, you went a step further than that to get on, it's only fair you should reap a reward.'

'And that's why I get to wear the pin.'

'Well, partly. There's another reason. It protects you. It means no one can ever do the same to you. You're safe now. You paid your dues. You're a protected species. What's the point of a club if it doesn't privilege its members?' He signalled to a waiter. 'Can we get some wine over here?'

She should have felt wonderful. After all, no one could ever find out that she hadn't exactly 'paid her dues', but had merely watched in drink-numbed amazement as Max suffered a ridiculous accident. As Alana pulled off her shoes beside the hotel bed, she only felt sick and ashamed that, in the final reckoning, this was all her working life amounted to, this was why all the sacrifices had been made. If she had chosen to push Max into an alleyway and knife him into a lonely anonymous death, she would still have been awarded the gold pin. 'Clearing the path,' Brent had called it, as if she had just helped to cut away under-brush that impeded the wheels of industry. Max had rocked a few too many boats, it seemed; no one in the upper echelons was sorry to see him go.

The pin got her appointments with people who until a few weeks ago wouldn't even return her calls. She made better deals and cleared higher profits without working as hard, and after a while it didn't feel so wrong. She began to think about taking a holiday. As she watched the planes taxiing along the rain-sheened Heathrow runway, she tried to decide where she could take Loic, somewhere far away, a place that neither of them had ever visited before. That was when she saw Brent's face reflected in the dark glass.

The American was standing behind her, but the customary smile that creased his face had vanished.

'Brent,' said Alana as a sense of guilt returned, 'are you going to Antwerp for the ceramics fair?'

'No, Alana,' Brent replied. 'I came to see you.'

'Me? I don't understand.'

'Oh, I think you do.'

'Would you like to sit down?' she asked nervously.

'No. This won't take long. Why didn't you tell anyone the truth about what happened between you and Max that night?'

Alana thought quickly. She'd been over it a thousand times in her head. There was simply no way that anyone could really know how Max had died. She could brazen it out. 'You know what happened.'

'I know now.'

'What do you mean?'

'I know because Max Harwood told me himself.'

'What are you talking about?'

'He's back with us once again, Alana.'

'But he's dead.' Her voice rose. Other people in the lounge were looking up at her.

'Max turned up at my hotel last night, having spent three weeks in a clinic with no fucking memory. The last thing he recalls is walking away from you after you tried to jump him for a fuck, and tripping over the end of his bed. Which means—' Brent leaned forward and reached inside Alana's overcoat, feeling for the pin and unclipping it, '—that you are not eligible to wear this. It seems you don't have what it takes after all.' Brent weighed the clip in his hand before slipping it into a pocket. 'It means you're not protected anymore.' His eyes were lazy with contempt. 'We thought you were the first woman through the glass ceiling who acted like a man.'

'I'm a threat to you,' said Alana, realising her position.

'Maybe, but not for very long.' Brent smiled. 'You'd better hurry. I think they just called your flight.' His smile returned in a shark grin. 'You learned one thing from this, Alana. You've seen us, so you know who to keep an eye out for next time.'

Even as Alana ran for the gate, she knew there would never

be any escape. If she thought her life was fast and frightening before, she had no idea how fast and frightening it was going to get in the next few weeks.

PERSONAL SPACE

They rang the doorbell, just like any normal people. How was I to know? It was ten past nine in the morning, just after the postman had been. I was dressed, you understand, just about to go down to the shop for a newspaper. I wasn't expecting anyone, and at that time in the morning you don't expect—

You don't expect.

A boy and a girl. She was too thin, he was liverish, not a healthy-looking couple. Down at heel, I thought, fallen on hard times. Or perhaps they had never known good times. She looked about sixteen, he was two or three years older. John and Amy, they'd come about the room. What room? I asked them. They pointed to the lounge. They'd seen it through the garden window, the room I still called the front room. Sleet was falling outside. The girl was wearing a pink cardigan two sizes too small, like a little girl. She looked so cold.

How could I refuse them?

Hard times, he said, something about hard times. Well. This whole neighbourhood has fallen on hard times. I like to think I'm a good Christian. The thing was, they had no money. Not right away, but they could get some. Just a room. What about the toilet and kitchen? I asked, you'd need to use those. You won't know we're here, said the girl, we're very quiet. It won't be for long.

I suppose I wondered then if they had done something wrong. But the girl's eyes were so blue and wide, and the boy's face was so pale and lean. He had a rash on his neck that needed treatment. You feel sorry for the younger ones, how can they get a start in life now?

I had the space to spare. This house has three floors. A Victorian semi-detached residence. Even when Sam was alive we hadn't used all of the rooms, they cost too much to heat. With him gone, and hardly anyone visiting, what need had I for a front room with a piano I had to keep polished every week, and so many ornaments in the glass cabinet, and the best china and the rugs, and the air so still you could see motes of dust hovering on sunny afternoons, not even circulating through the light.

I let them move in. This was January. How was I to know?

I gave them a key, the only one I had spare, Sam's old key. At first I hardly knew they were there, they were so quiet. One day Amy left me a cake, came upstairs and put it on my kitchen table. Shop bought, just sponge and blue icing, but a sweet gesture. Amy and I ate some together with tea, and she told me she was pregnant, and had been thrown out of her stepfather's flat. She had no money. He had no job. How were they to live?

I moved my things to the first floor so that they could have the kitchen and bathroom to themselves. I thought it was only fair. She said they would pay me back once they got on their feet.

John often went out late. I saw him go from the upstairs window. He left Amy alone, but I didn't go downstairs. I didn't mean to pry. Who wants an old lady interfering and making a nuisance of herself? Young people live differently now.

It's a quiet street, run-down and dirty, but you should have seen it after the war, smart and neat, with tidy front gardens, not like today with the kids yelling and screaming. Now they leave fridges and sofas on the pavement, and abandon their cars in the road. A woman was stabbed in the middle of the afternoon for no reason. How can you be stabbed for no reason? The council do nothing. I write and write, but all I ever get back is a form letter – thank you for bringing this matter to our attention, and so on.

It snowed in February, and John stopped going out so much. That was when the doorbell started ringing more often. At first it was just during the day. Strangers would call and ask for John. I would hear Amy answer the door, see her usher them in. They would stay for just a couple of minutes and then leave. People soon began calling at all hours of the night.

One night I remember the house was cold because someone had left the front door open. I wanted to check that everything was all right, and knocked on the front room but there was no answer. I could hear crying inside.

I still did my own hoovering then. One day I was vacuuming the hall carpet and found a hypodermic needle, a nasty-looking thing with blood on one end. I should have asked them what was going on. The lady from the social services came to call to see how I was, and I told her everything was fine. A neighbour called, the Methodist lady from across the road. I didn't mention my lodgers, I don't know why. I wanted to sort things out for myself. I hadn't seen Amy for a while, and neither of them had offered me any money. I had to sort it out, just to know where I stood.

I knocked at the door, and found myself confronted by a tall black man dressed in one of my husband's old shirts. He told me he was staying with John and Amy for a while, and who was I? Well, I hardly knew what to say. When I was growing up, no one would have ever behaved in such a way. I was trembling, but I demanded to see the room.

This man – I never found out who he was – opened the door. It was a shock to find the place in such a state, rubbish on the floor, pizza boxes and beer cans and filth, everything so dirty, and John lying on the floor half asleep, dressed only in a stained T-shirt and shorts, and terrible bruises on his arms. Amy told me he'd been in a fight, and apologised about the state of the room. She'd meant to clean it but hadn't been well. Her stomach was no larger, and when I asked her about the baby she didn't seem to recall our conversation. I supposed she wasn't pregnant after all, but couldn't think why she would have lied.

I went back to my rooms on the first floor to think things through. Obviously I had to ask them to leave, but how?

I decided to talk the matter over with my neighbour, and went over to see her, but she wasn't in. I was worried sick. The next day John came in carrying one of those portable music players, and started playing it all the time, even after I asked him to turn it down. I must have been blind.

I saw him go out, watched through the banisters as he shut the front door, then I went downstairs. Amy was sitting against the wall with a rubber cord tied around her arm. She and the black man were boiling something in spoons over Sam's old primus stove. Well, of course I knew it was drugs, I'd seen it on the television, so I had to put my foot down. No drugs in this house, I told her, I'm afraid I will have to ask you and your friends to leave.

The other man, his name was Lee, he told me to go away – only he was much ruder than that, he actually swore at me, told me to eff off and mind my own effing business. Told me not to come downstairs again, that it was off-limits from now on. Shook his fist in my face. I was shaking when I went back upstairs. I would not be spoken to in that way, in my own house.

I waited until the next morning and went to the police. I waited for ages to see someone, and this very abrupt lady told me I was to make a report, and she would deal with the matter, so I filled out a form, giving them my name and address, and came home.

When Sam was alive the house was filled with plants, aspidistras, ferns and palms in round white china bowls. Everything gleamed, silverware, crockery, my best tea service, the framed photographs on the walls. In the month that followed, everything disappeared, the cutlery, the pictures, the books, the silverware. They sold it all to buy their drugs, became quite brazen about it. Amy wouldn't talk to me anymore. She seemed distant and only half-alive. John avoided me. One day, I came back from the shops to find two new men, one with a scar right across his face, and another girl, a scruffy little thing with sores on her arms. The men said they were friends of Lee's, and had come to stay, but they would need my first floor.

I wouldn't have let them and yet – something – all I could think was that perhaps there were redeeming circumstances, perhaps there was still a reason to be kind, but I was determined to return to the police as no one had called to talk to me.

In the meantime, I moved up to the top floor. The stairs were more steep, and although there was a toilet, the kitchen was little more than a cubbyhole. They stole everything that was left out, laughing and fighting and crashing into things, and I realised then that I was scared, really scared. I had survived a war and lived through rationing and seen my husband die, so of course I wasn't scared for myself, but these harmful people hurt themselves and each other, they were so in the grip of their need, this thing they cooked and smoked, this thing that made them crack into pieces and behave like animals. The man called Lee, going to the toilet on the stairs in the middle of the night, the one with the scar holding his fist up to me, his fist! Just because I asked him to make less noise, I couldn't sleep. They wouldn't let me wash, or sleep. I became ashamed of myself.

The worst time was when I came out onto the landing (I would sneak downstairs to use the bathroom while they slept, I didn't want to have to confront them) and saw one of them cutting Amy's arms with a razor-blade. Blood was falling onto the threadbare Persian carpet like tiny red raindrops. I cried that night – buried my face in my pillow and pretended it was not happening. I would dream Sam was still alive, and the house was still nice, and would wake up with a terrible sinking sensation when I realised that all my fears were real.

It frightened me to leave the house, but one day I crept out, went back to the police and told them what was happening. They seemed surprised that no one had come to visit, and insisted on coming back with me, half a dozen of them. They said there had been complaints from the neighbours. I didn't know about that. I had hardly ever talked to my neighbours, a young couple working in television on one side, hardly ever at home, some rough people on the other. The police told me they had 'initiated eviction procedures', but when they left, the people in my house were still there. They won't do anything to you, love, said one of the policemen, just let us know if you have any more trouble, they'll be gone soon.

The next day one of them called to inform me that a county court eviction order had been applied for. The police returned with a drugs search warrant and evicted everyone from my house. One man jumped over my garden fence and broke it.

I was alone for the first time in four months. I had terrible nightmares. A lady from social welfare called and told me I could apply for compensation, and that I could get someone in to help clean up the mess, but that it would take a while for the application to be processed. She didn't think they would be able to get my belongings back. I only cared about the things that had sentimental value.

The next night, they moved back in. I heard them banging around, not even bothering to be quiet. They had nothing to be scared of. I was nearly eighty years old, and had no phone. I couldn't believe anyone could be so brazen. You hear about such things but never think it can happen to you.

The police came back later that week, and this time they were armed. Dealers, I had dealers in, said one of the officers, and they had to get rid of them. He made it sound like I had mice or an infestation of cockroaches. But these men and their women and their drugs, they still came back. This time Lee tied my hands together and carried me to the top floor, and told me to stay there if I knew what was good for me. Every night I heard them banging through the house, looking for things to sell until there was nothing left. They cleared out my wardrobe and took my jewellery, my wedding necklace, the earrings Sam had given me on our silver anniversary. They emptied out my purse, even took all my old dresses.

I couldn't go out, and didn't dare to answer the door because I never knew who might be there. One afternoon at the end of May I heard the knocker – the doorbell no longer rang because they had taken out the batteries – and tiptoed out into the hall to peer through the bannisters. I recognised the shape standing behind the glass because the lady from across the road is rather large. I didn't know what to do. Should I risk going downstairs? Finally I decided I had to be brave, and crept down as quietly as I could. The door to the lounge was shut, and the house seemed quiet because everyone had a habit of sleeping at odd hours, so I carefully opened the front door.

Dear God, said my neighbour, what's happened to you? When did you last have something to eat? You look terrible. Her voice was so loud that I was frightened she would wake them up, so I told her I had the flu, and would call on her when I was better, and quickly shut the door.

I made my way upstairs and went to bed. There was little point in getting up, not when the rest of my house was out of bounds. The next day I received a letter from the bank warning me about running up an overdraft, especially since I had asked to close up my account. I had never had such a thing in my life. My pension was paid in by direct debit, and I always had enough to see me through the month because I suppose I spent so little on myself – you don't, do you, when you're eating for one. It was a shock, and when I searched for the box I keep my cheque book in, I couldn't find it anywhere, so I had to go and see Amy. She was in her usual sleepy state, only worse this time. Her face was yellow with jaundice, and her eyes had sunk so deep that I could hardly tell if she was looking at me in the candle light.

She told me that John had drawn out my savings and paid

some men the money he owed them, if he hadn't they would have killed him, and now it was all gone, and what did I have that I could sell? I got angry and said, how can you live like this, what is wrong with you people? When I was your age nobody lived in this terrible way, lying and stealing and hurting each other, and soon she was crying and hugging me like a baby wanting to be nursed.

Then John came back with some men in hooded jackets, and I could tell they had been drinking, so I scuttled back upstairs, but I heard what they said to Amy. Do you think she's got more money hidden away? asked John. We really need it, Amy. You could get it out of her, she likes you. And Amy said no, leave her alone, she's so old she won't live if you hurt her, and then it was quiet for a bit. We could tie her up and leave her without food until she tells us, that's not like actually torturing her, is it, said another. Then I heard them coming up the stairs.

I held my breath. The footsteps stopped. Something distracted them and they started arguing. After a few minutes they went back downstairs and closed the front room door once more. That was when I decided I couldn't stay on the top floor any longer. I would have to move.

I quickly decided that the only place left was the cupboard in the top room. I hadn't used it for years because it was tucked in a corner and hard to get at. It went under the attic, but if I dragged my blankets in there I could make myself a bed. I could come out at night and take food from the kitchen, perhaps use the microwave because it was quiet and they hadn't sold it yet. I worked quickly and quietly, taking only the things I needed, and made myself a new little home. I pretended it was wartime again, and that I would be hurt if anyone found me.

I did a clever thing. I crept downstairs and left the front door wide open, so they would think I had gone out, run away for good. Of course I couldn't because I had no money and no clean clothes, and I couldn't impose myself on people I hardly knew. In my day you wouldn't consider doing such a thing.

Then I went back up to my cupboard. I found a tin of condensed milk, and an apricot, not very fresh but better than nothing. And there I stayed.

I thought for a while I would escape, but I became too weak to get much further than the toilet and the kitchen, and certainly couldn't manage the main staircase to the front door, it is far too long and the stairs are too deep.

They quickly overran the house, barking and chasing each other like dogs, and nobody thought of looking in the cupboard because you wouldn't it was so insignificant, and they hardly noticed such details. At night they smashed things up and screamed at each other, screamed terrible things, and once there were gunshots, but none of the neighbours ever came round to complain.

No one comes round to complain. I think they are too frightened. The other afternoon I got as far as the kitchen (I had found some tuna left in a discarded tin) and I noticed that the house next door, the one belonging to the television people, was now empty. They had given up.

I still live here in my old house. I've been here for a long time now. The worst thing is when the police come and throw them all out, because I can't tell how soon they'll be back, and I have no food until they do. I need them to feed me. But they always return, smoking their little pipes and leaving half-eaten pizzas on the floor, which I can take and reheat when they're asleep.

Of course I am scared. I've been scared before, but when you are scared all the time, the sensation fades away into a dull ache that you hardly remember anymore, like losing Sam or any other sadness that is always with you.

Sometime I remember the house the way it was. With polished lino and ticking clocks and china dogs on the mantelpiece, and the wireless playing, the smell of fresh baked jam puddings and lavender polish, washed net curtains, everything dusted and tidy and bright, but those days have gone, and I would rather be old and filled with memories and living in this little dark space than be downstairs in the bare hard light, young and raw and screaming inside, facing the daily terror of being alive in a world that no longer cares, or even notices if you are there at all.

HOP

'I'm the only one who can stop the hopping,' Nathan Charles told the police.

'And why's that?' asked the taller of the two ginger constables, not bothering to suppress his disgust.

'Because I'm the only one who saw it happen. I put all this in my statement last night.'

The tall ginger constable leaned close. He'd recently eaten a curry. 'What your statement tells us, mate, is that you're a nutter. Worse than a nutter. You know what they do to people like you in prison? The warders won't protect you.'

Nathan tried to stay calm. He thought carefully, imagining another way to explain. 'Do you believe in the soul?' he asked. The copper looked blankly at his short pal. 'I'm not a religious man, but I've come to believe that a wronged soul might seek redress. Haven't you ever tried to put things right? What if you were dead? Wouldn't your soul be in danger? Hop is an ancient name for the devil, did you know that?'

'Right, that's enough of this bollocks,' said the short one, spitting his chewing gum into its foil for later. He signalled to his partner. 'Let's get him locked away again.'

Nathan Charles decided he was wasting his time trying to appeal to their spirituality. Before his arrest for murder, no one ever noticed him. He was a quiet, unhealthy man with a bad back that caused him to move cautiously, in perpetual expectation of pain. He was the last person you'd imagine hurting anyone, let alone committing such shocking acts of violence. But in the last two years, he had tried to kill seven children.

He didn't do it to satisfy an aberrant desire, or for financial gain. He was attempting to save the lives of others. Nathan constantly had to remind himself that he was not mad. *I'm a good man who has been forced to take an unthinkable path*, he thought. *I am trapped on the horns of a terrible moral dilemma from which there is no simple solution. But I must fight to find one.*

The police, as they say, were baffled. How could someone have attacked children with such frequency and avoided detection until now, when he finally struck in a crowded street? They didn't know that Nathan had been keeping to a pattern that no one else could discern, that he was careful to leave no trace. He was always watching for an opportunity to commit murder, and his victims were defenceless. Of course, parents were much more mindful these days, so he still had to be careful, but with a little planning and forethought he felt he could achieve his aim.

What exactly *was* his aim? The two ginger constables watched him and waited for instructions, but never asked themselves what had led their prisoner down this path, from a comfortable married home life to a haunted existence in a squalid bedsit. To discover that, they would have had to turn back the clock.

Two years earlier, Nathan Charles had been a happily married man with a three-year-old daughter. He had married Chloe, the girl he had dated since his days at Warwick University. His wife had given birth to Mia, a precocious black-eyed child whose atavistic behaviour amazed and amused them both. Nathan saw a lot of his daughter, because Chloe worked while he stayed home and tried to finish enough paintings to furnish his second exhibition. The first had met with modest success, encouraging him to strike out in a new direction, but all too often he found it easy to drift away from his sketchbook and watch Mia at play. He was entirely happy in this role. It allowed him to view his daughter's development at close range.

It was around this time that he began to make drawings of her. He had in his mind a series of sketches that would chart the mysterious behaviour of her expanding intelligence. He drew without thinking, marking in the folds of her arms, the back of her head, not really studying his efforts until he had several sketches complete. He filed the sketches in folders, with the idea of waiting until several sets were completed before creating a large-scale composite painting.

This was a new area for Nathan. His first exhibition was very different, and had come about because of the location of their apartment. The Charles family lived in a wide grey street, in a house set diagonally opposite the entrance to Holloway Prison. The place had come cheap because it was difficult to get tenants to live within sight of jails and graveyards. The view didn't bother either of them, and the light was good because it was a top-floor flat. They never saw the people inside the vans that came and went; Nathan had no way of telling who were guards and who were prisoners, and didn't give it much thought until the day of the escape.

Holloway is a women's prison with a controversial history, from the imprisonment of suffragettes, the dubious conviction and execution of Edith Thompson in 1923, the hanging of Ruth Ellis in 1955, and accusations of racism that culminated in the suicides of black prisoners and former inmates in more recent times. Yet the prison also had connections with art. One of the most striking was the silver pin presented to all members of the National Women's Party who served time for picketting the White House for women's suffrage. The pin was modelled after Sylvia Pankhurst's Holloway brooch, which represented the portcullis gate of Holloway Prison, chained shut with a heart-shaped lock.

The prisoner who escaped was a girl called Jackie Langford. She had been incarcerated for the murder of her father, and while there was no question of her guilt it was generally felt that she should have been placed in C1, the psychiatric wing of the prison, rather than the offenders' unit, because medical reports pointed to her poor mental condition. There were those who said she had suffered terribly as a child, and did not deserve to be in prison at all.

On that day, Nathan was returning from the shops with Mia, and had almost reached the front door when he saw a slender, pale girl running across the road. A car screeched, there was a slam of flesh and bone against metal, and her body fell at their feet. As she landed, she threw up her arms and caught Mia in the mouth with her wrist, splitting the child's lip.

Mia screamed, more in surprise than fright, and suddenly they were surrounded by officers in dayglo yellow jackets. Nathan and Mia were hustled to one side as the police twisted the girl onto her stomach and locked her hands behind her back. It seemed inhuman to Nathan; she had not meant to hit his daughter, and he felt the police should check her first for broken bones before slamming their weight on top of her. He began to say something, but was warned into silence by an armed officer. Later, when the event was covered on the news, he was shocked to discover that the girl, Jackie Langford, was only twenty-three. She looked much older, but her ethereal appearance was due to the hunger-strike she had embarked upon several days earlier. She had fought her imprisonment from the outset, and just half an hour earlier that morning had put out a warder's eye with a plastic fork after agreeing to eat a meal.

Mia seemed none the worse for her fright. The cut looked worse than it was, and she soon forgot the incident. Nathan read about the Langford case because it was in the papers for days afterwards; she had died on the way to hospital, but there was some confusion as to the cause of death. Doctors' opinions conflicted: one said she had been fatally injured in the road accident, another said that her wounds had been caused by the guards on their journey to hospital. The journalist implied that she had been assaulted in revenge for the injury she had inflicted on their fellow officer.

THE GIRL WHO WISHED SHE HADN'T BEEN BORN was the headline of one melancholy article about Jackie Langford. Beneath it were two photographs, one of Jackie aged three, already damaged by neglect, clutching a pathetic bunch of small white flowers; the other showed her grim little grave, where no such flowers would ever be left to take root, where attention would be denied in death as it had been in life.

Certain facts had not been made available at the time of her trial: Jackie's history of sexual abuse at the hands of her father, her often-expressed desire to die, her attempts on her own life. Born to an alcoholic and a drug-addicted mother, she had first been abandoned, then placed in care and finally reclaimed by her father. The scandal was that social services had allowed her to be returned to her abusive parent, whom she had eventually killed. Public sympathy for Jackie was mitigated by the fact that at the time of his death, her father was crippled and all but helpless, and she had tortured him before he had finally slipped away. The whole affair was sordid and sad, but Jackie's death had not quite brought the cycle of violence to an end; a few days later, newspapers reported that her mother had murdered the baby she'd recently conceived with another drug addict, before taking her own life.

Nathan studied Jackie's downcast face in the blurred newspaper photograph. He had never seen such an image of misery and damage – could nobody have done anything? Such things happen, Chloe told him, and there was little that anyone could really do. She was upset that Mia had come into such close contact with a convicted murderess. She wanted them to leave the area, but a move was out of the question until Nathan had sold some paintings at the next exhibition, which was still seven months away.

The paintings were not coming easily. None of them satisfied him. Nathan felt as if he was failing to grasp the point of his life. Was this really the best he could do?

And he had a problem with his drawings of Mia. It was hard to keep her sitting still, but when he gave her some coloured crayons and a sheet of paper, he found that she would hold the same position for several minutes at a time. He had hoped for early signs of artistic talent, but was too optimistic, because she only ever managed looping scribbles, their colours decided by whatever crayons were at hand. For some reason (probably because the sheets he gave her were the same size as the ones he was using) he kept Mia's drawings sandwiched with his own, and it struck him that he might use the random elements from her doodles in with his own sketches. It might even provide the breakthrough he was looking for.

Then an odd thing happened.

At the end of an overheated, tiring day (the stormy August afternoon had drawn Mia into a state of fractious boredom) Nathan emptied out the drawings and began to assemble them in order. Although it still seemed a good idea to mix both sets of sketches, what upset the compositional balance was his daughter's profligate use of colour, so he tried to damp them down by overlaying coloured gels. The first few didn't work; they rendered the sketches invisible. Nathan threw the sheets onto the polished pine boards of the studio and dug out a crimson panel of acetate, laying it over the scrawls.

What the crimson did was knock out all of the reds, yellows, oranges and lighter tones, leaving blues, deep greens and blacks. To his surprise, he found himself looking at a legible sentence.

It read: I AM THE AVENGER OF ALL UNWANTED CHILDREN.

It wasn't possible, but the words were quite clear and spelled out in block capitals. They had simply been buried under many layers of crayon. As the weather broke and rain began to patter against the windows, Nathan dropped to his knees and pulled out all of the other sheets she had drawn on. Then he applied the same sheet of acetate. The following sentences were slowly revealed like coded patterns in DNA:

FOR ALL MEN THAT DO NOT LOVE.

WHO MUST TAKE THE BLAME.

FOR NO ONE WILL AVENGE ME.

I JACKELINE *(sic)* LANGFORD.

THEY WILL DIE AT MY HAND.

THROUGH THE HANDS OF OTHERS.

THEIR OWN OFFSPRING.

AM NOT THE ONE.

Rearranging these and adding the first drawing, he came up with:

I JACKELINE *(sic)* LANGFORD AM NOT THE ONE. WHO MUST TAKE THE BLAME. FOR ALL MEN THAT DO NOT LOVE. THEIR OWN OFFSPRING. THEY WILL DIE AT MY HAND. THROUGH THE HANDS OF OTHERS. I AM THE AVENGER OF ALL UNWANTED CHILDREN. FOR NO ONE WILL AVENGE ME.

It seemed as though someone was playing a grotesque trick, but try as he might, Nathan could not come up with a rational explanation. The drawings were his daughter's, and the block letters all matched. He could see that in every case they were carefully buried under layers of scribble. He had watched the child make every one of the pictures herself, beginning with a blank piece of paper. She had pieced the lettering together stroke by stroke, entirely out of order, as a medium might.

With trembling hands, he laid a fresh sheet before her. Delighted, Mia grabbed a handful of crayons and began to loop and scratch at the paper. Nathan watched for an hour, and could still not see the letters being formed. If they were there at all, they had been made up from hundreds of tiny disconnected lines. When he removed the sheet from her and placed it beneath the crimson gel, he could read:

THEY CANNOT CATCH ME FOR I WILL HOP.

This seemed to make even less sense than the previous

statements camouflaged in the drawings. Worse, it was the last sentence Mia produced. When he tried to get her to do the same thing again later that evening in front of his wife, Mia produced a little-girl daub with nothing hidden within. Nathan searched the sketch in every imaginable way. It was as though his daughter knew he was onto her, and had decided to call his bluff. When Nathan attempted to show the drawings to Chloe, she took Mia's side against him.

On those long afternoons while his wife was at work, he watched the little girl constantly. He knew that she was someone else. Her body language had completely changed. He watched her, and she knew when he was watching. A slyness crept into the corners of her eyes. She became preternaturally calm and intent upon her tasks, studiously ignoring him as if to say, 'I know what you're about, but you won't catch me out.' She was no longer his daughter, a small distaff form aligned to his emotions, but a Midwich Cuckoo of a child, something to be feared when they were left alone.

Curled against the far side of his bed at night he thought: *I love her. My daughter was never unwanted. She hates me. How can she hate me for not loving her?* He knew the hatred must come from the woman who possessed her, but it seemed impossible, insane to believe.

In the months that followed, the marriage began to break apart. Nathan was unable to provide enough paintings for the gallery, and lost his exhibition. All his energy was spent on studying his alien daughter. A strange pattern to Mia's behaviour had emerged. This sentient being, this guarded spirit, only appeared in the light of day. After dark when Mia was sleepy, she was quite herself. It was as though the thing – that part of Jacqueline Langford which had been denied sunlight for so long – could only thrive and take hold in brightness, even the grey-tinged sunlight of North London. He imagined her spirit operating like the phototropic cells of a plant, a purely chemical transformation, as impersonal and determined as a poisonous orchid, unfolding to release its spoor like a spreading cancer.

Chloe became mistrustful of leaving her daughter alone with her strangely behaved husband, but one winter afternoon, while she was visiting her gynaecologist, Nathan reached a decision and took the child to a lonely part of Clissold Park.

'I know you're in there,' he whispered to Mia as the insipid November sun flecked her face. She ground the toe of her Wellington into wet grass and gave him a new look she had lately developed, the one that said 'Daddy can't stop being silly'. She held his eyes for so long that he jumped when she suddenly ran off.

He caught her in a few easy strides as she tried to dive inside a straggly bush of gorse. She did not scream or fight to escape his embrace. He tugged but the thorns refused to yield her, snagging her clothes and striating her pale limbs with spidery crimson trails. Her body went limp in his hands, and for a moment he thought he had killed her.

He only realised what she was doing when he saw the boy, a self-consciously tough kid of nine or ten, his grey cotton hood up, a Silk Cut smouldering in a pinched mouth. He'd been mooching behind the bushes, and now stood frozen to the spot as the sentient spirit gathered strength in Mia's inert form, preparing to hop.

This time he almost saw it leap, as some filmy, fiery substance, the passing of raw energy, displaced the air between girl and boy. Now Mia was awake and screaming at him in shocked bewilderment, and the boy was staring at him with her crafty eyes, preparing to bolt. Nathan made a grab for the child, but found himself holding the grey hooded top.

The good news was that Mia, his daughter, had returned. She retained no knowledge of what had happened to her, and seemed none the worse for her distant interlude.

Chloe's coldness was harder to dismiss. She would not forget her husband's disturbing manner so easily. Nathan's last sight of the little boy running away across the sodden park returned to him each night, preventing sleep. He began to retrace his steps across the grass, searching for the boy. He had taken the first steps in a hunt that would last for eighteen months. Soon his wife and child were gone, but losing them was the price he paid for vigilance.

He came to feel that he had been chosen to protect the children of the city. He had no money, no friends. He followed the tormented spirit of Jacqueline Langford from the body of one child to the next as it hopped, tracing families from Balham to Tooting to Finsbury Park to Leytonstone to West Hampstead, and always the creature defeated him at the last moment. It only chose young children; perhaps teenagers were too closed, too knowing. He had no way of understanding the process. He only knew that such things existed.

He watched the children as they changed, and sometimes he managed to stop them before they hurt their fathers. But he was never sure what to do with any child she had hopped into. Should he kill it? Would that stop her from causing an eternity of harm to others?

On that final rainy Thursday in the Edgware Road, he trapped the little boy Amir, into which Jackie's much-travelled soul had hopped only a few minutes before. He strangled Amir with his tie, coming up behind the boy outside a shop. Amir had been choosing oranges, and held several in his hands. As the tie tightened around his neck, the oranges fell from his hands to the gutter.

When she saw that her child was missing, Amir's mother screamed in a way that only a middle-Eastern woman could.

Later, Nathan told the police everything, right from the start, but of course they didn't believe a word. They only wanted to know what he had done with the boy. When Amir was found alive in a nearby cemetery, tearful and confused, a doctor examined him and found no sign of abuse. What's more, the boy plainly had no recollection of the strange man whom witnesses had placed in the street just before his disappearance. The spirit had hopped once again.

The police released Nathan. What else, they told Amir's screaming mother, could they do? Just a few days earlier they had captured a man who had run amok in Oxford Street with an axe, yelling to his victims that he was the Devil's emissary on earth. These days there was a tendency to lump all the lunatics together; there seemed to be so many of them about. Nathan's case was unproven.

But Nathan Charles was no longer the man he had once been. His wife sued for divorce. She wanted to know what he had done with the child while they were in the cemetery. She had been in touch with Amir's mother. Eventually a case was assembled, spearheaded by the parents of children all across London who recognised his photograph in the *News of the World* and logged onto a website with testimonials. Chloe gave evidence against him. Although little hard fact emerged, Nathan did his case no favours by insisting that his story was true. He was placed under the supervision of a North London psychiatric ward.

After a further two years had passed, he was allowed to make local trips in the custody of his doctor. On one chilly Sunday morning in June, Nathan visited the cemetery where he had taken the boy Amir. After this trip he became quite calm, and never again tried to convince the examining board of his case. For he had seen the tiny flowers that now blossomed across Jacqueline Blandford's grim little grave, on the spot where he had shaken her spirit free from the terrified boy. The fresh white petals had transformed the site into a place of lasting peace, a small sign of thanks given to a man who had sacrificed everything to restore a single tortured human soul.

THE SCORPION JACKET

The pink minarets rose as slender as paintbrushes above the mosque in the deserted town square. There were eight of them, set amid 177 white domes, and could be seen, it was said, for seventy miles. But the paint was peeling now, and the latticed shadows of the courtyards passed across dried-up flowerbeds and dust-caked fountains.

Beyond, the Bosphorus was covered in brown cadavers, agitated at the pleasure of the winds and the waves. Sultan Seyfeddin Mehmet II cared little about the carnage his infidel wars had caused, and petulantly complained when his *pazar caique*, or imperial barge, had trouble nudging its way through the corpse-thick tides. His mother, the *valide* Dowager Sultana, controlled the city of the Golden Horn now (as mothers so often did in this region), and rarely left his side during the hours of light. At night she slept in a curved chamber of beaten gold-leaf, protected by twelve dwarves armed with scimitars taller than themselves.

The Sultan Seyfeddin had six brothers, but three had been garrotted, two banished to Albania, and the only one with any sense, the young favourite Beyazit, had been imprisoned in his quarters for the past eight scorching summers, to languish in his *kafes*, or cage, until his death, with only his sterile concubine for company.

The kingdom was, to put it mildly, in disarray. The Sultan's armies had protected its borders at a terrible cost; the court was in chaos, the peasants were eating tree bark to survive and even most of the royal swans had been snared and baked by desperate farmers whose lands had been taken to provide military camps.

But life – such as it was – had to go on. The towns and villages of the land were quieter now because people were weak, and it required too much physical effort to move around the dusty landscape. Those camels and asses that had not been boiled for their flesh were worked until death came as a happy release. Desperate mothers defied the will of Allah and smothered their children at birth rather than bring them into such a world of misery.

And the Dowager Sultana was preparing for a wedding banquet. She had taken such delight in ordering everything, from the bolts of fine blue damask filled with crimson rose petals, to the little round almond cakes dusted with yellow icing sugar, that one would have thought she was to be the bride, but that dubious privilege belonged to Aimee, the girl who had been selected to marry the Sultan and secure an alliance with the kingdom's southern borders.

It would mean that the Sultan Seyfeddin would have to turn his attention from the ladies of his seraglio, Circassian concubines on whom he nightly lavished amber wax and tulips, but it couldn't be helped; the Sultan would eventually need to father a child, and that was something he couldn't do with a slave girl. Aimee was ten, a little old as brides went in this part of the world (the Sultan's father had married a girl of seven at the age of fifty-eight) but the kingdom could not afford to wait too long for an heir. Seyfeddin had no interest in love, or marriage, or art, or politics, or even his people. He was a child in the body of a corpulent thirty-five-year-old man, and chiefly delighted in playing practical jokes upon those in his power.

Once he had arranged to have his harem dressed in new chemises of orange silk, then ordered them brought to the royal bath house, where he secretly spied on them from a screened window. His tailors had removed the stitches from the garments and lined the seams with glue, which melted in the bath house heat, causing the chemises to fall apart and leave his ladies naked, whereupon he took great merriment in their anguish.

The Dowager Sultana had been unhappy with the court tailors ever since, and when she was unhappy, terrible things could happen to a courtier. Soon the north wall of the palace was covered in a skein of blood that dripped in strands from its dragging hooks, and there were no tailors left in the palace to torment, so she summoned a Janissary and commanded him to ride into the first village he could find that had not been wiped out by cholera, and locate a tailor who would make her a beautiful gown for the approaching wedding.

The Janissary questioned the villagers and was directed to a young man called Abdul Paizar, who lived with his wife and daughter in a clay hut at the end of a cracked white lane, the sides of which were littered with the carcasses of starved animals. The Janissary was shocked at the state of decay and poverty within the town, and hoped that the tailor would prove skilled enough to earn a future for himself and his family, for the Dowager Sultana could be generous when served well.

'I understand you are the finest tailor in these parts,' said the Janissary as he tried to calm his skittering mount outside the tailor's house.

'Though I say it myself, sir, there is no garment I cannot make.'

'Then you have not been tested for a time, or at least you have not been rewarded,' observed the Janissary as he regarded the tailor's own ragged clothes and humble dwelling. 'You will come with me to the palace at the command of the *valide* Dowager Sultana. If you do well, it will be the making of your fortune.'

And so it was that Abdul the tailor attended the Dowager Sultana, who showed him plans she had drawn up for a gown of her own design, with a tight bodice of spun gold and a long train of dyed purple goose feathers. Her royal modesty prevented her from being physically measured for a fitting, for the hands of a peasant could not approach the flesh of one who had been chosen by Allah himself, so the tailor was required to guess her size, and given that the Dowager was prone to dressing in layers of different materials, his task was far from easy.

It was a tricky situation; Abdul knew that if he made the bodice too loose, the Sultan's mother would appear less attractive than her son's intended bride, and would demand a suitable revenge on the tailor, something traditional and lingering that involved sharp hooks. If, on the other hand, he made a gown which was too tight, it would cause her discomfort, and she would not look suitably radiant, with the result that the street dogs would soon be feeding on the guts of the hapless tailor.

But Abdul was a smart young man, and came up with a solution to the problem; although his time was limited, his resources were not, and so he resolved to have the palace seamstresses make not one gown but ten, each of a slightly different size, so that the Dowager Sultana might find a span of material that exactly suited her girth.

The plan appeared to be a great success, and work proceeded well on the dresses. When all ten were completed shortly after midnight on the morning of the wedding, the tailor inspected the work of the seamstresses by lamplight, and approved each gown only after examining it in minute detail. He noticed that one of the dresses contained a faint flaw in the material, barely noticeable to the closest eye, but a flaw all the same. However, it was too late to start afresh on another gown, and besides, the flawed outfit had but a one in ten chance of being chosen.

It was the tailor's misfortune to discover, several hours later, that the Dowager Sultana had picked the gown with the flaw.

Hardly anyone looked at the bride, for even though she was shy and slender, with the unblemished skin of a child not long removed from the womb, the Dowager Sultana had ordered her features to be hidden beneath a veil of dense reed-satin, and had refused her jewellery of any kind. She herself had been fitted in five-inch high *panttobles*, shoes which set her above the rest of the court, and braided plaits of gold wire laced with pearls.

The wedding took place in the orange-and-white-striped mosque, under a vast canopy of cerise velvet supported by four golden trees. Of course, the canopy was set at an angle, because no Ottoman wished to view his world with squares and corners and straight lines, for such arrangements smacked of death. Nothing was straightforward and direct in this world – not love, not war, not revenge.

The procession into the wedding banquet was led by the Provost and his officers, the judges, the Emirs, the Viziers, the Mufti, the Hautboys, the Musick, the Guardians of the Arsenal, the Treasurer, the Eunuchs and then the family of the bride, in order to show them their place in the pecking order of the palace.

Everything went well until the tailor noticed that the flawed sleeve on the Dowager Sultana's gown had become snagged on the gold wire of her armband. It was enough to start the back of the bodice – which was far too tight – unravelling at great speed. The more the Dowager Sultana's flesh shifted, the more the material was rent, until the courtiers behind her had begun to whisper and point. The mosque began to sink into unnatural silence, until only the Dowager Sultana was wondering what had happened.

To say that she lost face when she discovered what was happening is an understatement. She lost her reason, her dignity, her temper and finally her poise, collapsing off the high *panttoble* shoes with a crash.

After being flicked with wet rose petals in the seclusion of her bedchamber, she recovered sufficiently to order the tailor's death, preferably by being roped to stallions straining in opposite directions.

It was the Sultan Seyfeddin who came up with a better idea.

His practical joking had lately taken on a crueller edge – as the bridesmaids who had been made to cross a carpet laid over live coals could testify – and he had noticed that the tailor's greatest concern was for the welfare of his beautiful daughter, Mihrisah, for he kept her likeness etched in ebony around his neck.

'Tell me,' the Sultan asked his Grand Vizier, 'who is the ugliest man in the entire kingdom?'

'Why, sir, there is no one more grotesque than our own *munedjiin*, our royal astrologer,' replied the Grand Vizier. It was true; Ibrahim, the court astrologer, had been granted his powers as a child, when he had fallen from his father's horse while out riding in the desert. The poor boy had been dragged for a quarter of a mile across the hot sands. The sun-scorched sands burned against his skin like a million fiery cinders, and fused to his face like streaks of molten glass. Ibrahim had now reached the age of two and twenty. Although he was strong and pleasing of body, it was said that his face could stop the six-faced Italian timepiece in the clock-hall beyond the main courtyard. None of the concubines (whose rooms overlooked the astrologer's kiosk) would dare to peer out through their modesty-windows when Ibrahim was at work on his charts, for his desk faced their apartments.

So it was that the tailor's daughter was married, against her will, to the ugliest man in the Sultan's kingdom, as revenge for her father's ineptitude, it being a long-held belief within the Ottoman Empire that the creation of suffering was an art as subtle as any other. On the night before her wedding, Mihrisah sobbed uncontrollably, for she felt she had brought disgrace to her family by being born a girl. The marriage ceremony was a small affair attended only by the lowest courtiers, who reported back to the Sultan that when she saw the face of her husband, Mihrisah made no sound at all. Rather, she accepted the calamity of her fate with great stoicism. One of the courtiers delivered his report in such a tone of respect that the Sultan had him defenestrated for treachery.

The tailor was kept on at the royal court as the Sultan's personal tailor, and paid a handsome salary in order to give the Sultan's revenge more bite; for Abdul could not share his new-found wealth with his daughter, who had been given an adjoining apartment to his, nor with his wife, who was forced to remain at home without food in the cholera-stricken village. In addition, the tailor was forbidden from addressing Mihrisah in any way. Nor could he speak to her gruesome husband.

Without his family, the tailor felt there was little point in remaining alive. His poor workmanship had doomed them all to a life of wretchedness, but if he killed himself for his honour, he risked putting their lives at risk, and so he lost himself in his work, and tried hard not to think about the horror of his daughter's nights, or his wife's desolate, wretched days. The world settled back into a slow and soporific curve, while the tailer sewed and watched and waited.

Soon Aimee, the Sultan's young wife, was old enough to bear a child, and did so, producing a healthy son and an heir for her husband. A ceremony of celebration was announced, and the Sultan asked the tailor to stitch him a jacket finer than any made before, in order that he might impress his wife at the recommencement of their lovemaking.

On the morning of the celebration, Abdul presented his work to the Sultan. Carefully unwrapping the silken bag into which the jacket had been laid, he raised a truly extraordinary piece of work. He had seen the style on a painting that detailed the outfit of a Western visitor, and had noted the Sultan's smile of approval. Slim of sleeve and narrower of waist than was usual in court clothes, it consisted of a single unbroken piece, like a second skin, that the tailor suggested would fill Aimee with delight. Moreover, its finish was of bright orange panels, over-lapping like turtle scales, and it glinted in the morning sun, first ginger, then cherry, then hesperidian, light reflecting like a thousand phosphorescent sunsets.

Of course it found favour with the Sultan, for dark colours

suggested the finality of death, and sunlight the converse. Sey-feddin was entranced and demanded to try it on at once, but Abdul insisted on making the fittings himself, and in a rare state of agitated vanity, the Sultan allowed him to touch the royal corpus. Once the jacket was correctly laced and buttoned, the Sulton summoned his mother to gain her approval.

The *valide* Dowager Sultana was not a woman known to express delight in the pleasure of others, but even she was thrilled by the tailor's work. She circled her son like an over-fed hyena, admiring the jacket from every angle.

'It is magnificent, is it not? What incredible new material is this?' the Sultan beamed, catching sight of himself in the great beaten-copper panels of his dressing room. He summoned his eunuch. 'Bring my divan in here,' he ordered. 'I wish to rest in my celestial raiment until the commencement of the cele-brations.'

'I wouldn't do that, your royal highness,' warned Abdul. The Sultan was shocked – no one was allowed to speak out of turn in his presence.

'You would not do what, pray tell me?' he thundered.

'You may not take rest, sire. You see, I made the jacket from a thousand scorpion tails, and I have sewn you into it, so that if you should put pressure on the jacket in any way, the tails – each one of which is threaded with gold and still contains its poison sac – will be drawn forward to sting you through the lining, and I can promise you that it will be a lingering death, as the scorpions I chose were of a middling size, and therefore as painful as they are poisonous. Any pressure, anywhere on the jacket, will cause you to be stung, and stung, and stung again. Only the bite of the desert tarantula is more agonising.'

The Sultan examined his left sleeve, and gently squeezed the plated material, which was segmented like a shrimp's skin. As he did so, he saw the golden thread tighten, and watched in horror as one of the stings thrust itself through the silken lining of the jacket to press against the soft white flesh of his wrist and puncture it.

The tailor stepped back toward the doorway as the Sultan released a roar of horrified anger. 'Take it off me!' yelled Seyfeddin as the Dowager Sultana began to wail.

'I will do no such thing, sir, although I assure you that I – and only I – could attempt to remove the jacket, for only I know where every sting lies, but I will not unless you grant a guarantee to release my daughter from her marriage.'

'How dare you presume to dictate terms to me!' yelled the Sultan. 'Guards! Cut this traitor into a thousand symmetrical pieces!'

'Wait,' cried the Dowager Sultana, 'if you harm him, you will never find a way to remove the jacket. You must show strength and rise to the challenge of this infidel.'

The Sultan glared at the tailor.

Abdul glared back.

It was a stalemate.

'Very well,' sneered the Sultan. 'I'll show you the power of a chosen Ottoman heir to the celestial ruler. A Sultan has power to control his body in a way that mere mortals cannot imagine. I shall never sleep again, but will remain standing, in defiance of your traitorous intent.'

And he did, right through the ceremony, through the night (after he had banished his puzzled wife to her bedchamber) and through the whole of the next day. His Janissaries built him a special post to lean his hands on, but toward the end of the third day the Sultan's iron will failed him, and his eyes began to droop.

His mother ordered the apothecaries to mix chemical potions that would keep him awake, and when those began to fail, she jabbed him with pins, that he might be reminded of the deadly scorpion tails. The garment Seyfeddin had so admired glittered about him like the coils of a deadly snake, but still he refused to collapse. The Dowager Sultana confined the tailor to his quarters while she devised a suitably exquisite torture for him.

Who knows what might have happened? It seemed certain that the Sultan would eventually be overcome by the failings of his body, and that his mother would order the tailor's death. But this was not what came to pass.

Instead, on the fourth night, as black and starless as the dark at the edge of the world, as the Sultan stood propped at his post and the tailor remained tethered in his apartment, a knock came at Abdul's door.

'My father, I must see you.' Mihrisah stood on tiptoe to see the tailor through the shadowed stars of the door's sandalwood grille.

'My daughter, you must not speak to me.' The tailor's ankle chain would not reach far, so he called to her as loudly as he dared. 'Haven't I brought enough shame upon our family?'

'I have a favour to beg of you.' Her lips shone in the diamond-fretted squares that lined the grille. 'I want you to release the Sultan from his coffin-coat.'

'Why should I do such a thing after all that has passed between us?' the tailor asked.

'Because something extraordinary has happened,' Mihrisah replied. 'Seyfeddin may rule his kingdom with fists of iron, but even he holds no power over the human heart. You see, I have fallen in love with my husband. I know the court thinks him hideous, but beneath that deceiving surface lies the kindest disposition in all the world. You must not feel shamed for bringing dishonour upon our family, for you have brought me happiness, which I treasure above all other things.'

So the tailor called for the Sultan's Janissaries, and requested an audience with his master, who was now barely able to stay awake, and therefore eager to find a solution to the challenge without losing face. Abdul agreed to remove the jacket, first exacting a promise from Seyfeddin and his mother that neither he nor anyone in his family would be punished. The Sultan agreed to the terms of the arrangement, and the tailor called for his scissors, carefully cutting him out of the viperous suit with a few well-placed snips. Shaking with relief and overcome by days of wakefulness, the Sultan collapsed onto his palanquin and was carried back to his bedchamber, where he slept for two days and two nights.

But the Dowager Sultana refused to allow the tailor to leave. 'Only the Sultan can grant your pardon,' she exclaimed with a crafty smile on her face, 'and he is fast asleep, so here you stay.'

The tailor waited. On either side of him, palace eunuchs stared straight ahead with their swords folded in their arms. As the sun set, the smell of boiling almond rice drifted through the windows of the apartment, and the tailor pondered his fate.

When the Sultan finally awoke (and ordered an immense meal of goat baked with mandarins), he summoned the tailor to his council-room. Abdul began to fear the worst as soon as he saw the Seyfeddin approach with the Dowager Sultana walking behind her son. A thin, dangerous smile split her face like a knife-cut across an aged pomegranate. Both were dressed in fine black silk, the official shade of impending death.

The eunuchs approached in silent curving rows and placed a palanquin behind the royal couple. The tailor had heard that the ceremonial bench was used whenever an imaginative execution was to be ordered. As the Sultan produced a dark scroll from his shirt, Abdul's suspicions were confirmed. But Seyfeddin's revenge was to be even greater than he had feared, for he proceeded to read out two other names apart from the tailor's, those of his wife and daughter.

As the proclamation reached an end, the Sultan and his mother seated themselves to announce the method of death. Their eyes widened.

Abdul waited with his breath held behind his teeth.

The Sultan and his mother were frozen side by side. Then they began to scream.

Afterwards, the tailor walked shakily past the oil-sheened

eunuchs, who continued to stare straight ahead. They were forbidden to do anything without an order, so they stayed in their places, as they had been trained to do upon pain of death.

Nobody dared to follow him.

Eventually, Abdul reached a courtyard where he could no longer hear the screams of the Dowager Sultana or her son, and sat down in the sun before a pale dried-up fountain. One day, he decided, he would get all the fountains in the Palace working again, for he longed to hear the splatter of water on azure tiles.

He was a free man once more.

The scorpion jacket had proven such a success that he had experimented further while the Sultan slept. Upon his instructions, Mihrisah and her husband had ventured into the desert, and had returned with their wicker baskets filled. There were enough tarantulas within the baskets to completely cover the dark surface of the execution palanquin, even though sewing them into place had proven far more arduous than tailoring the tails of scorpions, because this time he was working with poisoned pincers, not single stings.

By now the blackened netherparts of the Sultan and his mother would be bloating with one of the most excruciating venoms known to the world's apothecaries. They would eventually die in a fearful extrusion of lethal pus, but only after they had had time to reflect upon the cause of their fate.

Abdul followed the smell of roasting fowl to the royal kitchen. He decided to partake of a good meal before setting off to release the young Beyazit from his eight-year prison, and taking his place as court favourite to the kingdom's first wise ruler in decades.

FERAL

The English countryside is no more. Since it became a single vast coach-blocked conurbation of ring roads and 'Village-Experience'-style housing interspersed with poisonous cows, satanic farms breeding mutant chickens and genetically tampered-with crops, somewhere to empty the car ashtrays and shop for discount computer software, you have a better chance of spotting wildlife in its natural habitat where it belongs, wandering the streets of inner cities. Here's a breakdown of some of the horrifying creatures currently stalking the night streets of the city.

PIGEONS

The city pigeon, or Flying Rat, builds its nests in the lighting above strip-clubs and massage parlours. Its bodily secretions are powerful enough to short out up to twenty metres of neon tubing in one sitting. Pigeons are the billy goats of the sky, eating over seventy times their own weight each day. Sardine tins, syringes, used prophylactics, pizza cardboard, they all spell dinner to Stumpy, the peckish smoke-owl. For this reason, city birds do not make good eating, and when dead should be poked down a drain with a stick rather than served on a pesto mash with raspberry coulis. Pigeons are only spotted on pavements when they are very ill, or when they have had their feet burned off by pungent chemicals left on the ledges of government buildings.

The best places to pigeon-spot are in tree-lined squares, where, attracted by the smell of chips and Tennants Super Lager, they can be seen dropping from low branches to carry off pension books and under-nourished children, or arguing trea-sure-trove rights with tramps over urine-soaked cheese rolls. At airports you can watch entire flocks getting sucked into the jet engines of 747s.

FERAL CATS

These lively, independent creatures are distinguished by their unusual markings – clumped hair, torn-off ears, leg-stumps and missing eyes. They have been known to fly onto the face of a home-going clubber from a distance of forty metres, and can eat an entire pensioner in under two hours. The best time to hear them is after 2:00am, when fighting pairs sound like siamese twins in a spin-dryer. Feral cats can be spotted vomiting fishbones outside takeaway food outlets, where they are often befriended by half-asleep crack addicts. Their high, hacking coughs are possibly a mating call, or an attempt to clear their windpipes of cigarette-packet cellophane. Beware of feral cats rooting about outside the exit doors of one-nighters, as these are often hyperactive and hallucinating, and will not slow down until they have eaten a Marks & Spencers spaghetti and listened to at least four hours of low-level trancey mixes.

INSECTS

Many of the city's top takeaway managers breed exotic insects as a hobby. Drawn by the pheremones inherent in rancid fat, these creatures are allergic to bright light, and you will find them dragging themselves across the floors of takeaways underneath polystyrene box lids. Some species stem from Agent Orange experiments conducted in the underground tunnels beneath Saigon, and are sexually attracted to the smell of disinfectant blocks in restaurant toilets. Others live in temperatures higher than a human being can stand, and can be found performing water-ballets in the boiling oil of hot-dog stands.

Occasionally you may be lucky enough to spot rare Stickle-backed Vegetable-Bin Beetles on their nightly forage. One of these shy, colourful invertebrates can carry a family-sized sliced loaf on its back, and will explode if you stamp on him. The Razorbacked Vindaloo Dung Bug will noisily drink gravy from an unguarded plate, and has been known to lift a diner's chair in its mandibles, while the Chip-Batter Mildew Mite can pass its entire life-cycle beneath the surface of a pickled onion. Other, more specialised bugs breed in frozen pink slabs of burger meat as they are defrosted on griddles outside nightclubs, and devour all forms of garnish, puking it back into the bun for their children just before you put it in your mouth.

TUBE MICE

You may not notice these shy brown-furred rodents until the alerting rumble of an approaching tube train sends them scur-rying for cover in their thousands. One often sees a homebound office worker, slightly the worse for alcohol, staring vacantly at the rails, only to suddenly start in terror as a Pied-Piperish squeaking carpet cascades over his feet. Tube mice are harmless, and only harbour old-fashioned diseases like Bubonic Plague and Dropsy. They can cause commuters to catch a weird kind of herpes from rubber escalator handrails, and work in teams to replace the chocolate bars in platform vending machines with silver-foil-wrapped assortments of droppings. A variant breed is the luminous orange tube-mouse, which gains its pigmen-tation from drinking the dregs from discarded bottles of Sunny Delight. The friendly cousins of . . .

RATS

You used to know where you were with a rat (or not – see p. 106). They came available in two varieties, black and brown, were responsible for thousands of plague deaths and attacked the baby in *Lady and the Tramp*. Kids thought they could sort of fly through the air onto your face and gnaw your eyes out in seconds, whereas they mostly just cowered or ran away squeaking. However, having grown fit on a diet of kebab droppings and half-digested McDonalds burgers vomited onto pavements after the pubs shut, they now have all the top jobs writing feature articles about 'How Staying in is the New Going Out' in 'style' magazines like *Dazed & Confused*, and fill pages with blurred pictures of bony girls who appear to have been dressed during bombing raids, train crashes and bad recreations of sixties' happenings.

FOXES

These adaptable mammals are nocturnal, and their eerie moans recall the sound of Victorian babies with whooping cough. You may see signs that they have visited your bin-liners in the night. Kentucky Fried Chicken boxes will not only have been cleared of bones; some foxes have learned how to open and use the moist towelette. The nesting fox's greatest enemy is the Falling-Over-Tramp, who frequently topples onto their young, mistaking them for cushions. Foxes drink from doorstep milk bottles, and have been known to change overnight orders for low fat yogurt to full cream.

SQUIRRELS

Most people know that the grey squirrel wiped out the red squirrel population of Great Britain, but did you know that many London squirrels can also pick your pocket and forge your cheque-card signature? Some hang around the entrances to parks making sexist remarks about passing girls and throwing nuts at old people. Teams of Gangsta Squirrels, or Squizzas, were behind the Great Hyde Park Conker Scam of 1998, and this year the ones in Regent's Park operated as ticket touts outside the open-air theatre, resulting in scenes of mob violence during performances of *The Pirates Of Penzance*.

ZOO CREATURES

These animals bear no resemblance to the beasts you see on wildlife programmes posing majestically on African plains. Most of them have lost the will to live, and loiter at the rear of their cages smoking high-tar cigarettes, listening to hip-hop bands or copulating with their food containers. Cages turn larger animals psychotic, and if you approach them incautiously they will try to force Unitarian Church leaflets and lucky heather onto you. Some smaller animals grow insignificant in zoos, blending so well with their surroundings that you cannot tell whether you are looking at a frog-eating lizard or some pebbles and a stick. Present-day ideology prevents zoo monkeys from being allowed to conduct tea parties. Instead they excite school-children by sticking their fingers up their bottoms and morosely sniffing them.

URBAN FLORA

During Easter, the windows of city florists fill with dazzling flowers that drop dead minutes after the Ascension. In the city's springtime, residents chain daffodils to their windowsills and trees leak Alien-acid-sap onto car bonnets. Some flowers are actually kept fresh by the chemicals found in car exhaust fumes, while others maintain their upright position in restaurant vases by the insertion of wires. Roses can be spotted on the roof racks of hearses stuck in traffic jams. Daffodils sprout in the wall-cracks of nightclub cloakrooms. Natural city greenery dangles from pub walls, courtesy of automatic watering systems. Some species of urban flora has adapted to carnivorous status, and can eat flies, bluebottles, nuts and the hard urine-stained peppermints people take from bowls in burger cafés after going to the toilet.

Although vegetables may be grown in the city, most urbanites believe that tinned food is the only food you can trust because it is sealed, whereas organic produce grows in dirt and is therefore harmful to anyone who still points from a car window when they see a cow.

GANG MEMBERS

Sixteen was traditionally a special age, the time of sexual flowering and personal growth. Now it is usually marked by a first conviction for aggravated assault. By the age of sixteen, gang members have reproduced often enough to become bored with the idea, and have moved on to the taking of life. Marked by their matching plumage of sportswear and baseball caps under grey cotton hoods, like large drab ducks, they huddle smoking in bus shelters, waiting for windfalls near senior citizens' hostels on pension day, noisily scoffing from plastic McDonalds boxes, the lids of which are good for holding used syringes. Their colourful cries increase as the pubs close and they set off clutching cans of Stella, hoping to kick someone to death for looking at them the wrong way. Few of these rituals are ever observed, as the city's million-pound CCTV systems are simply defeated by the use of a cheap hat.

BIN-BAG MURDERERS

These nocturnal creatures leave their spoor in various parts of North London, especially in the section christened 'Murder Mile', from outside Camden Town's *Prêt à Manger* (trainee

rabbi found hacked up in bin-bags), past Royal College Street
(whores chopped into pieces and dumped in bin-bags, identified
by their breast implants), along Kentish Town Road (where
Adam Ant threw a carburettor through a pub window and
threatened patrons with a fake gun), to Kentish Town tube
(man beaten to death for asking the way) and Tufnell Park
tube station (half a dozen assorted lethal gunshot victims). Also
near this site is the spot where Ken Livingstone, the Mayor of
London, allegedly pushed someone down a flight of steps at a
party. And so the city's Hogarthian spirit lives on.

Bin-Bag Murderers are the latest incarnation of London's
human ferality. While they are responsible for cruelly taking
human life, BBMs are, however, civic-minded enough not to
just shovel guts and limbs into gutters, leaving them where the
rats, mice, insects, cats, squirrels and foxes can gorge on them,
causing them to genetically mutate into something entirely
nastier, and they do have the appealing side-effect of ensuring
that the dustmen always turn up on time in hopes of recovering
the victims' jewellery.

If you spot any creatures that do not conform to any of the
categories mentioned in this guide, they might belong to another
species entirely, like homegoing clubbers or Golf Sale placard
holders, and it is best not to stroke them. And if you do go to
the countryside, remember that nothing on four legs can really
harm you there – the most ferocious creature of all will always
be man.

ONE NIGHT OUT

The night I took my father up west, he'd been dead for thirty-five years. I know that sounds strange, but what happened was this:

I was standing on a stool in the bathroom, stripping off the old paintwork on the linen cupboard with one of those electric hot blowers, and my mind was wandering. The paint was bubbling and lifting off easily beneath my scraper, but I still had an hour's work ahead of me, so I was running over the events of the day, thinking about the staff problems we were having at the showroom, when I suddenly remembered that tonight was Hallowe'en. And that immediately made me think of my father.

I admit that these days I don't think about him as often as I used to, but Hallowe'en was the date of his birthday, and although he wasn't one for celebrations, we always used to go for a drink together on that night, usually down at the Royal Oak.

The thought struck me, as I was burning away a strip of old green paint, that he'd be fascinated by the fancy gadget I was using in place of the old-fashioned blowlamp we used to have to pump into life for paint stripping. He'd been a great one for gadgets and time-saving inventions, fascinated by the way they worked. He hadn't any academic or technical training – it wasn't high on the curriculum in the days when he went to school – but most evenings he'd sit in the kitchen tinkering around with something, making a musical box or a clock-case, not saying much, just enjoying the simple precision involved in such a pastime.

I was just thinking of taking a break to open a can of beer when the doorbell rang. My wife had gone out to the cinema with a friend, and they'd only left an hour ago, so as I turned off the hot blower and headed for the front door I wondered if perhaps the film they were going to see had been cancelled.

When I opened the front door I nearly jumped out of my skin.

There was my father, standing on the step in his old brown leather jacket, with his hands in his pockets. For a moment I couldn't speak. I opened my mouth but no sound emerged.

'It's bloody cold out here,' he said. 'Can I come in?'

I was so shocked that all I could do was stand back and hold the door open. He stepped inside and passed me in the hallway. There was a faint smell of tinned tobacco, just as there always had been when he was alive. He looked well, the way he had at the end of the summer before he went into the hospital. Tanned, slightly gaunt, hair thinning a little, glasses perched above the rather lumpy nose he'd broken so many times in his youth. A very wrinkled forehead, just like mine, and creases running from cheekbone to jaw, just like the ones that were beginning to appear on my face. My wife always said that I'd be his spitting image when I grew older.

He stood there, hands still in his pockets, waiting to be asked into the lounge. I ushered him in.

'This is all right. Nice place. You must be doing well for yourself.'

He looked around the room before finding a straight-backed chair and sitting down on it.

'What – what are you doing here?' It was all I could think of to say.

'Hallowe'en,' he said, still turning around in his chair to

study the room. 'My birthday. I couldn't half do with a cup of tea.'

Stunned, I went and put the kettle on. When I returned, he was still sitting there with his hands in his lap, looking admiringly at the shelves.

'Blimey, you've still got that clock,' he said, pointing to the ticking box he'd made decades earlier. 'Does it still lose half a minute a day?' I just stared at him.

'How did you get here? I thought you were . . .' I couldn't bring myself to say it.

'I don't know,' he replied, a frown wrinkling his brow even further. 'I've never been back before, even on my birthday. I think I'm just here for the evening, like a treat. How's Kath? Keeping all right?'

'She's fine. She's gone out for the night.'

'Where are the kids?' He looked about for them.

'They're not kids anymore, Dad. Steven's married, and his children are grown up.'

'Well, I haven't seen them for a long time.'

'I still can't believe you're here.'

'No. I suppose not.' He rose and began to walk about the room. He never did sit still for very long. Hated the TV. Would rather be working out in the shed, making something on the lathe. The shed had gone now. The entire neighbourhood had gone.

'Dad . . .'

'Hmm?' He was examining the photograph frames arranged on the bookshelf.

'I don't know what to say. This is . . .impossible.'

He stood there for a minute or two without speaking. He never really talked much when he was alive.

'It's strange for me too. Before this there was . . . nothing. The hospital. A long time ago, mind.'

I was conscious of the minutes passing, frightened that he would have to leave without anything important being said between us. He seemed suddenly aware of what I was thinking. He ran a veined hand through his sparse brown hair and studied me long and hard.

'I think I can stay for the evening, old son. I don't know how long I've been away. Your mother's gone.' It was an assumption rather than a question.

'Yes. Not long after you.'

'Hmm.' He was holding the wedding photograph of Steven, my son, and his wife.

'You still got your old motorbike?'

'Uh, no . . .I haven't had that for years, Dad.'

'Pity, 'cause we could have gone up to Reynold's Place and had a look at the old house.'

I didn't like to tell him that the street stood alone now, since all the roads around it had been flattened to make way for a new ring road. Roundabouts and flyovers now covered the area where terraced houses once stood with bee hives and chicken runs in their gardens. As late as the end of the sixties the chickens were still there, in the suburbs of London. It seemed hard to believe now.

'What do you want to do, Dad?'

He replaced the photograph and turned to me.

'I don't mind. We could go for a pint down the Royal Oak.'

'They pulled it down. The Sun in the Sands is still there. You've been away for thirty-five years. A lot has changed.'

Just then, an idea came to me. It seemed to strike him at the same time. 'You want to see some of the new things we've got now, Dad. All sorts of things have happened.'

A light came into his eyes and he smiled broadly. He began to zip up his old leather jacket. I noticed he was wearing the clothes he had worn the summer before he died.

'Come on then . . . show me what they've done since . . . what year is it?'

'Two thousand and three, Dad.'

'Blimey. These old houses have lasted well. The way things were going, I never thought you'd make it this far.'

'Where do you want to begin?'

'Here, in the house.' He was prowling around the room, keen to be shown something interesting.

'Okay,' I started. 'Oh, guess what, we had a woman prime minister for years.'

'Blimey, you're joking, how was she?'

'Bloody awful. Let's see . . . lasers, and computers, they've come a long way with those.'

'I thought they would. Do you still make things in glass? Animals and things?'

'No, everything's done by machines now. I'm a showroom manager. There's no call for what I used to do. Have a look at this.' I showed him my old digital watch.

'Bloody hell, they're using mercury. Doesn't weigh much, does it?'

'Quartz crystal. It emits a pulse when you put an electrical charge through it.'

'Expensive?'

'No, garages give them away. Look at this, you'll like this.' I showed him my home computer, lighting up the screen, and then logged onto the internet. I opened a simple puzzle game, and explained how the thing worked.

'You mean they developed all this just as a children's toy?'

'Oh no. It has loads of practical applications. You can find out all sorts of things, it's just not as good as everyone thought it would be. Too much stuff nobody wants.' I showed him some websites, and let him tap the keys.

'It's a bit of a mess,' he said, fascinated. 'The boffins used to muck about with this idea during the war. Turing and that mob. What else you got?'

For the next hour I went through the house pulling out drawers and opening cupboards, finding all kinds of gadgets to tell him about. Looking through his eyes, I wondered if the world was less interesting than he'd hoped it would be. Only the small stuff had changed. The house still had old chairs and tables and beds and a TV. Silly things amused him, like a little robot dog that wagged its tail when I whistled. He was very interested in the CD player.

'It's like a record,' I explained. 'Covered in tiny holes which are read by a concentrated beam of light. It's been around for years.'

He turned one over in his hand, his fingers leaving no smudges of condensation on the surface of the disc. I touched his hand briefly. It was cold and dry.

I had a sudden thought, and pulled my mobile phone from my pocket, flicking it open. 'Look,' I said, 'a telephone small enough to carry in your pocket. No wires. And it can take pictures.'

He squinted at the tiny screen. 'What for?'

'I don't know.'

After we had gone through Steven's wedding photographs, I suggested we went for a beer. He wanted to know all about the instrument panel in the car, why it lit up like the CD player. It seemed too fussy to him, unnecessarily complicated.

'Who made this, anyway?' he asked, peering into the back seat and out of the windows as we headed toward Tottenham Court Road.

'The Japanese,' I replied, 'they make a lot of cars now.'

He stayed silent until we had parked the car in an underground garage off Shaftesbury Avenue.

'Lots of new buildings around here. They don't look very well finished to me. All this glass, no privacy.'

'Everything's made by machines in factories and assembled,' I explained. 'Nobody makes anything by hand anymore. Things don't break down like they used to.'

'That's good. The streets are very scruffy, aren't they? Roads all dug up, what's going on? There are more people than I remember.' He pointed at someone using a cashpoint to get money. I explained what it was.

'How do they know it's you and not somebody else?' he asked.

'You have this little card, see?' I removed mine from my wallet. 'And a special number that nobody else has.'

'Computers again. Hmm.'

'That's right.'

We walked into one of the older Soho pubs. I thought he would be more at home here than in a place with flashing lights and video screens. I found a brand of bitter which he was prepared to drink, and we settled down in a corner, away from the jukebox.

'They've still got all this loud music then. Blimey, look at them, all dressed up for Hallowe'en.'

Two goth girls had come in and were heading for the bar. Both were dressed in black plastic and leather, with white faces and chained noses.

'Oh, they're . . . a bit like Teddy Boys.' I couldn't think of any other way to describe them to him. 'They just dress like that when they're going out.'

'There must be something that's stayed exactly the same,' he said.

'Well, Cliff Richard's still around.'

He stayed quiet when the goth girls were joined by two boys in heavy makeup and strapped boots. The group spoke German. Some Rastafarians seated themselves in the corner, laughing and drinking.

'There's no one speaking English in here,' he said. It wasn't really a complaint, more an observation. On the whole he seemed less surprised than I thought he would be about what to him was a sudden leap into the future.

'Travel's cheap, Dad. You can go anywhere in the world now.'

'No more wars, then?' he asked as he drained his bitter.

'Yes, but they're different now, more to do with making money than taking land. Fancy another?'

'I'd get you one but I don't think I've got enough.' He pulled out a handful of old coins, tanners and threepenny bits.

'They're no good anymore, Dad.' I showed him the new currency.

'Too small,' he said, weighing some ten pence pieces in his hand. 'Too light. Doesn't feel like real money. Probably doesn't buy as much either.'

We had another pint, and I talked about some of the things I'd been doing since I last saw him. It all sounded so ordinary, so trivial. I had wondered before – as I suppose lots of people do – what I would say to him if we ever met again, and I knew I'd remember all the things I really wanted to say after he was gone. I looked up at the clock. It had just turned eleven.

'They haven't rung the bell,' he said, surprised. 'At least they've finally done something about the licensing laws, then.'

As we finished our pints, seated side by side behind the small brass-railed table, he stared off into the distance, listening to the music. He was tapping the fingers of his left hand on the rail, frowning. Then he grinned.

'Remember those rides on the old bike, down to Dettling and Box Hill?'

'How could I forget, Dad? Egg sandwiches in the meadow, and Mum lighting a primus stove for tea. We used to have a good laugh.'

'I was tough on you, though.'

'I turned out all right. It's just the way things were then. Life's very different for kids growing up these days.'

'Better?'

'In some ways. But they have more to worry about.'

Outside, walking along the street away from the lights of Leicester Square, the night air moved coldly around us, to draw heat from the windows of Chinese restaurants lining the far end of the road. I noticed that his old sheepskin gloves were thrust into his jacket pocket, unneeded. We stopped in front of an electronics store. A big sign in the window read: REMOTE CONTROL PTERODACTYLS NOW HALF PRICE. I explained how digital cameras worked. He nodded as I talked, interested, but realising as I did that his time was drawing to a close.

'When do people get time to use all this stuff?' he asked. 'What do they do with it all?'

'People own a lot more than they used to,' I told him. 'Life is faster now, people want to be amused all the time.'

'Why don't they just talk to each other?'

'I'm not sure.'

'All these things. Seems bloody daft.'

We had reached the corner of Cambridge Circus. There weren't many people about. I looked at my watch. It was three minutes to midnight. Opposite, a chicken takeaway was closing its doors.

'I'm sorry I missed Kath. She's a good girl. Funny, coming up west again. It looks the same, but more crowded together.' He took off his glasses and absently wiped the lenses clean.

'I'm very glad you turned up,' I said. 'I've had a good time tonight.' He was looking around, up and down Charing Cross Road, waiting for something. There seemed to be very little traffic heading north. In the distance, a bright empty bus was moving towards us.

'I think what it is . . .' he slipped the glasses back on the bridge of his nose, 'is that this is the birthday I missed. Being in the hospital so long. I think someone in the family arranged for me to come back.'

I could hear the bus engine idling as it waited for the traffic lights on the other side of the circus to change.

'That sounds fair.'

'I think it's just coincidence, being Hallowe'en. I can't be doing with that sort of thing. Your mother was the one who believed in fate, tea leaves and horoscopes.'

The bus had crossed the lights, and by rights should have

continued around the roundabout to the north side of Charing Cross Road. Instead, it drew alongside. I could see now that there were a couple of other passengers, a young Asian boy and an old lady. My father patted his pockets and turned to me.

'I think I've got everything.'

'Is this your bus?'

'Hmm.'

'Will you come back again?'

'I don't think I can. I think you just get one night out.'

I smiled as I watched him climb up onto the platform of the bus. Just as it began to pull out into the road, he turned back to me and grinned.

'I bet it was your aunt Nell,' he said, suddenly laughing. 'Well, when I see her, I'll be able to tell her you turned out all right, Billy boy. I'll bet she's still got that bloody mynah bird.'

'Wait.' I reached forward and gave him the digital watch. 'It's not much.'

He went inside to find himself a seat on the lower deck of the bus. But he looked back at me standing there, right until the bus lights had dimmed in the cold haze that blurred the road ahead, and the sound of its engine had blended with the rumble of the distant city traffic.

As I walked away, I began to look forward to visiting my son.

EMOTIONAL RESPONSE

The night Nell met the man with whom she fell in love, she was looking her absolute best-ever all-time peak, which meant that she would either have to face the strain of looking that good whenever he was around, or only ever see him after he'd been drinking.

Nell was attending a gala dinner for the funding of the Columbia Road Art Gallery in an area of such appealing local colour that the rents had been raised and the locals forced out. For this event, she had chosen a tight-fitting Bill Blass black gown that lengthened her legs. She balanced on a pair of ridiculous Manolo Blahnik heels that were instantly priced by every woman in the room. She'd had her hair coloured and cut by Daniel Herschesson (himself, not one of his henchpeople) and her décolletage glowed with a light tan from a business conference in Nice, helped along with a spray of Clarins Post-Sun Body Shimmer. She was on target weight. She had been using Slimfast liquid meal substitutes made with skimmed milk for two weeks now, and was consequently a little shaky and spaced. She was no longer retaining water, and had switched her carbo-conversion-to-muscle-tone regime from weights to pilates because she hated the endless hip-hop tapes they played in the gym, not to mention the weird-smelling men who grunted sexually on the abdominator and never remembered to wipe down the seat.

It had stopped raining by the time Nell climbed from the cab and headed for the gallery, which looked suspiciously like a restaurant converted for the evening and was surrounded by more uplighters than the Nuremberg Rally. The air smelled clean, an event so rare in London that you noticed when it happened. The night was dry, so her antiperspirant was still kicking in and she didn't look like she had fallen down a well on the way over. Her hair was exactly as Daniel left it, shaped but not unnaturally so. Nell lived in fear of turning into her mother, who had a tightly permed helmet of curls fitted onto her skull every second Tuesday and sported more costume jewellery than Ann Miller did in her eighties. She was wearing understated black-pearl earrings and a minimum amount of expensive wrist-silver, but knew she was still trying too hard to please men.

To be fair, she had been panicked into the temptress look by the fact that she recently passed her thirty-second birthday, an event that felt like it had been carved onto a marble slab instead of written in the greetings cards she received. Her best friend, an animator called Kerry Martinez who was straight but didn't fancy her, told her that thirty-two was a great age, and that when Seigel and Schuster created Superman they had designed him to look thirty-two, which they considered to be the best year of a man's life, at which point Nell reminded Kerry that a) Superman was male, and therefore not subject to the problems of accumulating cellulite, b) he had Lois Lane, Lana Lang and some kind of mermaid in love with him, and who did she have? And c) he was a cartoon character who nobody could identify with spectacles on, for Christ's sake. Nevertheless, when everything was taken into account, she looked damned good. What worried her was that she might never look this good again.

So falling in love with someone right now would not only boost her ego and restore her self-image, but might possibly save her life. And tonight, at precisely 9:10pm she met the man who changed her life and broke her heart. In the course of their time together three hearts were actually broken and mended, but you can't make an omelette . . .and so on.

But first came the art and more importantly, the canapés, which comprised transparent slivers of seared tuna and livid, sore-looking carpaccio cut so finely that you had to eat an entire trayful before reaching the calorific equivalent of an egg sandwich. Nell wished she had eaten first, but knew she would not then have been able to fix her dress without help, and until she could train Biffo, her cat, to do up a zip, starving was the safer option.

After two – no, make that three – glasses of a surprisingly acrid urine-coloured champagne, possibly a brand used by an economy airline, the kind that tasted faintly of sick, even the art started to look good. It was the kind of work that needed reams of explanatory text to go with it, otherwise there was no way of knowing that five lengths of rusted iron and a yard of blue nylon rope with a bell attached to one end was meant to empower women in the way they felt about their bodies.

It was not the kind of art Nell liked, the kind that made you feel a growing interest when you looked at it. It wasn't even the kind of art that shocked the English, who were so easily shocked, but the other kind, the kind that was anxious to change the way you felt by hectoring you. Nell was not in the mood to be lectured. She was here to look at men. Just to look. She expected nothing more, because for many years she expected too much.

She was content to smile and hope for a smile in return, to be noticed, to register in the eyes of others. It wasn't much to ask, an achievable goal within the realm of her possibilities, and that was fine. But she didn't think it was going to work out that way tonight. The walls were too white, the lights too bright, the room too hot and crowded. Just getting to the bar required an agility exceeding the stress-level of her dress, which was threatening to open at the back.

It was eight-thirty when she arrived, exactly three-quarters of an hour after the reception started, and forty minutes before she met the man with the emerald eyes. He was already in the vicinity; standing in the Royal Oak pub across the road having a row with a woman who had just accused him of flirting with one of the barmaids while he was meant to be apologising for his non-appearance at her birthday party the previous night. (I know it's complicated but nothing is clean-cut in life, more's the pity, otherwise Nell and the man would have met and fallen in love, and have been with each other for the rest of their lives, and there would be no story.)

So Nell looked at her Cartier Panthère, a gift from a grateful client, and sipped her bitter champagne, and pretended to be fascinated by a knotted length of fishing net stabbed into a wall with tin-openers, when a woman tapped her on the shoulder.

'I thought it was you,' said the woman, who was dressed slightly too young for her age in combats, back-pack and round-toe heels, and who Nell vaguely recognised and slotted into the gategory: *business dinner at Asia De Cuba, Alice or Amanda*, then, 'do you know anyone here?'

'Not on the artistic side,' Nell admitted, 'I'm working for the vendor of the property.'

'I can't believe how expensive this area has become,' said Alice or Amanda, and a conversation Nell didn't want to have got underway. Nell didn't like being an estate agent, the profession had a limitless capacity to embarrass her, yet she was perversely good at it, so good that she should really have set up her own company. But she was a partner in a thriving practice with six branches, and that way she could earn a good wage without the kind of anxiety attacks that left you hopping out of bed in the middle of the night to leave yourself Post-It notes for the morning.

'Which is a pity, because you never really get the smell of a dead person out of a room,' Alice or Amanda concluded wistfully, and Nell wondered which part of the conversation she had missed. She surreptitiously consulted her watch again, realising as she did so that this time-checking business had lately become a nervous tic, and accepted a sliver of strawberry glued to what appeared to be a triangular piece of chipboard from a passing waiter.

'I think the artist has a lot of issues to deal with,' sniffed Alice or Amanda, studying a protuberance of hexagonal lug-nuts covered in pink fur. 'Not sure I'd want one in my lounge, but there are quite a few orange stickers appearing.'

'It's corporate art,' offered a deep voice behind her. 'Look at the scale. It's designed to be seen in an office foyer, big, mildly provocative, non-threatening, intended to be bought by a middleweight advertising agency.' Nell turned to see who was talking, and became the surprised recipient of the Look.

Not many men could get away with the Look. It was a look that could melt the polar ice caps and raise the level of the sea. It opened cave-anenomes and unfolded the mysteries of women. It involved lowering the head a degree and raising the eyes so that they smile up from beneath the line of the brow in a manner that was both innocent and lascivious. This man had mastered the Look to perfection without looking entirely like a plonker. He knew it was a powerful weapon, and sensibly rationed its use. You should never point a loaded revolver at the same person more than once a night.

Nell's breath caught in her throat. A tanned hand reached forward, forcing Alice or Amanda to move to one side. He was wearing a fantastically dressy Thierry Muegler jacket over faded black jeans and Adidas Manchesters: a look that acknowledged the evening without obedience to it.

'Rafael DeNapio,' said the man, who had short black hair, wide shoulders and eyes the colour of an emptied Gordons gin bottle. Possibly he made his living in razor-blade commercials. In photographs he was a little too sure of himself, squinting into sunlight like a Mediterranean chancer whose desire to appear as a *consigliere* resulted in him being mistaken for a *barista* or a male prostitute. He looked Italian but was in fact half-Spanish and half-Luton. His mother never got over the shock of the weather in Britain and made use of the airport as soon as it started cheap fares. She left Rafael and his father to cope alone, and as his father could not cope with anything, Rafael learned to cope with everything.

'Are you enjoying the art?' he asked politely.

'We were just saying how disappointing—' Nell's friend started, before Nell cut across her.

'You're not the artist, are you?' asked Nell.

'No, but I'm a good friend of hers. She's over there.' He pointed out an elegant black woman in a leather sheath dress and African beads. 'She sells very well to banks.'

'But all that stuff about empowering women.'

'Well. It gives the buyer a story to tell his clients, paints him in a good light, makes him look philanthropic.'

'I'm not sure that's very honest,' Nell countered.

He raised an eyebrow. 'Do you think making money is a bad thing?'

'No, of course not.'

Alice or Amanda tapped the side of her glass with her wedding ring and muttered 'Refill,' then slipped away into the crowd, leaving Nell and Rafael to argue about art.

'Do you think people should have to be dead before they become successful?' said the man. *That's the second time someone has mentioned death tonight*, Nell thought. *One more to go*. She was irrationally scared of death, but then, wasn't everyone except Mexicans?

Nell couldn't catch her breath. 'Why is it so hot in here?' she asked. Her hand rose to her throat.

'Keep that breathless charm,' he told her.

'I'm sorry?'

'You know, the old Fred Astaire song, "The Way You Look Tonight".' He afforded her a further glimpse of the Look, and led her to the front door for some air. She felt his hand in the small of her back, guiding her, and wondered if he noticed the small but persistant roll of fat that she knew was there. There was something peculiarly old-fashioned and cheesy about his chat-up technique, but not in a comforting way. The conflicting emotions inspired by this tiny gesture made her realise that she should get out more.

Outside, the night was warm and so clear that they could hear a woman screaming outside Hackney Town Hall and fire engines rushing to Tower Hamlets. An old RKO feature could be heard playing on TV in the old people's flats across the road. It might even have been a Fred Astaire movie. A parked minicab, less a conveyence for transporting passengers than a bass-speaker for old school hip-hop, trembled at the kerb. An eye-watering odour of urine drifted past them. Londoners were forced to find romance in unlikely places.

'How's your breathing now?' he asked solicitously.

My breathing's fine, she thought, but my pulse rate seems to indicate that I just fell out of a plane. 'Better,' she told him, gazing away at what she tried to pretend was an attractive scene. But the dustbins of Columbia Road were not the palm trees of Tobago, and she found the pretence an effort.

'Is it possible for canapés to leave you hungrier after you've eaten them?' he asked. 'Don't you feel hungrier now than when you arrived?'

'You know, I do?' She looked at him and felt a light stab in the heart, as though someone just prodded her with an unbent paper-clip. He returned her look with surprise growing in his eyes, but then she realised he was looking past her.

'Now there's a sight you don't see every day. Isn't it some kind of omen?'

She followed his gaze to find herself staring at an adult male tiger padding softly down the middle of Columbia Road, stopping to sniff around the drains where the market traders empty their flower vases. It had a long, rib-sticker frame and patchy orange hair, like a childhood teddy bear.

Nell and Rafael watched in apprehensive disbelief as it placed its paws with great deliberation on the littered tarmac before stopping and coiling down into a crescent like any sleep-ridden housecat. It yawned immensely, its great pink tongue flexing and distending, and a deep purr rolled out like the ratchet of a turnstile. Above the creature's closing eyes, the bright neat windows in council flat canyons stood in for the star-swamped skies of India.

'Remember when we saw the tiger?' asked Nell a year and two months later, as they were lying in bed watching a terrible old horror film starring Joan Crawford as the world's oldest circus ringmistress.

'God, she looks like a drag queen,' Rafael murmured, barely hearing her. 'Good legs though. I've seen this one before. Diana Dors gets sawn in half.'

'Its eyes were so yellow.' Nell pulled the edge of the duvet over her nipples. She was still conscious of the age-gap between them, and rarely let him see her naked with the overhead lights on. She was a bit of a magician when it came to getting from the bed to the bathroom without letting him see her midriff from the side. She knew she shouldn't be like this, but he was so perfect that he made her feel too human. For a year and two months she had watched him sleep in her bed, his profile half-buried in the pillow, his mouth slightly open, a scruffy angel with shiny eyelids and thick, unruly hair the colour of a twilight wood. It seemed impossible for anyone to sleep so beautifully without knowing it, but Rafael managed to be unaware of her eyes following him as he awoke. He slept more than anyone she had ever met, and would have missed Sundays completely if she didn't wake him.

Nell's flat was situated in Primrose Hill, where the sun crossed the road from the park. The rooms were small, plain, mostly cream paint and reclaimed oak. She had paid too much but got a good deal because, after all, she was an estate agent, and how would it have looked if she hadn't? Rafael was a chef but had given up his job to become an artist. His work was intriguing, his drawings and sculptures winding strange narratives across half-hidden landscapes that only offered clues to his intentions.

Sex with Rafael was muscular, athletic, emblazoned with energy. He had this way of flexing himself inside her that sent her wild. He was young, of course, just twenty-three, and she was now thirty-three, which should not have mattered but somehow did. He made her feel younger and rather brave, and she needed to feel that way because her parents had made her sister their favourite – Karen was married and had two children – and nothing Nell said or did encouraged them to view her as an adult. Nell thought of herself as mature, cynical, dry-witted, but when her parents visited they treated her like a silly child who had let them down in a matter of responsibility. They made her feel that she had failed, although they would have denied this if confronted. They were unable to respond at all to Rafael, and talked to Nell as if he was not in the room with them.

Rafael had a small, gloomy flat in the Caledonian Road above a locksmiths. The only time she visited him at home, a headline in the shop window underneath his bedroom window proclaimed 'Cally Road Slasher Strikes Again'. She never went back, and he didn't move in with her because she didn't ask him. She was scared he would make an excuse to spare her feelings. Nell financed his career. She rented him a workshop, furniture, canvases and sculpting materials. She bought his clothes and – since she couldn't cook and he no longer had time – bought him many meals in pleasant mid-priced restaurants, for which he regularly expressed his gratitude. Sometimes he danced around the lounge with her, his tanned broad hand in the small of her back, guiding her steps into the line of his strong, supportive body.

Would you call this love? It worked for her. She didn't want the state to evolve, but worried that it would end, so she worked harder and started taking more classes at the gym, and Rafael ran her hot baths and gave her aromatic foot massages, and explained the effects of light on wood. Sometimes he spent the evening at his studio, and then, as he approached his twenty-fourth birthday, he spent the night there. Nell was not suspicious of him because Rafael did not appear to notice other women. They always noticed him.

Nell tried not to wonder how long this could last, but told herself that she lived for the moment. She was besotted, hopelessly, pathetically in love, despite his recent aloofness toward her. She abandoned her plans to set up her own property company, and instead accepted a partnership in the firm, which was run by a man who thought of himself as liberal but who was in fact as sexist as a seventies nightclub comic. She had done this because she wanted to make Rafael's dream come true.

The next day was Rafael's birthday, and Nell had planned a special surprise. She found a gallery that would exhibit his art. It was the room where they met in Columbia Road, and for two weeks in July it was to be his. She knew he had enough work stored up, and had already arranged for the invitations to be printed. She needed the addresses of his friends, and one evening, when he went to the studio without taking his mobile phone, she unlocked it and found the postcodes she needed. She also came across the text message that read *without your love i am only a shadow xxx rafael.* She sat on the corner of the bed, the moment she dreaded now made flesh, and the sun faded from her life. First she became ashamed of herself, for not being strong, but then she grew angry. She called the number. A girl with a babyish voice answered.

'Is Rafael there?' asked Nell.

'No, he doesn't live here,' said the girl tentatively. 'Who is this?'

'His wife,' said Nell. 'Who are you?'

'Oh my God,' said the girl, and hung up.

Nell just wanted to know one thing; how long had it been going on? She rang the number again, and again, until she got an answer.

The flat was in the basement of an Edwardian house in a

corner of Crouch End where the drives had been gravelled and filled with dustbins, and there were never less than four door-bells. Hope was no more than twenty-one, and answered the door in the kind of clothes Nell had never worn, pulling the unravelling brown cardigan tighter across her breasts as if to protect herself from the harm this older woman could do with her lies. Hope invited her in, clearing a cat from an armchair to offer her a seat.

'I've only got instant,' she apologised, eyeing her opponent's too-elegant clothes.

'That's fine.' Nell gingerly seated herself on cat hairs and watched Hope duck behind the badly-repainted kitchen bar to emerge with unmatched mugs. Hope needed a good conditioner; she had what the commercials used to describe as 'flyaway hair', but underneath the baggy waistless clothes, beneath the unruly fringe, was an appallingly attractive girl. Hope earned a pittance as a television researcher for a company that was surviving on verbal promises and gently failing. She and Rafael had been dating – her choice of verb – for nearly a year. He had promised to move in with her very soon. So fervent was Hope's belief in her boyfriend, so transparently innocent was she, that Nell found it hard to believe they were talking about the same man.

Hope reminded her of a beautiful actress playing a role in which she was required to spend the first part of the film as an ugly duckling. Her awkward shyness prevented her from raising her head to face Nell. She had obviously never confronted anyone in her life.

'Actually I'm not his wife,' Nell felt compelled to tell her. 'Where did you meet him?' She watched the cat cleaning itself while she waited for Hope to frame an answer.

'We were filming in a small art gallery in Hoxton, and he started talking to me about his work,' Hope explained meekly. 'Believe me, I had no idea he was seeing someone else.'

'Seeing is an understatement,' Nell felt compelled to point out, bearing in mind that she was financing his career.

Hope shook her head at her feet, mortally embarrassed to be forced into this conversation with a stranger. 'I help Rafael with his art. I gave him the theme that will provide the centrepiece of his show. It's a piece constructed of found items that represent the love we have for each other.'

'This just keeps getting better, doesn't it?' Nell found a space to set down her undrinkable coffee.

'To be honest, I wondered if he was seeing someone else because he's always working late, but then artists keep unusual hours, don't they?'

'If you suspected something, why didn't you ask him?'

'I'm not good at confrontations,' Hope admitted. 'I have no confidence in myself. Perhaps we should talk to him together.'

'I don't think that's such a good idea. We should talk to him separately. Whatever you do, don't tell him we've met. You should never reveal all your cards to a man.'

'I'd feel terrible if he had to choose between us,' said Hope, as faint as a winter shadow.

'Then let's hear him out without prejudice,' Nell suggested. 'The son of a bitch.'

Confronting Rafael on consecutive nights, Nell and Hope blamed his mobile phone for the discovery of infidelity, and insisted on an honest response, at which point he casually agreed to leave them both. He told them – with some relief, they noted – that he felt no real love for either of them, and furthermore that he believed a man was born to have as many partners as he could manage, and while Nell and Hope had been good for him, the time was right to part. In fact, he was glad this had happened because they were holding him back from achieving his full potential. His work, he explained, was already being tipped as the next big thing in the art world. He was unrepentant and cheery as he left, pecking each on the cheek as he went.

As well as trusting Rafael, Nell had given up her savings and her dreams for her lover, just as Hope had surrendered her belongings and her faith in men. The trouble, as Nell saw it, was that men didn't suffer in love as women did.

As Rafael advanced towards his first gallery show, the two women arranged to meet again. Eating ice cream on Hope's sofa, they watched as Rafael was interviewed on TV, hoping to see at least some sign of attrition. But the young artist was more appealing than ever, and to their dismay told the interviewer that his art was driven by his emotional honesty, and that without love he was nothing. He unveiled his masterwork, entitled 'Breathless Heart', and gave no credit to the women who helped him achieve success.

Determined to cheer themselves up, Nell and Hope went out on the town, and in the course of a night spent downing sweet overpriced cocktails in West End bars, came to realise just how cruelly they had been used.

'We've no legal comeback against him, you realise,' said Nell, ordering another round. 'We have to face the fact that we've been taken for a ride. We're older – in my case, much older – but no wiser.' Nell felt stigmatised by her age, just as Hope did by her shyness. 'I'm not going to let him get away with it. Our only advantage lies in the fact that Rafael has no idea we know each other.'

'At least we have our friendship,' Hope pointed out, a little drunk. 'Maybe something good will come of this.'

'You're damned right it will,' promised Nell as she bit the cherry from her stick. 'You and I are going to take him down.'

It took Nell a week to come up with a way of taking revenge on Rafael. She emailed Hope and informed her that they would place an advertisement on the internet for a young girl. Not just any young girl, but someone so young, thin and dazzlingly sexy that Rafael would not be able to resist. She would make him fall desperately in love with her, leading him on until he acknowledged that he couldn't live without her. Then she would publicly dump him and shatter his stupid breathless heart.

What they needed was a girl who hated men with a terrifying passion. They agonised over the wording of the ad, but finally agreed on a few carefully loaded sentences and placed them on a dozen websites. Then they waited to start interviewing.

It seemed to take forever. The emails and photos flew back and forth, but no one was exactly right until Miranda came along. She had a rough-edged London accent, but apart from that she fitted the job description perfectly. She was just twenty-one, at college and driving a minicab around Middlesex in her spare time to make ends meet. She explained that she had been incredibly hurt by lying, cheating rat-bastard men in the past, and now hated and distrusted the entire male species. She felt such deep emotional scars that she had given up her lucrative career as a model, because she no longer wished to pander to male fantasies.

For a handsome fee that would see her through college, Miranda agreed to take Rafael, emotionally speaking, to the cleaners. She readily agreed to abide by the women's rules, and felt revulsion when taken shopping for the kind of tarty killer outfits that Nell knew Rafael liked. She was briefed in fine detail about what the artist wanted and didn't want in a woman. The question of sleeping with him was broached; Miranda was ready to do whatever it took to enslave Rafael, in order to truly show him what a broken heart meant. Soon she was fully trained for her task, and set out on her mission to make a man suffer in love.

It was Rafael's big opening night. A large sign in the window read: 'The DeNapio Project – Emotional Response'. Apart from that, Columbia Road Art Gallery seemed to be decorated much as it had been the last time they had attended an opening; the guests and even the canapés were the same. But this time, Nell watched Rafael from a distance. She had forbidden Hope to speak to her. It was essential that no one knew they were friends. Miranda arrived in a separate cab, wearing a pair of diamond-chiffon triangles held together with silver chains. The room's conversation level momentarily dropped when she entered. Nell had warned her against making the first move. She glanced across the crowded room at Hope and gave her a reassuring smile. Rafael had noticed their protegée and was already moving in beside her. He and Miranda stood admiring the gigantic purple phallus of junk that dominated the centre of the room. When Nell looked back, they were no longer standing together.

'What happened?' Nell hissed at Miranda after signalling her to meet in the ladies' room.

'He's totally disgusting,' Miranda replied. 'Hit me with some crappy old lyric from a Fred Astaire song.'

Nell coloured with embarrassment as she remembered how she felt.

'I've never met such a total, utter creep.' Miranda fluffed her hair in the mirror as if trying to rid herself of his aura.

'So what did you say to him?'

'I told him his work was a load of cock, figuratively and literally, that he was using his ego to dupe people into thinking he had talent. He walked off.'

'You were supposed to make him fall in love with you, not alienate him.'

'This is too much of a challenge, Nell. He made my flesh crawl. Christ, he's so smarmy. What did you two ever see in him?'

'But you have to do it, Miranda. There's no one else who can help us. Please, you have to get back out there and seduce him. If not for the money, then do it for womankind. Think of all the others he'll get away with hurting if you don't pull him up short.'

That got her. Miranda touched up her warpaint and went back to the battlefield as Hope and Nell watched from the bar. This time she opened the conversation, and whatever she said appeared to do the trick. Rafael asked her to meet him in a few days' time, then took her to dinner, and Miranda reported everything back in detail. It was clearly a strain on her; of all the things she hated about him, the worst features were his insincerity, and the fact that he was only interested in her body. Miranda found herself dropping stupid statements into her conversation, just to see if he was listening, but it was obvious that her physical beauty had turned him deaf. On the third date he begged her to sleep with him. The more she refused, the more he fell in love with her. Nell was delighted by each report; Hope less so, because revenge gave her no pleasure.

The dates shifted from evening dinners to daytime outings. Gradually Rafael found himself forced to change his behaviour as he learned how to deal with this extraordinary young woman. After six weeks had passed, Nell had become anxious for Miranda to dump him, and the strain was showing on Hope. Miranda explained that she needed to string Raphael along a little longer; the deeper he was in love, the further he had to fall. She assured Nell that her resolve was as firm as ever, that Rafael had only strengthened her belief in the duplicity of men, and that the three of them would share in the pleasure of his downfall. He had entered the gift-buying stage, and was planning to introduce her to his parents. She was still refusing to sleep with him.

But too much time passed. Summer turned to autumn, and Nell grew impatient. The time had come to dump Rafael. Nell called a meeting with Miranda in her local Primrose Hill pub. The moment she saw Miranda, she knew that something had happened. They sat outside where the dying sun slung shadows across the cold grass. The girl looked sheepish and uncomfortable as she sipped a beer.

'I might as well tell you,' she said, unable to meet Nell's eyes. 'I've fallen in love with him.'

'How could you have?' asked Nell, aghast. 'You hated his guts.'

'He says he's going to marry me, Nell. Look, I'll find a way to refund the money you've spent on me—'

'This isn't about money, you know that.'

'He's changed. I've changed him. He's learned humility – even kindness. He's learned how to love, Nell. He admits he's been lousy to women all his life, especially to you and Hope. He's acknowledged his past mistakes. He's promised me that this time things will really be different.'

'But that's what he does, Miranda, he's just doing it a different way with you. Can't you see? You're falling for the oldest line in the book. He's covering himself from every angle so that he can get you into bed.'

'We're sleeping together,' Miranda admitted. 'Even a man like him lets out his true feelings when he makes love.'

Miranda was disgusted. 'Jesus, when did you get so naïve?' she asked.

'Look at yourself, Nell. When did you get so cynical? If you want the truth, Rafael found you too old and Hope too nervous, but he was too much of a gentleman to refuse either of you. Maybe the problem has been yours all along.'

Nell watched Miranda walk away across the darkening parkland.

The next day, Rafael called both Nell and Hope to tell them about his wedding plans. Both women were in shock.

'I warned you that this could happen,' said Hope. 'I wish I'd never listened to you. No matter how much somebody hurts you, taking revenge on them is wrong.'

'I'll call her, get her to hold him off,' said Nell. 'I'll prove to her that he can't be trusted around any woman.'

'Just give it up, Nell,' said Hope. 'Haven't we done enough?'

'You wait and see,' warned Nell. 'He'll fail her, just as he did before. He doesn't care for her any more than he cared for us. Men like that don't change.'

'Maybe you're wrong. Maybe they do.'

Nell refused to believe it. She watched and waited for proof of Rafael's duplicity. His first show had been a smashing success. Thanks to the piece he had created with Hope's memories and Nell's money, he found himself becoming a media darling. Charles Saatchi bought his art. The papers loved to carry his photograph. It didn't hurt that he was dating the most glamorous girl in town.

When Rafael announced his wedding date, Nell decided that what they needed to do was find a way of bringing out Rafael's worst side in front of his intended bride so that she could see the mistake she was making. An awful possibility had begun to dawn on them both: that Rafael really had changed his ways, and they had introduced him to the love of his life, when they could have remained blissfully ignorant and relatively happy sharing him.

As the wedding day approached, Nell played her trump card.

'I've convinced Miranda to tell him the truth about how we recruited her,' Nell explained. 'You watch, he'll reveal his true nature now. No man wants to admit he's been played for a fool.' She was drinking too much, and in all honesty, was starting to sound like a broken record. Hope no longer enjoyed the evenings they spent plotting in bars. Nell's bitterness increased according to the amount she drank. Hope was still angry and upset, but there was a limit to how long she could nurse a grudge.

'The Ride Of The Valkyrie' sounded from Nell's purse. 'That'll be her now,' she said, digging deep to extract her mobile. 'She said she'd tell him at nine, and it's nearly half past.'

Nell listened, and as she did, her face fell. She's looking tired, thought Hope. This business is eating her up, the sooner it's over, the sooner we can get on with our lives. She waited until Nell snapped the mobile shut and threw it into her bag.

'Miranda told him.'

'What did he say?'

Nell pulled an ugly face. 'She says he was hurt at first, told her he felt betrayed, but then he forgave her.' She threw back her drink and gestured to the barman for another. 'He even professed his undying love for her, says he's going to contact both of us to formally apologise for his past behaviour.'

'Oh.'

'That means more phonecalls from him. He's taken to calling me on a regular basis, as if he expects we can all magically be friends now. All this sweetness and light is killing me.'

'Maybe we can be friends, Nell. You know, eventually. Maybe he just wants to bury the hatchet.'

'Yeah, I know where I'd like to bury it.'

But this time, Hope decided to speak up. 'You know, perhaps the time has come to give in gracefully,' she suggested gently.

'You still don't get it, do you?' snapped Nell. 'He's lying. You can see the lies in his eyes, in the way he gives women that patented sexy look. Trust me, he's still using that look to get himself laid behind Miranda's back, I can feel it.'

'You have no shred of proof, Nell. Neither of us do.'

'I feel terrible,' Nell told her. 'After all, it was me who got her into this situation. He's broken through that tough shell of hers and fooled her.'

'It sounds to me like you're jealous,' said Hope, rising from her seat. 'You don't want Miranda to be happy. She's young and beautiful and finally in love. No one could have predicted it, it's just the way things turned out.'

'Maybe I am a little jealous, but I'm more concerned for her. You remember how Miranda was when we first met her. He's going to take away the trust she's rebuilt in men. She won't survive a second time. He'll ruin her life.'

'I'm going,' said Hope. 'You should too. It's late, and we're both a little drunk.'

'Wait,' called Nell. 'I've another idea. We could smuggle ourselves into his stag-night and catch him doing something inappropriate, wanking over a waitress in a broom cupboard – it happens.'

'Will you listen to yourself?' said Hope angrily. 'I can't take it any more, Nell. You have to let it go at some point. Goodnight.'

After that night, Hope stopped taking her calls. Worse, she called Nell just once to announce that she had been invited to the wedding as a friend of the groom. Unusually, the ceremony was to be held at midnight. British services usually took place before dusk, due to ancient laws aimed at preventing the substitution of brides under cover of darkness. For Rafael the midnight setting was an artistic statement, one which had already intrigued the press and encouraged them to run pages on the couple's lifestyle. The happy couple smiled out from the pages of colour supplements and glossy magazines. They appeared together on talk shows, hand in hand. Rafael and Miranda had joined that elite group of crossover stars whose opinions were canvassed on every topic of passing interest.

Nell made an effort to move on with her life, but everything seemed stalled. Her work had became more demanding as house prices slumped. She found herself trapped in a job she hated. She had missed her chance to get out, and blamed herself for compounding the idiocy of trusting a man like Rafael by trusting a girl as beautiful as Miranda. She should have seen that they were made for each other. Rafael, on the other hand, had learned from Damien Hirst's famous comment about it being easy to be a British artist, and was quickly becoming rich.

It rained hard on the night of the wedding. Nell drank alone, disgusted with Hope and the thought that she could happily celebrate with the man who had so cruelly deceived her. She left the bar at ten without any formal plan in her head, but found herself driving to Rafael's studio. The lights were off, and although the rear of the building was protected with bars, Miranda still had a set of keys. As she walked unsteadily through the darkened studio, she could smell Rafael's aftershave mixed in with the scents of plaster and paint. She searched for evidence, but after finding nothing, sat on the floor and cried. Her head was throbbing. In the slim streetlight she saw a new version of his most famous statue, another monument to his sexual ego. Frustration welled up as she lifted the fire extinguisher from its clip on the wall and smashed at the purple mosaic. Splinters of mirror sprinkled around it in a crystalline rainbow. She had broken the top clean off.

The dark hollow centre of the statue beckoned. She peered inside, then felt around with her hand. What had he put in here? Carefully she pulled at the square of cardboard with her fingertips, but couldn't imagine what it was. She could not risk putting on the lights, but found a torch in one of the cupboards. Carefully focussing the beam, Nell found herself looking at a Polaroid photograph pasted to the inside of the statue. The lurid picture, conveniently dated in felt-tip pen, showed Rafael kissing a naked girl with body makeup and cropped golden hair in his bed just two weeks earlier, at a time when he was supposed to be working late in the studio. He had even graced the photo with his signature.

It was shameless. It was obscene. More importantly, it was evidence. She called Miranda and told her what she'd found.

'You're drunk,' Miranda countered. 'I'm being dressed. Where are you?'

'I'm in his studio. Just come down here,' whispered Nell. 'He's been screwing around behind your back, and I've got concrete proof.'

'How can I come down there? I'm getting married in less than an hour! People can hear me. Listen, you're not supposed to be in there, you have to get out before anyone sees you.' She didn't know Nell had smashed Rafael's latest artwork nearly in half. 'What kind of concrete proof are you talking about?'

The literal kind, thought Nell, tugging hopelessly at the photo, which was firmly set in the huge concrete base of the statue. 'Fine,' she snapped, 'Go ahead and marry him. I hope you'll be very happy together.' She hung up, appalled. This, truly, was the death of love. Miranda knew her future husband couldn't be trusted, but was still going ahead with this sham of a marriage because she wanted him. The thought disgusted her. So much for sisterhood. So much for equality. If only she had some way of getting the evidence to the wedding ceremony. She looked at the statue. Then she peered out of the window at her car parked outside.

This was the only way. If she confronted him at the service or the reception, she would have to accuse him of lying without being able to offer up proof. He would accuse her of being bitter and jealous, and would have her thrown out of his gallery. She would be made a laughing stock. But she could haul the statue across town to the Charlotte Street Hotel, where the wedding was taking place, and show Miranda the truth before it was too late.

It was lighter than she'd expected, but was still a bugger to manoeuvre out of the back door and into the alleyway. It helped that the top two-foot section of the statue was missing. By the time she had managed to tie the damned thing to her roof rack, she was covered in concrete and plaster dust, her soaked clothes were torn, and she had managed to misplace her shoes somewhere.

The ride across the city proved hair-raising, as she was forced to hang onto the nylon ropes threaded over the statue and through the windows. She reached Tottenham Court Road and became snared in a traffic-choked diversion around a flooded slip-road. There was nowhere to park in Charlotte Street, so she paralleled the car beside the wedding limo, and dashed into the hotel. The desk clerk warned her that the service was already taking place in a function room, and that she could not be admitted, but the corridor outside the room was deserted; everyone was inside.

As Nell opened the door, a collective sigh went up from the congregation. Miranda and Rafael, dressed in matching midnight blue outfits that would have looked twee in the suburbs, were about to exchange vows in what appeared to be a souped-up version of a traditional non-religious ceremony, complete with African singers and an elaborate audio-visual screen presentation. Nell watched miserably as the lovers stepped onto a white dais and stared into each other's eyes. Hope stood on the groom's side, barely visible in a wispy beige suit. She appeared to be crying.

Nell could hardly bear to look. In front of Rafael's family, his friends, his peers, the film crews and the congregation, the groom said 'I do', and pledged his eternal love for Miranda.

Miranda turned him down.

Nell couldn't believe her ears. The girl actually said no. A murmur of disturbance rose from the gathering. Rafael was looking at his bride in disbelief.

'I don't love you,' said Miranda firmly, 'in fact, I hate everything about you,' and everyone started talking at once. Rafael appeared to be about to fall to his knees. He didn't get angry. He didn't scream and shout. He looked destroyed, defeated, humiliated. He still had the same look on his face as Miranda climbed down from the dais and walked from the room.

'I don't know why you're acting so surprised,' said Miranda. 'You always knew my intention. We went over it often enough.' She had pulled Nell and Hope into the bar across the road from the hotel, away from the questions of the press. 'We all agreed my actions at the outset. I never deviated from the plan. I broke his heart, just as I said I would, and you're paying my college fees.'

'But you told us – you told us—' Hope abandoned the sentence and drank her gin.

'I had to convince you because Rafael would have discovered the truth from Hope. No offence, Hope. I mean, he was ringing you day and night.'

Nell and Hope were silent.

'What's the matter?' asked Miranda, puzzled. 'You don't look very happy, either of you. You got exactly what you wanted.'

'I don't know.' Hope looked uncomfortable. 'Don't you think this whole thing might have – well, damaged you?'

'I'll admit it's done something,' said Miranda. 'It's got the anger out of my system. I have a feeling I don't hate men anymore. After all, we're equal now.'

A noise in the street drove Nell to the window. 'Oh God,' she cried, 'the statue.' The downpour had unsettled the chemical compound of the mosaic phallus, and it was crumbling into pieces. One half slid onto the bonnet in a pool of plaster. Nell ran through the flood and fished out the Polaroid as it came loose. The rain had blurred the felt-tip date and signature into illegibility. She brought the picture back into the bar.

'Oh, that's me,' Miranda told them as she studied the photograph. 'We were fooling around one evening. I tried on a wig. It brought my scalp out in a rash.'

'You mean—' Nell was suddenly overwhelmed by her own meanness of spirit. 'We've wronged a reformed man after all. Together we've ruined the life of a born-again innocent.'

'I wouldn't lose any sleep about it,' Miranda told her. 'He's really not so innocent. I knew from the moment I met him that he'd eventually cheat on me. It was a race to see if I could get him to the altar first. The way he gives gullible women that look is such a total tip-off.' She ordered another round of drinks. 'Damn, I feel good. There's something very enjoyable about being able to beat the odds just once.'

Back at the ceremony, the photographers and friends dispersed as Rafael picked himself up, dusted himself down and shot the maid of honour his patented look. She glanced around first, but smiled back.

As Nell surveyed the evaporating mess on her car, Hope and Miranda gave her a hug. 'You realise that if anyone of us ever decides to marry, the other two will be watching her partner's behaviour very carefully,' Hope warned. 'If I was a man, I really would not want to mess with us.' The others were forced to agree.

They've started dating again, the three of them, Nell, Hope
and Miranda, and they're all out there, somewhere in the city.

CAIRO 6.1

'This is your big day, isn't it?' said the bottle-blonde Croatian girl in Coffee Republic, smiling as she tipped boiling foam into his cardboard cup. A splash of milk flicked onto her bare midriff but she didn't flinch. 'You must be very excited.'

'You've got a good memory,' said Mark, secretly pleased.

'You've been coming in every weekday for over four years. I saw your name on the list.' They published the list every day in the *Evening Standard*. She didn't seem to disapprove, which was unusual. The girl pressed the tips of her silver nails on the white plastic lid until it popped into place. 'I'll miss the custom, but I hope it goes well for you. There's no charge today.' She waved his money away, then handcuffed the cup in a corrugated cardboard sleeve and passed it to him before switching her smile to the next customer. He wondered if the knowledge that he would never set foot inside the coffee shop again had briefly changed the way she looked at him. In another life he might have fucked her. Nothing like that could happen now.

Outside, another working morning was underway. Motorcycle couriers were sprawled across their bikes, relaxing in low sunlight. The sprinklers misted the trampled grass in Soho Square. Girls in short skirts stood outside Barclays bank having a smoke, as furtive as delinquent schoolgirls. He turned into Bateman Street and shouldered the door to the grey concrete reception area, his office for the past seven years.

'We weren't sure if you were going to be in today,' said Bianca behind the counter, a phone cradled under her ear. 'I heard you made the list.' Her radio was on, playing a song about perfect true love.

'You've had your hair cut. It's nice. I thought I'd look in just to say, you know. I didn't want a big song and dance. Just clear out my desk and, you know.'

'Of course. If it was me I'd feel the same. No cakes and cards, just go, sort of thing.'

'Why, you haven't got your name down, have you?'

'Me?' Bianca pressed a hand to her chest, offended. 'Oh no, it's not my cup of tea at all.' She hastily corrected herself. 'But obviously it suits some people, what with everything being so – you know.' She played with the ends of her hair, distracted by the idea. She had slept with him once after a party, an event which his memory had not retained for some reason. Maybe it hadn't been very good.

Mark went up to his desk and emptied the drawers into a bin-liner. A few people came up and made awkward farewells. Some made light of his departure, as if he was merely going on holiday. Others were careful to stay out of his way.

'Trish, what do you think I should do with these?' he asked, indicating his desktop collection of novelty snowstorms – Paris, Rome, Barcelona, Budapest, Nice, Berlin. Cairo was notable by its absence.

'You can leave them with me if you like. I'll make sure a child gets them. He doesn't have to know where they came from.'

'Thanks, that's sweet of you.' There was a stigma attached to passing on belongings from someone who had joined the list. The process had already created its own mythologies. He trudged upstairs to say goodbye to his boss. It felt odd, actually going. He had butterflies in his stomach.

Sturman had been expecting the visit. He didn't mind talking to Mark, so long as the conversation remained practical and unsentimental. He'd never dealt with a situation like this before, although it had been covered in management meetings. A lot of people talked about doing it, but few were brave enough. 'I've filled in all your paperwork, Mark, there's nothing to worry about.'

'Thanks. I've enjoyed being here, you know it's not about that. I've been waiting to get on the list for a long time.'

Sturman walked to the window and looked out. 'It's a beautiful day.' He meant it as a rebuke.

'I know, but my mind was made up a long time ago.'

'So there's nothing I can—'

'No. I appreciate it, though.'

'What time are you on?'

'Midday.'

'I suppose that's something.'

'They're at half-hour intervals right through the day.'

'So I understand. Incredible how popular it is, especially with young people.'

'Hardly surprising, though, with things the way they are. I've got to be there fifteen minutes beforehand. For the preparation.'

'I'd better not keep you then.' Sturman shook Mark's hand, and had already returned to his computer before the door had closed. Communing with his screen made him feel more comfortable. It was easier than dealing with people.

Mark walked back to his bare desk. The morning dragged past. He had wanted to make the appointment for first thing, but the earliest slots cost more, and had all been taken. Finally, he decided to ring his mother. He'd put off making the call as long as he could. She listened to him, then started to whimper. 'I've read about this, who hasn't, it's been on television for weeks, I just don't understand. Your father and I were good to you, it's so unfair, we only ever wanted the best—'

'This isn't about you and Dad,' he explained with as much patience as he could manage. 'It's something I have to do for myself.'

'There must be some other way.' Her voice was so small. 'Can't we just meet and talk? Please, Mark.'

Now she wants to talk, he thought. 'I love you, Mum. Be happy for me.' He closed the phone. He wondered if he should call Anna, but they had only been out four or five times together, and he doubted she would miss him. She went out with a lot of guys. One less was no big deal.

It was raining thinly, just enough to darken the streets. Packed buses in Tottenham Court Road, a scrum of English language students milling beside the tube station – everywhere was crowded, and he was late. He ran past the rancid kebab stalls, sex shop windows filled with bald mannequins and cheap red nylon fetishwear, past the beer-sticky entrance to the Astoria blocked with queues of dead-faced teens. A vast illuminated poster hoarding showed a tropical beach, impossibly idyllic, heavily retouched. The tramps, slumped against this paradise in unruly symmetry, seemed unaware of their intrusion.

When the mass of the crowd forced him off the kerb and through the traffic, he had no choice but to run the gamut of dealers in Crack Alley, past the stagnant litter-filled fountain at the base of Centrepoint. The area beneath the tower block had become a no-go zone, a dark wind tunnel filled with junkies. He wondered how it had looked on the architect's model, a vale of shaded tranquillity peppered with smiling couples and small round trees. The grand social experiments, the elegantly planned palisades of leisure and commerce, none had worked. The world was on the move, running into darkness, and all dreams collapsed before the devouring dollar. In this frame of mind, he knew he shouldn't have bothered to go to the office at all, not on this day. A walk in the park, a visit to a museum, a stroll beside the river, all would have been nicer.

The protest group was smaller today. It was usually moved on by the police. He recognised some of the angry faces from last time. The hard core were dug in for the long run, and sat in little makeshift camps of 'Choose Life' sheets and placards.

Everyone wants to tell us how to live, thought Mark. He climbed the white steps and checked in, using the pin number they had given him.

The man, Dutton, was sitting behind the desk at his computer, exactly where he'd been when Mark first came to fill out the forms. He appeared to be wearing the same shirt and tie. Perhaps he never went home. Mark wondered if he was happy in his job.

'Mr Cox, you're a bit late but we're running behind, too. Take a seat. I know you signed everything last time, but you have to sign one more clearance form, just to certify that you haven't changed your mind. It's just a precaution. People do back out.'

'Of course.' Mark barely bothered to read the type-filled sheet before he picked up a ballpoint and signed his name. Dutton checked the signature. 'Good. Now if you'd care to follow me.' He rose from his seat and led Mark along the corridor. The white walls were lined with old railway posters, chocolate-box views of an unimaginably picturesque city. 'You haven't eaten?'

'All I've had is a coffee.'

'Good. Obviously it works quicker and more effectively if you have an empty stomach.'

'You explained that to me before.'

'And you've had adequate time to sort out—'

'Everything's in order. There wasn't much to do.'

'No, we find that with most customers. People think that more preparation is needed, fears have to be faced, mistakes have to be corrected, wrongs have to be put right. But in reality, that sort of thing hardly ever gets done.' He pushed open the door at the end of the hall and ushered Mark into a dimly-lit room, switching on rows of pencil spotlights before moving to a steel counter and slipping into a white doctor's coat. Mark was surprised to see a young nurse standing motionless in the room. She looked about seventeen. Her white outfit had smart red piping, and seemed designed like a theatrical costumier's version of a medical uniform, the way nurses in private practice dressed. He wondered if she had been standing there in the dark, waiting for him. He tried to memorise how she looked, in case he wanted to take her to Cairo.

'This is Karen. She'll be assisting me today. If you'll just take a seat over there in the armchair and make yourself comfortable. We produced a CD that I think you'll find has everything you requested.' Dutton raised a plastic case and opened it, discreetly slipping the disc into a slim steel tray. He handed Mark a set of cordless headphones.

'Pop these around your neck, but don't put them on yet, the sensors are on and I'm not quite ready to transmit readings. And roll up your right sleeve, please. What did you decide on, people, memories, abstract colours or a destination?'

'Destination,' Mark murmured, barely hearing himself.

'Of course.' Dutton withdrew a slender vial of colourless liquid and flicked it lightly as he snapped off the plastic cap. 'Did you have somewhere specific in mind?'

'Cairo.'

'Cairo? Fond recollections of the place, eh?'

'Not at all. Quite the reverse.'

If Dutton was surprised, he didn't show it. You could never tell what people would say at this stage of the game. Karen stepped forward and tied a plastic tourniquet above the elbow joint of Mark's right arm.

'You'll barely feel this.' Karen smoothly injected the vial into Mark's vein. She withdrew the needle, removed the tape and threw the syringe into a bright yellow 'Contaminated Materials' bag. 'I want you to put on the headphones now,' Dutton instructed, 'then stand up and come over to the car.'

Mark raised himself from the armchair and began to place one foot in front of the other. He felt his sense of balance shift as the drug swiftly began to take effect.

'Very good, Mark, you're doing very well.'

The car reminded him of an old ghost train vehicle. It was

more low-tech than he'd been expecting. Its exterior sparkled with red and blue speed stripes. Around the wheels, yellow worms of grease extruded where the maintenance men had deployed their guns with too much enthusiasm. The car sat on a sloping steel track that extended forward by about eight feet, ending against the far wall.

Karen held the door open and he climbed inside. It was a soft red leather bucket seat, and there was no safety belt. When Mark had finished studying the interior, he looked up to find that Karen had gone.

Dutton was at his console, programming in the final sequence. 'The drug is simply a psychotropic enhancer, with a couple of little things mixed in to keep you calm and chilled. You might like to start thinking of your destination now.'

'It works that quickly?' asked Mark.

'Oh yes, improved formula, program upgrade, much quicker than the old methods. OS 6.1. They change it every few months and we have to buy new software.'

Karen stepped forward and fitted a soft black leather patch over his eyes. She gently adjusted the strap behind his ears.

'Comfortable? Okay, we go in exactly one minute.'

The music began, and it only took a few moments for the first abstract images to start swirling into place around him. It seemed that Dutton had suddenly turned up the lights, and they were bleeding prismatically through the blindfold, because the colours grew very bright. As the car's brake was released, he felt himself starting to roll forward.

The sudden acceleration, similar to that of a looping roller coaster, shocked him until he pressed his head back into the cushion and relaxed, at which point sound and vision moved smoothly into synchronisation. The music, an unfashionably lush orchestral version of a recent club anthem, was not exactly what he'd requested, but at least he detected the pseudo-Egyptian instrumentation that had been overlayed on the track. He felt himself turning over, and opened his eyes to look down between his feet. As warm thermals rushed about him, his winter clothes were torn away, born across the sky like ragged birds. He was far above the passing earth, the sky's breath fluttering across his bare skin. England, a dull and damaged mess below, was lost beneath scudding cumulus clouds as the horizon gently curved.

When the vaporous grey curtains next parted, they did not return, and he found himself travelling in a clear dome of sky reflected through a fierce, luscious ceiling of Yves Klein blue, the glittering ocean forming a complementary azure bowl below. Logically, the approaching coastline should have been that of France, but when it arrived, the distant ground was yellow in every direction, with tiny emerald clumps of oases shimmering as the sun caught them.

Now he was hand-springing through the heavens, buffeted from one air current to the next. As the rushing wind dissolved into silent softness the music enveloped him and he rolled slowly over, his head tucked beneath his heels, watching as the undulating ground rolled by.

The wedge of the great city stood in the distance, proud and angular, at a hundred different levels, a mosaic of hot white rooftops, with the pyramids and the Nile in the distance. He glimpsed the chaos of Bulaq, the curving streets of Garden City, the walled compound of Babylon, Cairo as it had been in his childhood imaginings, in his dreams, his hopes, his fantasies – not the traffic-choked maze of freeways, garish neon signs and crumbling grey apartment blocks that had wrecked his romantic notions on the dysentery-riddled trip of his gap year. Cairo, like the railway posters in the corridor, like the streets of London, had lied. The place he had been promised did not exist, at least not in his lifetime. The pleasure of promenading those broad dusty thoroughfares had belonged to his grandparents; they had wrecked it for the generations to come, and now this was the only way to get back to the places he had been promised as a child.

His body was sloping forward now as he started his descent, cutting through the high zephyrs like a hawk descending on its prey. He could feel the blood flushing to his face and neck. The city became more distinct; there were no office buildings, no battered taxis honking in the streets, no tattered plastic palm trees around the Giza squares, no pulse-light party boats on the Nile, only fly-flecked donkeys and dromedaries, market traders, traders in djellabas, veiled women in flowing skirts. He was looking at a brightly-coloured picture book brought to life. The sand-coloured minarets were no longer restricted to the City of the Dead; they covered the entire delta, down to the tip of its southern valley. The ancient city came closer, then closer still. He saw it as his Victorian forebears had imagined it in paint: slim quadrants of light and shadow, merchants arguing in sun-sharp pools, slouching in dim doorways, laden with baskets and bolts of cloth, vanishing beyond the tops of steps. Cairo as it should have been, filled with unamplified prayer-calls and the graceful curvature of Arabic speech. He was free, for the first time in this toxic barren life he was free to fly unshackled through a world of clean hard sunlight and infinite possibilities . . . he would live forever in his unrestricted incarnation. Cairo 6.1 approached.

The picture fuzzed and broke up as the disc stuck.

He looked down at stalled wet traffic in the grey rain of Tottenham Court Road.

He saw an empty, filthy skip roaring toward him.

He screamed.

Dutton removed his finger from the button, and the exit-car retreated to its starting position with a sigh of gears. The seat lowered from its tipped-forward angle, locking smoothly back into place. The final section of the program engaged, and the outer wall closed shut once more. Dutton ejected the skipping CD and the lights came up.

'This equipment's a piece of shit,' he told Karen, tossing the

CD into the bin. 'His last moments couldn't have been pleasant. Just as well he won't be asking for a refund.'

'There's this mental case on Death Row in Missouri, some fucking place like that,' said Harry, the driver. He had to shout above the traffic passing around the one-way system to make himself heard. 'They're going to give him a drug that makes him normal for a few hours, just so they can fucking execute him. Can you believe it? Give us a hand.' He locked the lid of the skip and hauled at the iron catch of the dangling chain, but it wouldn't clip around the skip's handles.

'Hang on.' His partner came over and kicked at it with his boot. The handle locked with a dense clang. He waved to the driver and watched as the chains took up the slack. They strained at the skip and slowly raised it onto the truck as the vehicle behind waited to lower an empty container in its place.

'Be a fucking sight easier if each one didn't need a separate skip,' said Harry, coughing around his cigarette.

'Health regulations,' his partner explained. 'We had one miss the fucking target completely over in Hackney. Smeared all over Old Street in the rush hour. Guts everywhere. Some old dear found his dental plate in her shopping.'

'What do you expect when the fucking council runs the PES.' He knew he shouldn't complain; Personal Exit Strategy was a big money-spinner for the London boroughs. They were talking of going twenty-four seven, which would jack up his overtime. He looked over at the chanting protestors. '*Choose Life*, yeah, you lot can fuck right off for a start.' Harry flicked away his damp cigarette. 'Tell me this life is better than being chucked into a fucking skip.'

'They live inside their dreams forever,' said his mate. 'That's why it costs so much. He's wherever he wants to be now. At the end, the only important thing left is to pass from this world in a state of euphoric grace.'

'Don't be a cunt.' Harry raised his face to the the low clouds and the falling rain. He closed his eyes and tried to shut out the cacophony of dirty noise, and feel only the wind and water on his cool grey skin. For a moment he tried to pretend that he was somewhere far away, but as he had never been anywhere else, he could only recall the poster of the tropical beach on Tottenham Court Road. With a shrug, he gave up and set off for the dump.